AWAKENED ROYAL

CLUB ROYAL, BOOK SIX

ELOUISE EAST

CONTENTS

DEDICATION

To all of my readers
Who've read and loved my boys as much as I do

SUTCLIFFE ROYAL FAMILY

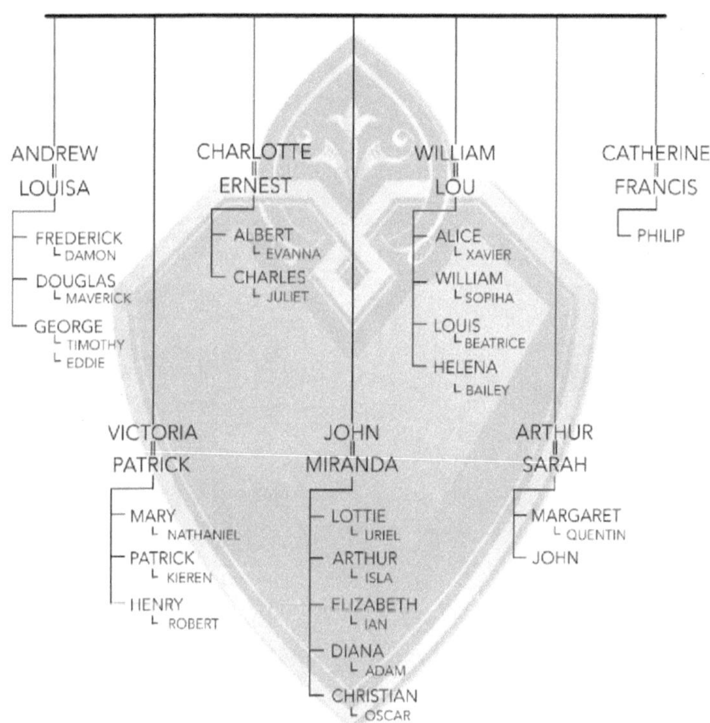

LIST OF CHARACTERS

(ALPHABETICAL ORDER)

Andrew, King of England, Patrick's uncle

Charles, cousin, Charlotte and Ernest's child

Charlotte, Frederick's aunt

Christian, Frederick's cousin, Oscar's boyfriend

Clarice, Club Royal's receptionist

Damon, Frederick's best friend

Douglas, Frederick's brother, Mav's boyfriend

Eddie, barista, George and Timothy's boyfriend

Elizabeth, Frederick's cousin, Christian's sister

Frederick, Damon's best friend, heir to the throne

George, Frederick's brother, Timothy and Eddie's boyfriend

Henry, Frederick's cousin, Robert's boyfriend

Hudson, Damon's bodyguard

John, Frederick's uncle

Kean, Henry's best friend

Kendal, friend of family, submissive

Kieren, Patrick's boyfriend, security
consultant

Locke, Frederick's bodyguard

Louisa, Queen Consort, Frederick's late
mother

Maverick, social media manager, Douglas's
boyfriend

Neil, Christian's boss, ally

Oliver, Club Royal bartender

Oscar, owner of Book Drunk, Christian's
boyfriend

Owen, Frederick's bodyguard

Patrick, Frederick's cousin

Quinn, friend of family, submissive

Randall, King Andrew's assistant

Robert, florist, Henry's boyfriend

Timothy, teacher/therapist, George and
Eddie's boyfriend

Victoria, Frederick's aunt

William, Frederick's uncle

AUTHOR NOTE

If you would like to see any potential triggers for this book and any other books I've written, please go to this link on my website: https://elouiseeast.com/triggers

AWAKENED ROYAL

1

FREDDIE

"It's New Year's Eve! I want to spend it with my brothers like I always do!" Frederick Sutcliffe clenched his jaw, not wanting to say something he might regret.

Damon's expression tightened, his eyes glittering. "I know you do, but you can't. There's a threat against the event, Freddie. You know this! If something happens, and you're there, they will take out *all* of you." His mouth flattened. "As much as I hate saying it, someone has to survive, and it needs to be you."

Freddie's stomach churned, and he turned away, pacing across the expanse of his living room. He inhaled and exhaled several times, trying to calm his heartbeat. Damon wasn't wrong, but Freddie hated that they put his life above others, especially his brothers' lives. Any other family would sacrifice themselves to save other people, but he wasn't "allowed." As if his life was worth more.

It definitely wasn't.

Each of them had found someone, or two someones, to share their lives with—except him. If that didn't make their lives more important than his, he didn't know what did.

Damon sighed. "I know you want to be with them, and you can be. *After* the event."

Freddie spun around, throwing his arms in the air. "Yeah, after midnight!"

"Freddie—"

"No! I'm going. I'm celebrating with my brothers because I'm not letting that...that..." Freddie worked his jaw and swallowed hard. "I'm not letting her win," he continued in a calmer voice.

He strode for his bedroom. His suit was ready to go, as always, and he needed to get dressed if he was going to be there on time. Damon had delayed him enough. He'd already showered, which was a bonus, and while he fastened his shirt buttons, he thought about his best friend. Damon was between a rock and a hard place in this situation. He didn't have to be part of Freddie's life, but he threw himself in regardless of the danger that surrounded them. It made Freddie proud and terrified at the same time. Having been best friends since they met at pre-school at three years old, Damon had been by Freddie's side ever since. No matter what. Freddie didn't know what he'd do without him.

His stomach fluttered, and he stared at himself in the mirror, remembering how it felt to be held in Damon's arms at Christmas. They had hugged before, but that had seemed different. They'd survived a mass assassination attempt, granted, but something that had already been shifting inside Freddie had roared to the surface, and he barely kept it contained. Even now, it bubbled in his veins, but he didn't know what to do with it. So, in true Freddie fashion, he ignored it.

Sliding his jacket on, he exited the bedroom and came to a stop.

"You're not going. That is an order if I have to make it one."

Freddie held his tongue against the words that he wanted to rail at his father. King Andrew was a force to be reckoned with, and if Freddie had even a quarter of his might, Freddie would still be a good king. Great even. His father was on a whole other level of greatness.

Except at this moment.

"There's enough security at the event. We'll be safe!"

"Safe is relative," Andrew said. "Everyone is safe until they're not."

"You could say the same thing about walking out of the front door every day," Freddie argued.

Andrew nodded. "You could. But there's a difference between not knowing if you're heading into danger and purposefully going where there's a threat."

"You let George and Douglas go!"

"You're the heir, Freddie," Andrew stated.

"So are they! They're your sons. As I am. Why is my life worth more than theirs?"

Andrew sighed and rubbed his chest. "They're not. Not to me. You're all the same, and I love you all with my heart. But we need you safe. *They* need you safe."

"Am I ever going to be able to make my own decisions without being vetoed at every turn?" Freddie asked. "Because it seems like I'm in a cage at the moment, with no one respecting my choices."

"That's not how this is." Andrew stepped forward, clasping Freddie's shoulders.

For the first time, Freddie shrugged his hands off and moved back. He clenched his jaw and slid his glare to Damon, the man who had tattled to his father, and Damon lifted his chin and stared back. But it was what he saw in Damon's expression that had his shoulders slumping and his head dropping forward.

"No order necessary," he said, turning back to the bedroom, trying to forget the fear glittering in Damon's eyes. He paused, gripping the handle, and glanced over his shoulder. "Happy New Year, Father." He slid inside his room and closed the door, leaning back against it.

Murmurs met his ears, but he ignored it and stripped back out of his suit. Hanging it back up, he dressed in joggers and a T-shirt, something he rarely wore except for when he exercised. He considered going to the gym but couldn't find the energy after the conversation he'd had.

A knock sounded, and he paused. Should he ignore it or answer it?

"Freddie, *please*," Damon said.

Freddie sighed. "Come in." He could no more deny his best friend than he could a starving child some food.

The door opened slowly, and Damon poked his head and shoulders around the edge. "I'm sorry."

Freddie nodded slowly. "Pulling the big guns out was unnecessarily harsh." He tapped his fingers against his thigh.

Damon slid into the room, closing them in the room, and rested against the wall beside the door, crossing his arms over his chest. "Would you have listened to me otherwise?"

Butterflies took flight in Freddie's stomach as he took in Damon's body, but he ignored them. "Doubtful."

"Then your wrath is worth it."

Freddie stared at him before snorting. "I can't believe you called my father on me!" He shook his head and grabbed the remote for the TV.

Damon grimaced. "Yeah, me either. I'd say I'm sorry, but..." He shrugged.

"It's a good job you're my best friend, asshole." He shook the remote in Damon's direction.

"Is that a new job title? Best friend asshole?" Damon stepped closer, and Freddie's stomach rolled, his breath catching.

"Should be," he said, clearing his throat.

Damon stopped in front of him. "I'll take it." Freddie couldn't look away from him. "I *am* sorry, but not for calling your father. I'm sorry I hurt your feelings."

Freddie sighed and closed his eyes. "It's fine."

"It's not, but thank you for saying that."

Arms came around Freddie carefully, as if Damon wasn't sure Freddie wanted to be touched. Freddie dropped his head to Damon's shoulder and sank into him, a position he'd taken several times since Christmas—the first time Freddie had totally fallen apart. The feeling of being safe in his arms was something Freddie ached for. Nothing could touch him when Damon held him like that. Freddie gripped the fabric of Damon's shirt at his hips and inhaled, the scent of the outdoors flooding his senses. Damon always smelt as if he'd spent hours outside, and Freddie loved it.

The thought had him lifting his head and pulling back. "Watch a movie with me?" he asked and climbed onto the bed, shoving a pillow behind his lower back, hoping to ease the ache in it.

"I'm not in the mood for sappy." Damon rounded the bed, kicked off his shoes and laid beside him, propping two pillows beneath his head and crossing his feet at the ankles.

"Sappy? If you want sappy..." Freddie pointed the remote at the TV.

Damon lurched upright, grabbing for the remote. Freddie held it out of his reach, and they tussled until a spasm wracked Freddie's body, and he couldn't hide his gasp of pain. Damon paused, lifting off him.

"What's wrong? Did I hurt you?"

Freddie shook his head but kept his mouth and eyes closed, trying to breathe through the pain in his back.

"Is it your back?"

Freddie nodded, exhaling as he moved to sit. "I'm okay."

Damon knelt beside him, hands on his hips, one eyebrow raised. "You're still having pain? I thought it had gone."

Freddie hadn't told him he'd been having problems with his back ever since the helicopter crash three years prior. He'd mentioned his back had occasionally been twinging, but he didn't know the cause.

Freddie glanced at him, and Damon cursed. "How long has this been going on, and why didn't you tell me?"

"An ache in my back is low on the agenda with everything else we're dealing with." He reached for the remote, which had fallen to the floor, and hissed when his back spasmed again.

Damon climbed off the bed and crouched in front of Freddie. "Let me help you. Lay on the bed on your stomach with your head towards the TV. I can give you a massage while we watch a non-sappy movie."

Freddie gritted his teeth while Damon helped him remove his T-shirt and lay down. "There you go asking for a sappy movie again. I'm getting concerned." Being on his stomach didn't hurt as much, but it might when he moved to get up afterwards.

"I think the pain has addled your brain. I'm in charge of the remote now." Damon plucked it from Freddie's hand without issue and set *Equilibrium* playing. "I'll grab some stuff."

He disappeared into Freddie's bathroom, and Freddie dropped his head to the bed. Maybe he should explain what was going on with his back. The doctor had said he might have issues with his back for the rest of his life. After all the years he'd been in the Royal Air Force flying planes and helicopters, it was a quick trip to Sandringham on a helicopter that had made it next to impossible for him to board another flight.

Memories of crashing, flames licking at the mangled metal while he dragged himself free of the debris bombarded him. The smell of fuel and smoke clogged his nose.

He lifted his head and exhaled, brushing aside the images for the gunfight onscreen. The investigation had deemed the crash to be a mechanical failure, but Freddie had never understood why. He'd checked everything himself before he'd taken off, and it was all perfect. Only now, since everything had begun with Aunt Charlotte, he wasn't sure someone hadn't tampered with it to *make* him crash.

"I'll kneel beside you, but tell me if it hurts too much."

"Mmhmm."

"Cold." Freddie inhaled shakily when the cold gel hit his back. "I'll do the same I did last time."

At Damon's words, it took Freddie back to when Damon had given him a back massage at Club Royal. Freddie had finished a shift, and Damon had followed him to the changing rooms, having noticed Freddie was in pain. Damon had massaged his back, but at the end, Freddie had seen Damon's cock pressing against the zip of his jeans. Would the same happen this time? Freddie blinked away the thoughts and focused on Damon's hands.

"Where does it hurt most?" Damon murmured, his hands smoothing across Freddie's shoulder blades.

"Lower back." Freddie's eyes drifted closed, relaxing into the massage.

Having Damon's hands on him was magical, and not just because of the release of the pain. He couldn't understand when his feelings for his best friend had begun to change but change they had. He had no idea what he was feeling if he was honest with himself. It didn't make sense to him to be aware of Damon when they were both straight. Or rather, Freddie was. Damon had never been with a man, from what Freddie knew, but he didn't think Damon was completely straight, either. He'd seen Damon eyeing men before, even though he'd never played with one at the club.

The twinge that time had nothing to do with his back and everything to do with the pumping organ in his chest.

"Are you okay?" Damon asked.

"Yeah." Freddie glanced over his shoulder and frowned. "Can you even see the TV from that position?"

"It's fine. I can hear it. It's not like I haven't watched it a thousand times." Damon chuckled, the deep, dark sound vibrating through Freddie.

Freddie was going to hell for his next words. "Straddle my legs. It'll make it easier for you. Easier on *your* back, too."

Damon paused, his hands resting on Freddie's skin. "Are you sure it won't hurt you more?"

Freddie ignored where his brain went with that and

answered, "No. I'll be fine." His back would. He wasn't sure about anything else.

Damon manoeuvred his legs on either side of Freddie's thighs and continued his massage. "I think this is a better position to do the massage, too. I can reach better."

Freddie huffed a laugh. "We know for future reference."

"You expecting more of these?"

"I wouldn't say no. Did they teach this in graphic design or something?" Freddie dropped his forehead back to the bed.

Damon chuckled, his thumbs digging into either side of Freddie's spine. "Yeah. In between the chapters on typography and the colour wheel."

Damon's hands slid up Freddie's back to his shoulders, and Freddie groaned, the movie forgotten. As Damon's hands moved down to his lower back area, Freddie's body melted into the bed. Freddie's endorphin fuelled brain hoped Damon would continue further down than he needed to. Freddie's cock hardened against the bed, and he bit his lip. It was the actions that were doing it, not because it was Damon.

But Freddie couldn't deny it completely.

He wanted to move his ass to find out if Damon was hard. He wanted to feel it pressed against him, rubbing against his ass cheeks while Damon kissed his neck and slid his arms beneath him, holding him close.

Freddie couldn't help the breathy moan that left his mouth, but he snapped it shut and cleared his throat, lifting his head to rest his chin on the back of his hands and facing the movie again. It took everything in him to stay still and relaxed. If nothing else, his back was no longer hurting. Whether that was because he was too busy thinking about Damon in a way he shouldn't be or because Damon's massage had helped, he wasn't sure. He knew one thing. There was no way he'd be able to get up from the bed without showing exactly how he felt at that moment.

"Are you okay?"

"Fine. Thanks for the massage. It's feeling much better." He glanced at the time. "Don't you need to get going?" He tried to keep the pout from his voice.

Damon removed his hands and sat back, his weight transferring fully onto Freddie's legs. "I better. I don't want to be late."

"Definitely not. Your tardiness will be a reflection on me." Freddie tried to make light of the situation.

"We wouldn't want that." Damon paused and then climbed off Freddie and the bed. He held up his hands, and Freddie kept his gaze on his best friend's face. "I'll..." He disappeared into the bathroom again, but not before Freddie saw the telltale bulge in his trousers.

Freddie closed his eyes and muffled his groan in the covers, not daring to move until Damon left, scared even a thrust against the bed would make him come like a teenager. He lifted his head when Damon returned.

"Will you be okay? I can call someone to stay with you."

Freddie glared at him. "I don't need a babysitter."

"I didn't mean it like that. It's New Year. We usually see it in together…"

Freddie stared at the TV, ignoring the ache in his body from not being with Damon to see in the new year. From being alone for the first time on New Year's. "I'll be fine. Go. You need to bring back the gossip."

Damon chuckled. "Will do." He turned for the door, pausing before opening it. "For what it's worth, I'm sorry."

Freddie sighed. "The only person who needs to be sorry is Aunt Charlotte. You're doing what Father has asked you to do. Me being on my own is inconsequential in the grand scheme of things."

"Doesn't make me feel better about it."

Emotions overwhelmed Freddie, and he ignored the possibility of showing everything he had and climbed off the bed, striding for Damon and stopping toe-to-toe. "Promise me one thing." Damon nodded. "Be safe. If I can't be there because of the threat, that means it's serious. If you're in danger, run." Freddie swallowed. "Come home to me," he whispered.

Damon grabbed Freddie and hugged him, tightening his grip until it hurt, but Freddie buried his face in Damon's neck and held on. "I promise I'll come home to you," he murmured in Freddie's ear.

Damon pulled back and smiled. He cupped Freddie's face and then whirled around and left, closing the door behind him. Freddie stared at the door. His body trembled from head to toe, and he clenched his fists at the need to stop Damon from leaving him. When it was his life in the balance, he didn't care, but Damon's? George's and Douglas's? Their partners'? His cousins'?

No one else should be hurt in this treasonous endeavour, but he could guarantee they would be. But who would pay the ultimate price this time?

2

DAMON

Damon Winchester wanted to kiss Freddie to prove he was coming back, but he couldn't drop that on him with everything else Freddie was going through. Damon had hidden his love for his best friend for this long. If he was ever going to admit to it, it wouldn't be when there was a chance he wouldn't return.

Everyone involved with the event was taking this potential threat to the next level. They had no way of knowing if anything was going to happen at this event or not. The list of potential targets Christian's late mother had given them was exactly that—*potential* targets. There was no other evidence to prove anything would happen, but security was assuming it would, especially because it was a highly advertised and attended event. The least of whom were Princes George and Douglas and their partners.

Damon shook his head, striding for the security room.

Having two princes in one place was a nightmare at the best of times. At this point, it was worse. Especially because they were the closest in line to the throne after Freddie.

He wanted nothing more than to spend New Year with Freddie, but the king had declared all hands on deck, and that meant Damon, too. For reasons Freddie didn't yet know.

He knocked on the security door. Felix opened it and nodded when Damon slipped inside.

"Ah, Damon. Glad you're with us on this one. Your training is almost complete, and after your reactions at Christmas, I don't think anyone here has a problem with bringing you on board as security for this event." Brett glanced around the room at the extensive number of body-guards, none of whom spoke up to argue. "Good. Take a seat, Damon. We're doing a final run-through before heading to our designated person. Although yours is slightly different." He winked.

Damon sat and caught Kieren's eye. The man nodded at him though he wore a frown. And there was the problem. Damon, Kieren and Andrew, not to mention the entire security team, were hiding something from everyone else. For the last three years, Damon had been in training as a bodyguard. A secret bodyguard. Someone who could go under the radar and not give away their knowledge and ability unless it was necessary. Keeping people safe while providing people with the feeling of being free.

Freddie had no idea.

He was going to kill Damon when he found out. Because he *would* find out. He was Freddie. He always found out.

Damon was going to this event under the guise of seeing if there were any people he recognised from his "auditing" job. The job Andrew had given him to find any inconsistencies within the royal family's businesses. Inconsistencies that might point towards something untoward.

But Damon was going as an extra pair of security hands in the event something happened. He and Kieren, who was not a secret bodyguard, could get their group to safety easier than official security guards could because they had the ultimate trust of those people. Something Damon was putting at risk by hiding his actual job—Freddie's personal bodyguard.

"Kieren, although you're back as security for this event, you'll be a guest. Patrick won't be there, but you're there to support his family and show a link *to* Patrick. The same goes for you, Damon. You're Freddie's ambassador if you like. Both of you need to keep your wits about you, as usual. Don't drink, don't bring attention to yourselves, just be there like you usually would. If anything happens, you grab a prince each, and you move towards the designated room. Got it?" Damon nodded. "Okay. We know what we're doing. Go do it," Brett said. "Damon, Kieren, wait behind."

The rest of the security team filtered out, and Damon and Kieren approached Brett. The boss was Christian's bodyguard, but how he managed to balance that with being the boss of the entire security team was beyond Damon's understanding.

"Right, here." Brett handed them a badge with the royal crest on it. "Wear this on your jacket or tie. It's a radio transmitter and locator. All you need to do is press it to activate it, and it will send out a locator signal and pick up any and all conversations nearby. You don't need to hold it to speak. Just talk." He handed them an earpiece. "Do not put this in your ear unless you have to press the locator. I don't want you distracted by security chatter. If you press the locator, put this in your ear, and you'll be able to hear us. It isn't the same frequency as everyone else. It has a direct link to me." He sighed. "I hope you aren't needed, but good luck."

Damon inhaled and followed Kieren out of the room. He stared at the two small electronic items in the palm of his hand and realised they could be all he had to keep George safe. It was an immense responsibility.

"Damon," Kieren said. He glanced up at his friend's boyfriend. "You're ready. Christmas proved it. That instinct is inside of you now. You won't have to think about your reactions. They'll be there, leaving your brain free to either listen to orders or to figure out what to do next."

"Will I ever be able to tell anyone?"

Kieren exhaled. "Hopefully. There's no reason for your job to be a secret from those you're protecting, only from the public. But I'm not the boss." He clapped Damon's shoulder. "I'll be there with you. You'll be fine."

Damon was scared he wouldn't be able to protect

anyone. Physically, he could do it, but mentally? Was he too close?

He smiled at Kieren. "See you later."

Heading for his room, something Andrew had insisted upon during his teen years when he spent the same amount of time at Windsor with Freddie that he did at his own home with his parents, Damon thought about how the conversation might go with Freddie when he broke the news. He didn't think it would go well. Freddie was already sick of the number of secrets Damon had kept from him over the past few months. Would this secret be one too many, or would it be too big to forgive?

By the time he was ready to go, he'd pushed all other thoughts aside. He met up with George at the entrance when they were getting ready to leave.

"Hey, you! How did Freddie take it?" George asked, looking every inch the prince in his black tuxedo.

Damon rolled his eyes and exhaled. "As good as could be expected." He grimaced. "I had to call your father."

George's eyes widened. "Oh, shit." He patted Damon's shoulders and arms. "You still seem to be in one piece, so he couldn't have killed you."

"It was a close call."

"I can imagine." George brushed a hand down the front of his jacket and sighed. "Time to face the music." He gave a small smile, betraying his nerves. They headed for the car once the bodyguard said they could.

"Timothy and Eddie are meeting you there, aren't they?" Damon already knew the answer, but talking about George's boyfriends was the best way to distract him.

George nodded. "Yes. Security's orders." He settled into a seat in the back of the car. "Would feel better if they were with me."

"I know. You have me." Damon grinned.

"That I do. I wish Freddie could be here. It doesn't seem fair to leave him alone."

Damon nodded, having had those exact thoughts. "I'll make it up to him somehow."

"I bet you will." George chuckled, and Damon flushed.

He decided to face the music. "Does everyone know?" he murmured.

George didn't pretend not to know what Damon was talking about. "Pretty much. Except for Freddie. He seems clueless, and not only about your feelings for him. What I don't understand is why haven't you told him?"

Damon snorted. "He's straight, George. You know that. Have you ever seen him even look at a man like that?"

"I've never seen you play with a man, but I know you're not straight. He plays with men, but he could not realise. Maybe he only likes you."

"There are no indications of him returning my feelings, George. I'm not ruining what we *do* have to assuage my heart." He stared out of the window.

"I don't think you'd have to worry, Damon. From what I see when you're together, Freddie is not quite straight."

Damon didn't answer. He couldn't get his hopes up because it would slowly kill him. It was bad enough having these feelings in the first place. There was no hope for him. Freddie couldn't have a relationship with a man.

He needed to continue the bloodline and marry someone worthy. If he could help Freddie do that, then Damon would be happy. Well, maybe content was the right word. Having his hands on Freddie earlier that night was something he could file away and bring up when he needed to be reminded of what he was doing. Ensuring Freddie's happiness was the reason Damon was on this earth.

When they pulled up outside the building, Damon's eyes darted around the journalists waiting outside with flashing cameras. Scenes from *The Bodyguard* flashed through his mind, with the shooter being someone with a camera, and it didn't help his nerves.

"You ready for this?" George asked.

Damon rolled his eyes again. "Are we ever?"

George accepted the answer and climbed out when the guard opened his door. Damon met the guard's gaze and nodded as he exited. The shouting of questions and names rose to ear-splitting levels. George and Damon made their way to the doors and inside without a single answer being given. They removed their coats and handed them to a staff member, and then the guards led the way to the event location.

"His Royal Highness, Prince George," the man at the door announced when they entered as if they were in a period drama and everyone needed to know who had arrived. "Damon Winchester, on behalf of His Royal Highness, Prince Frederick."

The words shouldn't have sent a dart of pleasure through Damon's body, but they did. Having his name attached to Freddie's was a dream of epic proportions but would never happen outside of events like these.

He stuck by George's side during the greetings and gradually guided him to where he could see Timothy and Eddie were waiting. Douglas and Mav didn't seem to be there, but they wouldn't be far behind.

When George saw his boyfriends, he pulled them into his arms, whispering in their ears before kissing them chastely. There had been a conversation with Andrew about personal displays of affection, and the king had declared that anything was acceptable, providing children could watch. Anything more than that was unacceptable unless out of public sight. Everyone had taken it to heart and listened to the reasoning behind it without argument, which had shocked Damon. He'd expected at least one of them to argue about being allowed to fondle their boyfriend whenever they wanted. When he'd asked Freddie, his best friend had said it shocked them that Andrew hadn't forbidden them to give any displays of affection in public like the royals usually had to. He'd said the royal family was moving forward, although it wasn't fast enough for Freddie.

"His Royal Highness, Prince Douglas and his partner, Maverick Houghton. Kieren Young, on behalf of His Royal Highness, Prince Patrick," the announcer said.

"About time, too," George grumbled.

"Are you in a rush?" Damon murmured.

"Only to get drinking." George frowned. "How come they could come together?"

Damon shook his head. "They didn't. Mav arrived earlier but waited in a side room until Douglas got here."

"They never told us that was an option," Eddie grumbled, holding onto George.

"We know for future reference," Timothy said, pressing his lips to Eddie's temple.

"Are we ready for the new year!" Douglas said when he joined their small group.

"As ready as we can be without drinks," George replied. "Let's remedy that."

They headed for the bar area, stopping for greetings and conversations. When they finally arrived at the bar, Damon was exhausted from keeping himself alert and attuned to every potential threat. He downed half a glass of water the moment the bartender set it in front of him and then ordered a lemonade. It gave him something to hold and fiddle with while he was "working."

A couple of hours passed before the time neared midnight. He wished Freddie was with him, or he was with Freddie. Either way. The best he could do was call him, but he didn't know if he should because he was supposed to be on alert.

"Kieren, can I call Freddie?" he murmured.

"Yes." Damon raised his eyebrows, and Kieren smiled. "I thought you might ask, so I cleared it with Brett first."

Damon chuckled. "Thank you." He pulled his phone out and dialled Freddie's number. It rang for so long he didn't think Freddie would answer, but when his best friend's silky, smooth voice said his name, it was all Damon could do to say hello.

"I didn't expect to hear from you," Freddie said, and Damon pressed the phone closer to his ear, wanting to catch every word.

"I know I couldn't be there with you, but this is better than nothing, right?"

"Definitely." They stayed in silence for a moment. "How long—" Freddie's words were cut off by the start of the countdown. "That answers that," he finished louder.

"FIVE, FOUR, THREE, TWO, ONE! HAPPY NEW YEAR!" the announcer called.

"Happy New Year, Freddie."

"Happy New—"

The building shook while screams tore through the room and debris rained down on them. Damon dropped his phone and grabbed George, covering him with his body as they ran for the door. Damon pressed the locator on his lapel and fumbled for the earpiece in his pocket.

"Oxford is on the move," he said, squinting against the raining dust while he led George through the mass of moving bodies towards the room they had secured for George's safe exit. If everything went according to plan, Kieren would head to another room with an exit for Douglas.

"What the hell was that?" George asked. He glanced over his shoulder and tried to stop, but Damon wouldn't let him. "Where's Timothy and Eddie?"

"They're with the security team being taken to safety," he said after hearing the information from Brett. "And to answer your first question, I have no idea."

"Where's Isaac?"

"I don't know."

Brett's voice filled his ear. "Isaac's not responding to his name. Continue alone."

Damon hoped Isaac was all right. They traversed the hallways until they reached the room Brett had told Damon to head for. He pushed George against the wall and opened the door, checking inside before dragging George inside and slamming the door behind them.

"Oxford at base," Damon said, heading for a drawer and grabbing the gun that had been stowed there for this situation. He checked the clip and held it at his side before facing George, knowing what would be awaiting him.

"Wait..." George stared at him, eyes widening. "*What?*"

"Head to the exit door. There's a car waiting with a blue dot near the handle. Do not approach if this dot is not present."

"Understood," he said. He stared at George. "I'll explain everything later, but for now, we need to go." He grabbed George's arm, and the man came with him without argument.

"You're in such shit when this finishes, man," George warned.

"I know." He paused at the door. "Wait here."

Damon cracked the door, peeking to see a black car waiting. He peered at the side of the car and saw the blue dot. He opened the door further. "Come on. Hold the back of my jacket and stay behind me." He held the gun outwards, scanning their surroundings, and reached for the door handle, opening the door and crowding George inside before following him. He recognised the guard driving and nodded at him.

"Oxford secure," he said when the car screamed away from the event. He collapsed back against the seat, breath heaving, the adrenaline flowing through him.

"Good job, Damon," Brett said. "Douglas, Mav, Timothy, Eddie and Kieren are safe. We have found Isaac. He got knocked out by flying debris, but he's fine."

"Thanks." George glanced at him, and Damon gave a small smile. "Everyone's fine. They're all safe."

George closed his eyes and covered his face with his hands. Damon dropped his head back and then lifted it again. "Oh, shit!"

George snapped his gaze to him, and Brett said, "What's wrong?"

"I was on the phone with Freddie when it happened."

"Fuck!" Brett said. "Hold."

It went silent, and Damon held George's wide gaze. Damon's heart raced. What would Freddie be doing? Would he put himself in danger?

"Locke and Owen are with him. Just in time, though. He was on his way out of Windsor."

"Stupid asshole," Damon murmured.

"What?" George asked.

"Freddie was on his way. His guards stopped him in time."

George stared at him hard enough to send Damon squirming. "You have a *lot* of explaining to do."

Damon nodded but said nothing. There was no getting away from the questions coming his way. Had it only been a few hours since he'd wondered if he needed to keep it a secret? That wouldn't happen now. His time was up. And he was glad. He was tired of hiding things, and Freddie didn't deserve it. It wasn't keeping him safe like Damon had pretended it was to help him sleep at night. It was building a wall between them, and Damon wanted the wall gone. He was going to expose all his secrets.

Well, all but one.

That one secret would be taken to his grave because it would make that wall a steel structure unable to be climbed or torn down. It would destroy everything they'd ever had. And Damon couldn't live his life without Freddie being in it.

Even if it meant having to let Freddie find someone else to marry. To have kids with. To love.

3

FREDDIE

"Happy New Year, Damon," Freddie said. He heard a bang and thought the fireworks were loud, they came through the phone, but then he listened to crashes and screams tearing through the phone line. "Damon! DAMON!"

Freddie scrambled from the bed, holding the phone to his ear and trying to hear what was happening. His heart pounded, and goosebumps rose over his skin when the call ended. Images raced through his head of Damon lying dead on the floor while people ran screaming from the building. What the hell had happened? There was a potential threat, but Freddie hadn't believed Aunt Charlotte would go ahead with it because they thought she knew they were onto her plans. Who would still go ahead with an attack like this when every eye was on the event?

Freddie scrubbed a hand over his face. Aunt Charlotte would. "Fucking bitch is going to get what's coming to her. I'm telling you now." His words flung into the empty room, echoing back at him. He dialled Damon's number again and only reached his voicemail. Damon's recorded voice floated through the speaker, and Freddie closed his eyes and bowed his head. "Please, please, don't let this be the end," he whispered. He swallowed hard and ended the call, not wanting to hear Damon's voice when he couldn't see him. Instead, he tried Douglas's number, which went to voicemail, George's number, which did the same, and then Brett's busy number.

He wanted to throw his phone across the room, but he couldn't. Someone might need him.

"Who the fuck am I kidding? Damon needs me."

Freddie threw on a jumper, slammed his feet into trainers and ran through his room for the door. He'd get to the event if he had to walk. He wouldn't leave Damon alone any longer than he needed to. He raced down the hallways to the exit, where two bodyguards intercepted him.

"You need to stay inside, Your Highness," one said, holding out his hand to stop Freddie from leaving.

"You need to get out of my way," Freddie said, anger tinting his voice into a tone he never used on the people that worked for them.

"I'm sorry, Your Highness. You can't leave."

Freddie clenched his jaw, his body trembling, and he closed his eyes to regain his control.

"FREDDIE!" Freddie spun around at his name. Locke and Owen ran towards him. "He's fine, Freddie. They're all fine," Locke said.

It took a moment for the words to sink in, and by that point, they stood in front of him.

"He's okay?" he whispered.

"Yes." Locke nodded, reiterating her answer.

Freddie's knees buckled, and Owen caught him around the waist. Freddie leaned against him, Owen steering him back through the hallways. His brain was a jumble of images and conversations, years of memories whirling through his head. By the time he shook himself free of them, they were back in Freddie's suite. He sat on the sofa, and Locke sat opposite him on the coffee table, a frown on her face.

"What happened?" Freddie asked, licking his dry lips.

Locke rubbed her palms together and sighed. "Some kind of explosion. We don't know the details yet, but other than superficial injuries, every attendee is alive. Douglas and George are on their way back now."

"What about the others?"

"Timothy, Eddie, Damon and Kieren are coming back here, too. His Majesty wants everyone checked out before they go home."

Freddie nodded and closed his eyes, leaning his elbows on his knees and covering his face with his hands. He concentrated on breathing, needing to be alive and alert when Damon got back. What had he been thinking? How would he have reached Damon even if he escaped Windsor? Why put himself in danger like that?

He stood. "I need..." He thumbed over his shoulder towards his room.

"We'll be right here if you need us," Locke said.

He closed himself behind his bedroom door and crumpled to the floor, breaths heaving from him while his body shook. He could've lost them all—his brothers and his best friend. All gone because of some mad woman hellbent on changing a world that didn't need changing. At least not in the direction *she* wanted it to go in. He crawled over to the bed, leaning his back against it and his head against the bedside table. The movie he'd been watching was still playing, but he stared at the door. The emotions battling inside of him were confusing. Was what he felt the result of Damon being his best friend or because he'd begun to mean more to Freddie? He'd never felt like this about anyone. Was he mistaking it for more when it wasn't? He didn't want to deny his feelings, but how could he talk to anyone about them when he didn't know what they meant? Besides, it wasn't only his feelings he had to think about. He had to think about the crown. His responsibilities. The public's reaction. Being bisexual wasn't an issue because his father had come out to the public the previous year, but his father was already king. Freddie was supposed to be next in line, but what was to say the public wouldn't cause enough of a problem that they wouldn't let him become king when the time came. Was Aunt Charlotte right about the royal line needing to be pure?

Freddie closed his eyes and banged his head against the table. Of course, she wasn't right. Bloodline didn't prove that someone could lead the country. People only had to see what a mess the government made of their "leading" to see that wasn't true.

A knock sounded, and Freddie's breath caught. He opened his mouth, but he couldn't answer, scared it would be bad news instead of good.

"Freddie?"

Freddie stopped breathing when Damon's voice came through the door, and tears overflowed, but despite that, he couldn't move.

"Freddie? I'm coming in."

The door opened, and Damon poked his head in like he had done earlier that evening—or the previous evening, if he was going to be picky, but now wasn't the time. Damon's hair was messy, sticking up in all directions, and his face had smudges of dirt on it, but his eyes caught and held Freddie's. Damon came all the way inside and shut the door, racing across the space and dropping beside him. Freddie's gaze didn't waver, taking in every bit of Damon he could.

"Breathe, Freddie. Breathe for me," Damon coaxed, wiping at Freddie's cheeks. Freddie inhaled, his lungs screaming and his head spinning, and oxygen flooded his body. "That's it. Breathe."

Freddie reached for him, gripping his dusty shirt, and rested their foreheads together. Then Freddie dropped his head to Damon's shoulder and slid his arms around him, grabbing at his back while trying to hold back his sobs.

"I'm here. We're all fine. I'm here. I'm here." Damon tightened his hold, rocking them side to side.

Freddie didn't lose minutes this time. He was aware of every second Damon held him, and he didn't want it to stop, but the feelings bombarding him were too much.

Enough conflicting emotions that he was on a waltzer. Damon and his brothers could have died. Damon had been lying to him about his job. His father had been lying to him about Damon's role. Aunt Charlotte was throwing them for a loop. The ups and downs of attending events. His potential new feelings for his best friend—if they were more than just friendship. The weight of the crown on his shoulders. The public. The journalists. The club. Everything. It was too much.

He pulled away from Damon and paced to the door, wiping at his face and clearing his throat. "I'm glad you're okay." He swallowed hard, facing Damon, who was still on the floor beside his bed. "Get some rest, okay? I need to check in on Douglas and George." He nodded as if Damon had said something and sent a small smile his way before exiting the room and heading for the door.

"Your Highness?" Locke said.

Freddie sent a smile her way. "I'm going to see Douglas and George. You're welcome to come with me if you need to." From the corner of his eye, he saw Damon come out of his bedroom.

"If you don't mind. For now, at least," she said.

He nodded and exited the room, letting his bodyguards fall in behind him. When he saw Douglas, he threw his arms around him and held him closely.

"This has to fucking stop," Freddie said, his throat aching.

Douglas held his shoulders and nodded. "It does."

Freddie hugged George too. "What happened?"

George raised his eyebrows. "Haven't you spoken to Damon?"

"I checked he was okay, but then I came here. Why?" Freddie frowned.

George shook his head. "I thought he would've explained, that's all."

"I suppose I didn't give him the chance." And for good reason, though he didn't say that aloud.

"Well, we don't know the cause of it yet, but there was an explosion of some kind. Debris and dust rained down on us. People were screaming and running for the exits. Luckily, Kieren got me to safety. Some of the other guards grabbed Mav, Timothy and Eddie, and Damon grabbed George."

"Why did Damon help you?"

George glanced towards his partners. "Isaac got knocked unconscious. He's fine, but he couldn't help."

Freddie could see Damon taking it upon himself to help Freddie's brothers. They were as close as family, and Damon had a heart of gold. Of course, he would help.

"They don't know where the explosion came from?"

Douglas shook his head. "I've not had an update, but it seemed to be from somewhere within the room. It sounded too close for comfort." He slid his arm around Mav, pressing his lips to his temple.

The door slammed open, and their father stormed in, eyes crazy until they rested on Douglas and George. Freddie stepped aside and let Andrew reassure himself about his sons. As he did, his phone rang.

"Hey, Paddy. Are you okay?"

"No, I'm fucking not! Robert's been arrested!"

"What! What the hell for?" Freddie stared at his father, who met his gaze after Freddie's outburst.

"For the explosion. The police say the explosions originated in the flowers that Robert provided for the event. They think it's him. Henry's in pieces."

"Fucking hell! When will this end?" He relayed the information to his father.

Andrew pointed at him. "Call Kean. He'll help with Henry while I speak to Brady. There has to be a mistake." He pulled his phone free and stepped aside to make the call.

"Do you have Kean's number, Paddy?"

"No, but I can get it from Henry's phone. We're going to need all the help we can get."

"We'll head over to you."

"No," Andrew said, putting away his phone. "Brady says we need to stay where we are. He's taking the threat seriously, which means he has reason to believe Robert is the right villain in this. We know otherwise, but until then, we can't go anywhere because it might cause problems with the investigation." Andrew shook his head. "We *know* Robert didn't do it, but until we can prove it, we have to be careful. If Charlotte is pointing the finger at him, this might not be the only thing she's done."

"You mean she might have another plan to put the proverbial nail in Robert's coffin?" Douglas said.

"Possibly."

"Did you hear that, Paddy?" Freddie asked.

"Yes, and it's fucking shit." He sighed. "I'll call Kean.

Kieren is with us, the guards and Mother and Father. We'll be fine."

"Keep us updated with whatever you hear," Freddie said.

"You, too."

"Chin up."

"Same."

Freddie ended the call and stared at his father. "What the hell is going on?"

Andrew blew out a breath and put his hands on his hips. "She either doesn't know we know about the events, or she knows we know, and she's doing them anyway, but making it so they point the finger at those closest to us."

"Payback for Charles?" Freddie asked.

Andrew frowned. "Maybe." He rubbed the back of his neck. "We can't do anything else until I hear from Brady, and that probably won't be until early tomorrow. I want you all to get some rest. I have a feeling this is going to be a long few days."

After a few more minutes, Freddie left to go back to his suite, both hoping Damon was and wasn't there waiting for him. He wasn't, and Freddie ignored the twinge in his chest when he realised. He said goodnight to Locke and Owen, who said they would stay outside his suite for the rest of the night and climbed into bed. His TV had been turned off, and when he flicked off the lamp, darkness covered him. He kept his eyes open, wishing his brain would settle, but it didn't. It kept going in circles, the problems, the potential answers, the potential outcomes from those answers, and nothing seemed the right choice.

He cared for Damon. That much was true. But what kind of "care" did he mean? Did he love him like a brother? Did he love him like a lover? Was it something completely different? He could only remember how he'd felt when he thought Damon was dead—a scarily similar feeling to what he'd felt when he'd found out his mother had died in the car bomb. Like a missing limb with phantom pains that didn't cease, as a veteran once explained to him. Even then, he wanted Damon by his side, but he owed it to them both to figure out what the hell was going on in his brain and body before doing something he might regret.

Being the heir to the throne, he didn't have the luxury of making decisions without thinking through every road it may take him on. He also had to have discussions with his father and any relevant people before they could confirm it was the right choice of action. And everyone thought being a prince was a blast.

Despite it being a Sunday and the first day of a new year, Commissioner Brady Thomas did his job and cleared Robert of any wrongdoing in the explosion. Experts had deemed the explosion as having come from the vases the flowers were in, not the flowers themselves, and the hotel supplied the vases, not Robert. After a harrowing seventeen hours in custody, they released Robert with an unblemished record, and Commissioner Thomas was hunting for who supplied the hotel with the vases.

Freddie watched when Henry and Robert were reunited at Bagshot Park, still unable to face Damon. He hadn't seen him since before he'd made sure his brothers were all in one piece. The trials of the day were getting to them all, and Eddie had tried to cancel their plans for his birthday the following day. No one would let him. They needed to remember they were all alive and well, even if they were dented a little, and a night at Club Royal was perfect for them.

Freddie asked Locke to drive him to the club, knowing he wouldn't be able to concentrate enough to drive himself. When he arrived, he pressed his thumb to the sensor for the lift. The doors opened, and he stepped inside, waving to Locke before being taken to the reception area.

"Good evening, Your Highness. I hope you're well," the receptionist said.

"I'm doing well, Clarice. Thank you for asking." He pressed his thumb to the sensor on the desk, logging himself present. "Anything I should be aware of tonight?"

"No, Your Highness. I won't say the 'Q' word, but things are going smoothly so far." She smiled.

"Any changes to the Monitors' schedule?" Every night, the club insisted on having at least four Monitors in the building to keep an eye on things. Usually, there were six of them, but depending on the number of attendees that night, one or two of them might be relieved of duty.

"No, it's still Princex Alice, Princesses Elizabeth and Mary, and Princes Albert, Douglas and Arthur."

Douglas got the short end of the stick that night

because he couldn't officially get the time off to join them for the party, but to be honest, most of them would separate and do their own thing, anyway. Especially the birthday boy and his two men.

"Thank you, Clarice. Have a good evening."

"You, too, Your Highness."

Freddie escaped to the changing room, entering the Monitors' only section, and headed for his locker. The club used thumbprints throughout to ensure restricted areas were only opened to those with access and also to let the staff know if a member wasn't allowed to play. If any member drank alcohol on the premises or arrived inebriated, the bartender took them off the "play" list. Club Royal would not take chances with anyone's apparent consent—they made sure everyone was clear-minded in making their decisions. There was too much that could go wrong if they didn't.

Freddie changed from his trousers and shirt into leather trousers and a leather shirt with fasteners across his chest and thighs. Whenever he strapped himself into the clothes, he felt completely different to a prince. It was as if he was playing dress-up, but the prince was the disguise, not the Dom. He inhaled and shut his locker, heading for the main club. He waved at Oliver, the bartender, when he passed through Douglas's aptly named "conversation area," not stopping for a drink, and entered the club floor. The sounds of slapping skin, moans and music met his ears. He had to find someone to help him get what he needed.

He wandered around the floor, trying to find someone

he had played with before, to no avail. If he couldn't find someone, he wasn't sure what he'd do.

"Hey. What's wrong?" Douglas asked when Freddie met him at the steps, where Monitors stood to be able to see over the heads of the members.

"Can't find anyone to play with."

It was a problem for his specific talent. Medical play was not for the faint of heart, and few people enjoyed it to the extent Freddie did.

"I'll do it."

Freddie froze.

4

DAMON

amon hadn't planned on volunteering, even though it was something he enjoyed, but the needy tone in Freddie's voice wasn't something he could deny. He'd never played with Freddie. Ever. He'd watched, don't get him wrong, but he'd never been in the scene with him. It was too much like tempting fate, but Freddie needed this, and Damon could give it to him. He doubted Freddie would agree.

Douglas's gaze met his over Freddie's shoulder, and the corner of his mouth kicked up. *Bloody princes think they know everything.* Freddie, on the other hand, didn't turn around straight away. He tensed up so much that Damon thought he'd break at the slightest touch.

Finally, Freddie glanced over his shoulder, his face a blank mask, which advertised more than anything that he needed this release. "You don't play with men."

Damon shrugged a shoulder and swallowed hard.

"Only because I haven't found someone I want to play with." The words, outing his orientation to his best friend, hung between them, and Freddie stared at him, a slight crease between his eyebrows. When Freddie stayed quiet, Damon shrugged again. "Offer's there if you need it. I'm grabbing a drink. Want anything?"

"I'm good, thanks," Douglas said, tilting his head towards Freddie and nodding at Damon. He took that to mean he'd speak with Freddie, but he didn't hold his breath.

"No problem."

He exhaled and walked away, wishing he'd kept his mouth shut. Before he pushed through the door to the conversation area, someone shoved him against a wall, and he instinctively went on alert, lifting his elbow, ready to retaliate, when words stopped him.

"Are you sure about this?" Freddie breathed into his ear, his hands resting on either side of Damon's head against the wall.

The heat of Freddie's body against his back had Damon's eyelids closing. He inhaled a couple of times before nodding. "I am."

"There's no going back from this. It's crossing the best friend's line. I won't go easy."

"I don't need easy," Damon murmured. *I need you.*

Freddie dropped his forehead to Damon's shoulder, and Damon didn't move until Freddie lifted his head again. "Follow me."

Damon swallowed hard. "Yes, Sir," he breathed, hoping he wasn't about to make a huge mistake.

Freddie's heat left his back, and Damon pivoted to keep him in sight, weaving through the members towards the arch to the left of the stage where Douglas stood. He met Douglas's gaze, and the man nodded with a small smile. They followed the hallway around to the left again and to the two rooms dedicated to medical play. Both were empty, the windows and doors open. Freddie entered the second room and headed for the window, pressing the button to darken and block anyone from seeing inside. Damon glanced over his shoulder, but no one seemed to be paying attention to them. He slid inside and locked the door behind him.

"What's your safe word?"

Freddie knew what it was, but he was a stickler for the rules. "Cheesecake, Sir."

"I know you have experience with some medical play, but what are your hard limits?" Freddie asked, opening a cupboard and removing some items Damon was familiar with.

"None that I'm aware of, Sir."

Freddie glanced at him. "None?"

Damon shook his head. "No, Sir." He hadn't found anything that didn't do *something* for him.

Freddie's Adam apple bobbed hard, and Damon felt the urge to feel it against his hand, but he refrained, waiting to see what Freddie would do next. This was so new he had no idea what to expect from him.

"Strip and get on the exam table."

Damon inhaled through his nose and followed the orders, his skin heating while his fingers fumbled against his shirt buttons. He'd been naked in front of Freddie before, but not like this. He slipped the shirt from his shoulders, folded it and placed it on top of the cupboard. Repeating the action with his trousers and boxers, he faced the table. The point of no return loomed before him, and he couldn't find it in him to worry about the consequences. Not if he could have Freddie like this. Even if it was only one time.

He climbed onto the cushioned table, the paper crinkling beneath him, and rested his head on the thin pillow before stretching his legs out. He stared at the ceiling and waited, choosing not to watch what Freddie was getting ready for him. No matter what it was, he could take it. He *would* take it.

Freddie stepped to his side, his hands hidden beneath the table. Damon met his gaze, seeing a brief flash of uncertainty before Freddie hid that, too.

"Hold your arm out to the side and fold it back in until your hand touches your shoulder."

Damon swallowed and did what he'd been asked. Freddie lifted a red rope, and Damon's heart raced. He loved being tied up, and the art of shibari was something he enjoyed seeing against people's skin. The talent it took to make the patterns, to tie the knots, to have the patience to create something beautiful was highly sought after.

"Let me know if you have any problems with this," Freddie murmured.

He wrapped the rope around Damon's arm, tying it around his thumb before beginning the process of creating a work of art. Damon closed his eyes, losing himself in the motions of Freddie's hands and fingers while he threaded, wrapped and tied. His body relaxed, his spine moulding to the table.

Freddie's fingers caressing his shoulder had him opening his eyes. "How does that feel?"

"Green, Sir." Damon wasn't sure that was the right answer but *was* sure his words were slurred.

Freddie's mouth twitched. "Is it too tight?"

"No, Sir."

Freddie rounded the table, sliding his fingers down Damon's chest, his side, the outside of his thigh and calf, across the top of his feet and then up the other side of his body. Tingles followed in his wake, making Damon a live wire, electricity bubbling beneath the surface of his skin. Freddie stopped on the opposite side of him, lifting a green rope.

"Red and green, like Christmas." Freddie smiled. "I know I'm a little late with it being New Year, but…" His gaze swept down Damon's exposed body. "A Christmas gift is just what the doctor ordered. Touch your shoulder."

The moment he did, Freddie tied the rope. This time, Damon watched, the intricate braiding tying his forearm to his upper arm, the soft and gentle movements ensuring Damon didn't feel any pain, the seductive release of control. Trust was important in this scenario because Damon was now completely devoid of any ability to get himself free. And Damon trusted no one more than he did Freddie.

"Colour?" Freddie asked when he finished the last knot.

"Green, Sir." He rolled his head on the pillow, and Freddie moved towards his feet.

Freddie touched the top of his foot, making him jump, but the warmth of his hand soon bled into Damon's skin. "Now for these." He pushed Damon's foot higher until it reached his ass, the paper beneath him ripping. "Hold it there."

Damon blinked, and Freddie produced another rope, blue this time. Freddie repeated the braiding on Damon's leg, and Damon let himself float, closing his eyes and enjoying the feel of Freddie's hands on him and of the loss of control. He didn't have to think about hiding his reactions, tempering his words or actions, or the emptiness in his chest. None of it mattered at that moment.

"Damon," Freddie murmured when he finished both legs, and Damon stared into the crystal blue depths of his best friend's eyes. Freddie stroked a hand through Damon's hair. "Colour?"

"Green, Sir," he whispered.

Freddie smiled. "Good. We're going to start with the TENS machine." He paused. "What are we starting with?"

Damon blinked, allowing the words to filter into his head until he understood. He licked his lips. "The TENS machine, Sir."

"Good." Freddie disappeared, and Damon's heart rate increased until he returned. "Here. Have a sip of water." He held a straw to Damon's lips, and the refreshing liquid calmed his parched throat. "Tell me again. What are we going to start with?" he asked once he removed the drink.

"The TENS machine, Sir."

"Good. Stay nice and still for me now."

Damon almost chuckled because where would he go when he couldn't straighten his arms or legs? His calves were now tied to his thighs, knees spread and tied to the raised sides of the exam table to allow access to his extremely exposed genitals. Which is where Freddie now stood. He pulled a trolley over and settled onto a stool between Damon's thighs.

Damon swallowed, eyes locked on his best friend and what he planned to do. Freddie pulled on some gloves, the thwack sound as he let go sending goosebumps over Damon's skin, and picked up a small electrode pad. He checked it over and then focused on Damon's privates. Damon tensed as if to close his legs and hide, but the ropes stopped him. Freddie glanced up at him, a small curl to his mouth, before sticking a pad to one side of his pucker. Damon closed his eyes and exhaled, realising what was coming. Freddie placed another electrode on the other side.

"Let's start slowly, shall we?"

Freddie flicked a switch. Damon felt a small hum across his hole, but nothing that would do anything if it stayed at that level. Freddie stared at him, turning a dial. The hum increased, a warming sensation settling inside him until his anal muscles repeatedly twitched with sharp stings. Damon blew out a breath, unable to look away from Freddie, the sting continuing to rise. This was just the beginning.

Freddie switched off the machine and removed the pads. "I think we need something more." He smirked up at Damon and grabbed his cock, holding it upright before putting a pad at the base, above his balls, and another pad on his frenulum—that bundle of nerves beneath the head that was always sensitive to touch.

Damon swallowed hard and met Freddie's gaze. There was a question in Freddie's eyes, but Damon wasn't going to answer when he hadn't been asked aloud, and he certainly wasn't going to stop him.

"Let's warm you up again." Freddie flicked the switch again and turned the dial, the hum immediately racing through his shaft. The sting increased, and Damon's breath caught, his cock twitching as the current ran through him. "That's it. Beautiful," Freddie murmured, and Damon's body heated at the praise.

Damon's eyes closed, his legs and stomach straining every time it intensified. He jerked when something cold touched his pucker, his eyes flying open. Freddie was focused on his actions, and Damon relaxed as much as he could when Freddie's gloved and lubed finger breached his entrance. His cock twitched and not from the current. This was more than he'd expected from his best friend. Was having this going to break Damon when it ended?

He closed his eyes again and pushed the thought aside, uncaring for his own issues when Freddie needed him this way. He'd give up everything for Freddie. *Everything.* Including his chance to be with him.

Tears pricked behind his eyelids, trying to take in every sensation, every feeling, every scent and taste he could. The sting increased again, his dick repeatedly pulsing while Freddie's finger thrust and withdrew in his hole.

Another finger joined the first, and Damon felt the first frisson of climax heading down his spine. It was still a little way off, but the continual electric current and anal probing would get him there eventually, even if nothing else happened.

He would've been stupid to think that was the end. A third finger breached him, and this time, Freddie curled them and pressed against Damon's prostate as he increased the current at the same time. Damon's entire body seized, his breath heaving from him as he squirmed and stared at the ceiling. The intensity died down to nothing, and he panted. Freddie removed his fingers, and Damon bit his lip to stop his whine against the emptiness.

"Colour?"

"Green...Sir."

Freddie removed the electrode pads and replaced them with more, putting them on the top and bottom of each of Damon's balls. Damon watched him, and he reached for something on the trolley, the clink of metal against metal sending shivers through Damon. He couldn't see what Freddie had hold of, but he heard the squirt of what he assumed was lube. Something was going in his ass.

"Wiggle your toes for me," Freddie said, resting a hand on Damon's foot. Damon did and repeated the action on his other foot. "And now your fingers." Damon did. "Good. Now, relax for me."

Damon almost scoffed. There was nothing "relaxing" about this, and that had nothing to do with it being Freddie doing this to him. Damon inhaled and exhaled slowly, trying to do what Freddie asked, even if it was next to impossible. Something cold and hard pressed through his ring, the muscles clenching instinctively to push out the intrusion, but Damon breathed through it, bearing down and helping the toy to enter. It flared, stretching him, and then his muscles closed around it. But Freddie didn't stop. Damon panted, his ass stretching again, spreading around another nodule on whatever toy it was.

"That's it. Keep going. Almost there," Freddie murmured, eyes focused on Damon's ass.

Damon gritted his teeth and breathed through, continuing to bear down until his ass clenched around it again. He hadn't been that full for a long time, and he hoped that was all he needed to take. At least for the moment.

"Well done. You took that well. Colour?"

Damon licked his lips. "Green, Sir."

Freddie stared at him, a small smile on his face, and nodded. He refocused on his trolley and picked up a wire.

"Oh, fuck," Damon breathed.

Freddie chuckled, the sound dark and deep. "You should enjoy this."

Damon felt the dildo move inside him, and Freddie clicked the wire into the end of it. Would he survive this?

"You know what to do if it's too much," Freddie reminded him.

"Yes, Sir." Freddie raised his eyebrows, and Damon silently cursed his need for vocal confirmation. "Yellow for slow down, and cheesecake or red for stop."

"Good."

The click sounded loud despite Damon's heavy breathing, and the slow hum was warming, but it wouldn't stay that way. The current increased, sending gentle, then not-so-gentle spikes through his balls and his ass. Damon's toes curled and stretched while the intensity rose, his fingers digging into his shoulders, his lungs forgetting how to work properly. Sweat beaded on his skin, and tingles ran down his spine towards his groin that had nothing to do with the electricity currently shooting through him.

"A little more," Freddie said, and Damon's mouth gaped as he took what Freddie gave him. "A little more," he repeated.

Damon closed his eyes and arched his back, trying to hold back his orgasm. If the current continued at this level, he would come, but he hadn't been given permission yet. He gritted his teeth, beating back the fire licking at him.

Suddenly, the sensation stopped, and a whimper left him, his orgasm dialling down again, leaving him breathless and exhausted. He licked his lips and panted, not wanting to open his eyes in case he sent a glare to his best friend. As submissive as Damon was, he had an attitude with it, and it often got him into trouble with the Dominant who was with him.

Wheels rolled across the floor, but Damon kept his eyes closed.

"Colour?"

Damon paused for a second to ensure his tone was respectful. "Green, Sir."

Freddie chuckled. "The end is worth the journey. I promise."

Damon exhaled, his body humming with the leftovers of his potential orgasm, but still aroused beyond anything he could remember being. Was that because it was Freddie doing this to him? It surprised him he was still coherent, but he assumed it was because he wanted to memorise everything about the situation, knowing it was unlikely to ever happen again. A pang of pain shot through his chest, but he pushed it down.

Metal clinked, and Damon squeezed his eyes closed despite wanting to remember everything. He didn't want to *know* what Freddie was going to do—he wanted to *feel* it. The sounds continued and then paused. Damon swallowed and jerked when a gloved hand wrapped around his cock. He ignored the urge to open his eyes. The hum of the current began again, tingling through his balls and ass, setting fire to his already inflamed arousal.

"Stay completely still," Freddie ordered.

At that, Damon opened his eyes, meeting Freddie's gaze. He took in his best friend, standing between his legs, Damon's cock in his hand and a sounding rod in his other hand. Damon's breath left him, but he didn't waver. Freddie must've seen his acceptance in his eyes because he focused on his ministrations.

The moment the rod touched his dick, he tensed, but he didn't move. Freddie's concentration was completely on his movements, and so was Damon's.

5

FREDDIE

It was only Freddie's training that stopped his hands from shaking while he stood before his best friend, inserting a sounding rod into his cock. The power of being in control was nothing compared to having Damon completely at his mercy. Showing Damon exactly what Freddie liked and needed at times like these.

He pushed those thoughts aside, concentrating on carefully sliding the rod into him. Sounding was extremely pleasurable when done right, but it could cause problems if someone did it wrong. Concentration and slow, gentle movements were essential to ensure no one got hurt.

Damon hissed an indrawn breath, and Freddie paused, knowing the tingles would've begun with how far he'd inserted the rod, and flicked his gaze to him. "Colour?"

"Green, Sir."

Every time Damon said "Sir," it sent a wave of heat

through Freddie. It didn't stop his conflicted emotions from battering him.

Freddie continued, lowering the sound until it could go no further, and Damon's breathing had become choppy and raspy. He held his cock and the sound still, letting the sensations flood through Damon. Having electricity flowing through his ass, his balls and now his cock would wreak havoc with holding back his orgasm. But Freddie didn't want him to hold back this time. He wanted the climax to be *his*. He waited, letting the current do its thing, and when a particularly hard tremble went through Damon, Freddie couldn't wait any longer.

He pressed the sound against Damon's prostate. "Damon, come for me." He kept the rod in place for a few more seconds and then withdrew it a little.

Damon's gaze met his, and within seconds, his entire body tensed before spasming in hard contractions. Freddie dropped his focus to Damon's cock, watching his come dribble around the sound, escaping despite the obstruction. He slowly withdrew the sound, more and more releasing until the rod was free and come spurted. Freddie stroked Damon through the extensive contractions, bringing him down slowly and lowering the current, too. When he switched it off completely, Damon's body sank into the table, except for the occasional spasm, jerking his muscles.

Freddie removed the pads from his balls and the dildo from his ass, biting his lip at the gaping hole he felt the urge to fill with himself. He ignored it and concentrated on Damon, making short work of cleaning him up and untying his right leg. He massaged the muscles, knowing he needed to get the blood flowing again but not wanting to cause too much pain in the aftercare stage of their scene. He moved the bottom of the table to lay Damon's legs straight and untied his left leg, repeating the massage.

While focusing on Damon's arms, he monitored Damon's breathing, pulse and the colour of his skin. Everything seemed fine, but he wanted to get Damon onto the bed and wrapped in a blanket while Freddie fed and watered him. He massaged both arms and shoulders, happy with his vitals. He left him for a few seconds, getting the blanket from the bed and throwing it over him. Then he slid his arms beneath Damon's back and thighs, lifting him easily from the table, and carried him to the bed. He settled him down, tucking another blanket over him, and reached for the energy drink and fruit from the small fridge beside the bed.

Freddie settled on the edge of the bed, staring at the long lashes resting against Damon's cheek. He couldn't help but brush a hand through his untidy, sweat-soaked hair. The gift Damon had given him was worth more than anything Freddie could give in return. They'd crossed a line in playing this scene, and Freddie couldn't help but think this changed things between them, whether or not they wanted it to.

Damon's eyelids fluttered, and Freddie held his breath. Damon blinked a few times and smiled. "Thank you, Sir," he mumbled.

Freddie's heart missed a beat, but he smiled in return. "Here, drink this." He held a straw to Damon's mouth, letting him have his fill. Damon didn't usually eat anything after a scene—it was information they had talked about when generally discussing scenes and how it worked for them and others—but he wanted to give Damon the option. He held out a piece of strawberry, but Damon shook his head. Freddie put the bowl aside and focused on the drink.

"Anything else you need?" Freddie asked, wanting to make sure he hadn't forgotten what Damon needed.

"Just you," he murmured.

Freddie frowned. "Me?"

"Hold me."

Freddie paused because Damon appeared half asleep and delirious already, and he wasn't sure if that was what he truly wanted.

"Don't let me go," Damon whispered, eyes closing again.

Freddie's heart pounded, but he listened to his instincts—and that voice inside him that coaxed him to climb onto the bed and wrap his arms around his best friend, tucking his head beneath Freddie's chin. He sighed in contentment, inhaling Damon's scent as he closed his eyes, relaxing into what he wanted, even if he couldn't say it aloud.

At that moment, he let himself feel everything. Conflicting emotions of confusion, uncertainty, longing, fear, and, yes, desire. In that place, where no one else could see them, he could admit to wanting more. How could he ever find someone who understood him as Damon did? Who was always there for him like Damon was? Who could meet him at his level and keep him from going down the wrong path? Damon was all that and more.

He drifted with the warmth of Damon in his arms, and he forgot his fears, allowing himself to imagine what his life could be like if he had the confidence they would be accepted. Days spent with Damon working alongside him to better the country, evenings with their friends and families filled with laughter and love, nights with Damon wrapped in his arms while they tumbled towards sleep.

It was a rude awakening when Damon pulled free of his arms, and Freddie blinked away the sleep that had accumulated while he'd inadvertently slept.

"Are you feeling okay?" he asked, his voice hoarse.

Damon gave a tight smile and rounded the bed for his clothes. "Yes. I'm good." He pulled on his boxers, and Freddie tried not to notice his tight ass. His trousers were next, then his shirt, socks and shoes.

"Are you sure you're okay?" Freddie sat upright, one knee on the bed, one foot on the floor, his hand raking through his almost guaranteed messy hair.

"Yes."

Damon's movements proved otherwise, and usually, Freddie would push, but they'd been through a life-altering, line-crossing event, and he wasn't sure *what* to say.

"Thank you," was all he could give him.

Damon paused, resting his elbows on his knees with his head lowered. Freddie didn't think he'd reply, but when he lifted his head, Freddie's lungs stopped working.

"*Whatever* you need, *whenever* you need it. I'm here. No

matter what." He stood. "But I need to go now." He nodded, not looking at Freddie. He started for the door.

"Damon?" His best friend stopped but didn't face him. "I don't want to hurt you."

When Damon answered, Freddie wished he hadn't.

"I'm hurting myself more than you ever could."

With that, he walked out, closing Freddie in the room alone with those last words. Freddie stared at the door, rubbing at his chest.

He had no idea how long it had been since Damon had left, but a knock at the door had him coming back to himself. He unfolded himself from the bed, the ache in his limbs showing him he'd been longer than he thought. He opened the door, and Douglas stared back at him.

"Can I come in?" Douglas asked.

Freddie widened the gap and closed the door behind him, resting his back against it and gazing at the floor, not wanting to see what he and Damon had experienced, especially as Damon wasn't there.

"Damon asked me to look in on you," Douglas said.

Freddie crossed his arms over his chest. "I'm fine."

"So is Damon, apparently, but I don't believe either one of you."

Freddie tapped his fingers on his upper arm. "I knew things would change the moment I agreed to this. I should've said no."

Douglas stepped closer. "Yes, things would change, but you both needed this." He sighed. "I told Mav I wouldn't interfere, but I can't not." He gripped Freddie's chin and lifted his gaze. "You've been dancing around each other for years. I didn't realise it until recently, but when I think back, I can see all the signs. You've never found a partner because *you already have one*. Damon has been in love with you for longer than anyone can tell, and if I'm not mistaken, you love him, too. Figure it out because you'll both lose something if you don't."

Freddie's eyes filled when Douglas let go, but he blinked to stop them from falling. "I don't know how," he whispered.

"Talk. Flay your emotions bare. Whatever it takes. Don't lose him."

Freddie swallowed hard. "I…I don't know if I can."

His brother gripped Freddie's chin again, but this time, it was gentler and with his forefinger, sliding his chin upwards. "Chin up, brother. You can do anything you set your mind to." He let go and gestured to the door. "Let's go and meet everyone else. You need a drink, and it's still Eddie's birthday."

Freddie cleared his throat. "I need to clean up."

"I'll ask Oliver to sort it. You don't need to deal with this now."

Freddie nodded absently, his mind a jumble of thoughts, images and sounds, none of which he could decipher. Douglas slid an arm around his shoulders and guided him through the club until they exited into the conversation room. He pushed Freddie into a chair and disappeared, returning quickly with two shot glasses and a glass of whiskey.

"Drink," he ordered.

Freddie didn't object, downing the shots, one after the

other, and cradling the tumbler to his chest. He didn't care about getting drunk that night. He needed to get free of his confusing brain.

"Let's raise a toast to the birthday boy!" Douglas said, holding his glass high. "Happy birthday, Eddie. Wishing you all the best, even though you have to put up with these two." Douglas tilted his head to George and Timothy, and everyone laughed.

"Happy birthday!" everyone shouted.

Freddie glanced around the room, surprised to see Kean, Quinn and Kendal sitting with them. Kendal hadn't returned to the club since their attack. Had he missed them returning because he was lost in everything going on with himself?

Kendal glanced at him and smiled, but Freddie could see it was strained. Quinn reached over and clasped Kendal's hand, grabbing their attention, and Freddie watched the interaction. Quinn whispered something to them, and Kendal nodded, then shook their head. They drank their drink and smiled. Kean leaned forward, saying something Freddie couldn't hear, and made them laugh, loosening their shoulders. After everything Kendal had been through, Freddie hadn't thought they would ever return to Club Royal, but he was glad they had. He would hate for something Kendal enjoyed to be tainted completely because of one or two assholes.

He tried to make conversation, but he mainly sat there and listened while others spoke, laughing along with them. But there was an emptiness inside him—and *beside* him. Damon was nowhere to be seen, and Freddie felt the loss.

That loss continued over the following days. Freddie was supposed to have flown to the Caribbean for a week of talks with the government there, but his father had postponed the visit due to the problems they were having with Aunt Charlotte. Nobody wanted Freddie falling out of the air again, least of all himself, when he could barely persuade his body to climb up the steps of an aircraft, anyway.

And Damon was supposed to have gone with him, but other than the odd text message saying he was busy, Freddie had seen nothing of him. The longest they'd ever gone without seeing each other was a week when Freddie had flown to America and Damon had been stuck in England ill.

The impromptu free time had made Freddie uneasy. He didn't know what to do with himself, and not having Damon there made things worse. Especially when he received another message.

DAMON: I'm heading out for more audits today. Kean is with me. I'll see you when I get back.

Freddie almost threw the phone at the wall but squeezed it in his hand instead. His finger hovered over Damon's name, ready to call him when a knock sounded.

Exhaling, he said, "Come in."

"Hey, bro," George said. "Father wants to see us all."

Freddie frowned. "What about?"

George rolled his eyes. "If I knew that, I'd tell you. I'm not a mind-reader."

"Sometimes, I wonder how old you are," Freddie grated, striding to the door and nodding at Douglas and Mav.

George reached up to wrap his arm around his shoulder, having to go to his toes with their four-inch height difference. "You love me, really."

"Unfortunately." Freddie disentangled himself and continued down the hallway to their father's office. "Morning, Randall. How are you?"

Randall stood and bowed his head. "Your Highnesses. I'm good, thank you. Your father is waiting."

"Thank you." They headed for the door, and Freddie knocked and entered. "Good morning, Father." He raised his eyebrows. "Good morning, Uncle William, Aunt Victoria." He leaned down to kiss his aunt on the cheek.

"Come on in and sit down," Andrew said, waving his hand towards the uncomfortable sofa.

"Father, isn't it about time you replaced this behemoth?" George said, groaning as he took one side.

"Absolutely not! Don't you realise it's used as a weapon?"

George frowned. "What?"

"If my furniture is comfortable, people will not want to leave. If it's uncomfortable, people will be happy to finish our meetings quickly." Andrew grinned.

"But what about when it's family?" Douglas said.

"You're welcome to stand." Andrew raised his

eyebrows, the same expression he'd seen on Douglas's face many times.

Douglas sat, and Mav perched on the arm of the sofa next to him. Freddie took the centre cushion, squeezing between them.

"Okay." Andrew glanced at his siblings. "I've had a meeting with the higher management of the club." By that, he meant he'd spoken with his brothers and sisters.

"*All* of them?" Freddie asked.

Andrew grimaced. "Not quite. All those who matter." He cleared his throat. "We've decided on some changes to the club."

Freddie leaned forward, resting his arms on his knees. "In what way?"

The corner of Andrew's mouth curled. "Good ways, I believe. *We* believe."

"Spit it out!" George said.

Andrew narrowed his eyes at his youngest son, who muttered an apology. "For the past two decades, we've been working at getting things changed on a foundational level within the club. It's not easy to change things, and it's taken time. Finally, we're able to let you know what those changes are."

Freddie couldn't decide if his father's words were accidentally or purposefully vague, but he held his tongue.

William sat forward. "We're going to remove the mandatory membership for royal members."

Freddie stopped breathing. "Why?"

"It's unnecessary," Victoria said. "Not everyone is into this lifestyle, and forcing them into it could make them feel antagonistic towards the family. Although the requirement was there to help bond us together and help with certain teachings needed to strengthen a royal, we feel this downside is more potent. There are other ways to teach those who do not want to be part of the club."

"Everyone will still be told about the club and, therefore, NDAs will be needed no matter what," Andrew explained. "As for keeping the family together, I don't think we have too much of a problem with that part of things." He smiled.

"We would like to keep the royal members as the Monitors, but we're not making anyone learn anything they do not want to. If they want to be submissive, they can be. They do not have to train as a Dominant or train in any speciality if they don't want to." William nodded. "Obviously, we might have to revisit this if there are fewer family members who want to be part of the club. We might have to go further afield for Monitors if that happened."

Freddie couldn't believe they were making these changes. He glanced at his father, who nodded at him with a small smile. Everything Freddie had come to Andrew about, the problems he'd seen and experienced, the issues brought to his attention, had all been listened to.

There was one thing they hadn't mentioned. "What about...?" Freddie halted.

Andrew stepped closer, crouching in front of Freddie, tears glistening in his eyes. "We're going to allow certain people within the judicial system to know about what we do. It will allow us to prosecute those who need to be without worrying that it will expose the information to the media and will take the weight of punishing them ourselves from our shoulders."

Uncaring about how he usually hid his feelings, Freddie hugged his father. He'd been trying to figure out a way to get people the justice they deserved without involving the police, and it was a tricky subject. People like Kendal and Umar, who were put into situations they shouldn't have been in, but because of the club's rules, weren't as easily supported as they should've been.

"I can't believe you've done that," Douglas said.

Freddie pulled back, grinning at his brother. "Helping subs became a whole lot easier."

His father settled back in his seat, wiping his face. "We still have to be careful," he cautioned. "No white knight complexes, please."

Freddie nodded. "Understood."

6

DAMON

Staying away from Freddie was slowly killing him. Damon hadn't heard his voice for three days, but it was a necessary evil, as far as he was concerned. He'd gone to his meeting with Andrew without dropping by on Freddie, even though his feet wanted him to take him that way. When Andrew had seen him, he'd asked Damon to visit a few more companies for their audits, not wanting to make it seem like they weren't bothering with them now. Damon had jumped at the chance, even more so when Andrew told him Kean would join him.

Their driver had picked Damon up first and then Kean.

"Morning," Damon said with a smile. "Any clue what to expect?"

Kean chuckled. "Not really. Andrew asked me if I wanted to learn something about the royal businesses, and as my background is in business, I couldn't resist. I'm not really sure what it is."

Damon opened his suitcase. "Well, I have some news for you. Auditing these businesses is only the tip of the iceberg." He pulled some files free.

"Andrew mentioned an extra benefit to the audits but not what that benefit was."

"He's given me permission to let you in on what's going on."

Damon spent the two-hour journey filling Kean in on the problems with Charlotte and John, the not-so-accidental accidents, and everything else they suspected. He told him about the three companies he'd found, which might be nothing at all, but it was what this visit was about.

"These companies are listed on four separate companies' accounts, and we need to figure out exactly who they are and what they do. Whenever I've tried, I've been taken in circles until I can't think straight. We need to see if we can link these companies to any other businesses within the royal family."

"Wow. I didn't realise things went so deep," Kean said, staring at the documents Damon had given him.

"Deeper than you believe. We know it's Charlotte's doing, but we can't prove it yet. The moment we can, all bets are off." *And everyone is safe.*

Freddie's face came to the forefront of his mind, and his heart jumped. Removing Freddie from the path of danger was what made Damon agree to this whole charade in the first place. Now, though, it was keeping himself away from Freddie that he needed to do. The scene from three days ago was always at the edge of his thoughts, waiting to press in on him and make him remember what it felt like to be Freddie's sole focus. To be held tightly in his arms. To be taken care of. But the emptiness he felt in his chest and stomach told him it was a fleeting moment. One that couldn't be repeated because Freddie had too many people relying on him. And an heir with a male partner wasn't something the country was ready for, despite Douglas and George having them. The only way they would become king was if something happened to Freddie, and Damon refused to consider that option.

As he sat beside Kean, discussing their plans, he relinquished the hope that he could be more than Freddie's best friend. Freddie's first responsibility was to the crown, and Damon's couldn't be part of that as anything more. He pushed aside any optimism he had and focused on providing Freddie and his family with the ammunition to bring Charlotte down. If that was all he could do, he'd be happy because it meant Freddie would be safe.

"Do you want to talk about it?" Kean asked two days later.

Damon huffed a laugh and shook his head, continuing to stare out of the hotel window. They'd spent two days at the first company, being given the runaround until Damon had put his foot down. They'd finally been given complete access two hours before the end of the day on Friday.

Damon had shown his displeasure by forcing the bosses to work that weekend to make up for the wasted time. They spent eight hours going through the files, and they had more to do the following day, too. Then on Monday, they planned to travel to the next company.

This would be the first time he'd spent more than a week without seeing Freddie because he wasn't due back at Windsor until the event in eleven days. It hurt his heart, but they needed the time apart. Freddie, to forget about what they'd done, and Damon, to push it all down and lock it in a box, not to ever bring it out again. That was the only way they could stay friends.

"Damon?"

He sighed. "There's too much to even go into. Life never turns out how you expect it to." He turned from the window and faced Kean in time to see his cheeks redden.

"True," he mumbled.

Damon raised his eyebrows. "Something *you* need to talk about?"

Kean rubbed his cheeks, ducking his head. Then he lifted his head. "Do you know what? Yes, I do. I'm completely up shit creek without a paddle."

Silence greeted his words, and then Damon started laughing, the belly-aching kind that had him leaning on his knees. Kean joined in, and after several long, hilarious minutes, they subsided. Damon reached for the minibar.

"I think we're going to need this." He grabbed several small bottles of alcohol and put them on the table, sinking into a plush armchair beside it. He waved towards the other chair. "Come on. Drink and spill."

Kean took a vodka, cracked it open and downed the entire bottle, coughing a little when he finished. "I'm in love with Andrew."

Damon stared at him, the bottle of whiskey halfway to his mouth. He threw the drink back, grimacing. "Okay. Not quite what I was expecting, but okay."

Kean drained another bottle. "I'm also in love with Kendal."

Damon had taken a drink, and he coughed it back up, spluttering into a wad of napkins. He wiped his eyes and winced when he swallowed, his throat raw. "Not quite simple, then. And I thought me being in love with Freddie was a problem."

Kean smiled at him and shrugged, holding up another bottle for a toast. "Brothers-in-arms?"

Damon laughed. "Definitely. Welcome to one hell of a ride."

They clinked glasses and swallowed another drink, the burn seriously hurting his sore throat, but Damon didn't care.

"What arc you going to do about Freddie?" Kean asked, settling back with a beer instead of anything stronger.

"Nothing. He has the weight of the crown on his shoulders, and being with me would cause more problems than it would help." He hadn't censored his words, but he wished he had when Kean's shoulders slumped. "Sorry," he whispered. "If you see a way out of this shitstorm, let me know." He sighed. "Do you know how either of them feels about you?"

Kean shook his head. "I hate to use the word, but Kendal's emotional state is too fragile to mess around with. Being their friend is the best I can hope for, but I would do anything for them. Anything."

"And Andrew?" Damon prompted when Kean went quiet.

"To quote someone I know, 'the weight of the crown is on his shoulders.' How could a relationship with me make things any easier for him? Plus, the age difference itself would cause an uproar. I'm younger than all three of his sons."

Damon winced. "It's not impossible, but I know what you mean."

"Neither has shown any sign they feel the same way. The best I can do is help protect the crown and be there if either needs me."

"I hear you."

They dropped into silence, each lost in their own thoughts. But Damon's were alive with possibilities for the first time in a long time. If Kean, Andrew and Kendal got together, they could pave the way for the rest of the royal family. No one would need to worry about their orientation when the king was in a relationship with men. It was unheard of, but Andrew had already made headlines by becoming the first out and proud bisexual king on the throne. Why not hope for more?

He had to be careful. Finding out Andrew's feelings for Kean was the first port of call because if Andrew felt nothing, it was a moot point. Maybe he could speak to Brett or

Kieren and get their opinions on it. Which reminded him…

He pulled his phone free and dialled.

"Locke."

"Hey, it's Damon."

She sighed. "You should really call him, you know."

"I know, but it's tricky. How is he?"

"In high spirits. Not sure exactly what's happened, but they're having a celebration of some sort."

Damon frowned. "Who?"

"The Thirsty Thirteen. Well, minus one." Her tone told him how she felt about that.

"I'm glad they're having fun. They need it." He sighed. "Thanks, Locke."

"Call him, and soon. Otherwise, I'll tell him you keep checking up on him."

"You're evil." His tone was dark, but he grinned.

"The worst. Bye."

He put his phone on the table and sighed again, rubbing at his jaw. What had happened? It couldn't have been anything to do with Charlotte because Andrew would've called him off the search. Maybe it was time.

He picked up his phone again and dialled, barely giving him a chance to talk himself out of it.

"Hey!" Freddie said, the smile in his voice apparent.

"Hey. What's going on?"

"You should be here! It's a celebration of the changing of the times."

Damon frowned. "What?"

"Father has changed the rules for the club. It's

making it easier for everyone. He listened to my—our—ideas about what they should change. We did it, Damon."

He placed his hand over his mouth, staring at the floor. "Why?"

"They'd been working behind the scenes for years to change things, but they needed us to decide what we wanted the club to be going forward before they could bring in any particular changes. When we started going to him with our thoughts and the complaints from members, they started putting the changes in place."

"All of them?" he asked.

"*All of them!*" Freddie said.

"Holy shit."

It wasn't until the silence descended between them that he realised they had spoken without thought to their situation. He didn't want to bring Freddie down by reminding him and kept quiet.

"I wish you were here with us," Freddie murmured.

"Me, too." Damon closed his eyes. "I'm sorry for—"

"No. No more sorrys. Do your job and come home. That's all I want."

Damon wanted nothing more than to see Freddie's face at that moment because his tone of voice wasn't advertising whether his meaning was more personal or that he wanted to celebrate with Damon. Usually, Damon could tell if he was physically with Freddie.

"I'll be back as soon as I can."

"Glad to hear it."

They fell quiet again, something unusual for them, but

Damon didn't know how to fill it for a change. It didn't feel uncomfortable, but it wasn't their usual state.

"Anyway, I better let you get some sleep. I hear things are tricky over there."

Damon snorted. "You could say that. I love being able to throw my weight around."

"I thought you preferred having control taken from you?"

Freddie's voice had deepened, sending Damon back to the room they'd used. Damon's breath caught, and he breathed through the ache in his throat that had nothing to do with coughing strong spirits. "Only in certain circumstances," he murmured and glanced at Kean, who was busy on his phone, pretending not to hear the conversation.

"Hmm," Freddie said. "Don't be a stranger, D. I couldn't stand it."

"I won't. I promise."

"Get some rest."

"Yes, Your Highness." Damon grinned when Freddie cursed at him. "Goodnight, Freddie."

"Night."

Damon didn't want to hang up, but he made himself press the red circle. The conversation had gone easier than he'd expected, but it made him want to be back with him, and he needed to stop thinking like that.

"Everything okay?"

Damon blinked at Kean and smiled, nodding towards Kean's phone. "I'm sure you've heard the news by now."

Kean grinned. "Henry couldn't wait to tell me. I'm not

sure I understand the ramifications of it because I've not been part of the club that long, but I can see it's a big thing for them."

"It is. It's a huge step forward in accepting everyone as they are instead of trying to squash them into certain characteristics where they don't fit. I know there will be backlash, but all in all, it's a good thing." He glanced at Kean. "Andrew might need your support more than ever."

Kean sighed. "I'll be there no matter what." He stood. "I'm going to bed after drinking far too much in too short a time. If I have a headache tomorrow, I'm blaming you."

Damon chuckled. "Blame me all you want, but you still have to work."

Kean held up his middle finger and strode for the hotel room door. "Don't stay up too late."

"Yes, Mum."

When Kean closed Damon inside his room, the quiet seemed loud. Damon returned his gaze to the window, staring at nothing and getting lost in his memories.

A week later, Damon was ready for his job to finish. The companies, however approachable they appeared, were not happy when it came to him checking their work. Understandable, but as far as Damon was concerned, if they had nothing to hide, they shouldn't worry about it. From experience, most companies had *something* to hide, even if it was that they weren't filing their paperwork correctly.

Damon and Kean exited the hotel entrance, heading for

the car that waited to take them to the last company to look at for this round of audits. It was a Monday, which meant they'd be working extra hours again because they only had until the following day, and each visit took between two and four days, depending on how "open" they were. They might have to come back to this company if they weren't helpful.

"Do you have any questions?" Damon asked Kean as he always did first thing in the morning when they first settled into the back of the town car.

The car pulled away, and Damon checked his phone while waiting for Kean's answer. He and Freddie had messaged back and forth over the past week, and they'd even had a few brief conversations, but Damon hated not being able to see him in person.

"Not really. I understand what we're looking for now and how to find it. It makes it easier when I'm swimming in data." Kean huffed a laugh.

"Yeah, those numbers swim too often when I'm staring at them." Damon put the phone back in his pocket and sighed. "One more to go."

"How many more are there to look at after this?"

"There are still at least eight more we need to audit, but I think we've found what we will. Unless we were really unlucky and left the most beneficial ones to last." Damon snorted. "I wouldn't put it past us. Our luck doesn't seem to have been on our side for most of the past two years."

"Things are looking up," Kean said. "We'll figure it out."

Damon nodded and stared out of the window. "We will." He frowned, studying their surroundings. "Kevin, I think the satnav is taking us in the wrong direction," he said to their driver. Kevin had been Patrick's driver until Patrick stopped working for his father, and then Brett had moved him to help Damon with his visits.

"Kevin isn't here right now," an icy voice told him.

Damon glanced into the rearview mirror, meeting the glacier-blue eyes of someone who wasn't their driver. "Where's Kevin?"

"He's taking a long-needed nap."

Goosebumps ran down Damon's spine, and he swallowed through his constricting throat. "Where are you taking us?"

The eyes crinkled at the corners, and the voice sent chills through him. "It was as easy to get to you as it was to get to Timothy. You think you're invincible."

Kean tugged at Damon's arm, and he glanced at him. Kean showed him his phone, which had no signal at all. Damon peered out of the window again, seeing fewer and fewer buildings. What the fuck were they going to do? They could jump out of the car, but they'd be hurt by how fast the car was going. They'd have to fight their way out when they get to their destination. He stared at Kean, the fear in his expression sending an ache through his chest. Brett had trained Damon in hand-to-hand combat and weapons training, but Kean had none of that.

"Where are you taking us?" Damon repeated.

"Somewhere no one will find you until we decide they should. Somewhere not even the king knows about."

Damon swallowed hard, knowing what they were about to experience would put his training to shame. Were they even going to survive? His thoughts went to Freddie, and a sense of calm fell over him. If this was the end of Damon's life, at least he had given himself to Freddie, and he was leaving him to find someone he could love. He'd done everything he could to protect the crown and its descendants. It was fate's turn to help now.

When the car pulled to a stop, and the driver got out, Damon covered Kean's hand. "Whatever they ask, tell them. It doesn't matter if you think you're causing problems for anyone. You won't be. Tell them whatever they ask. Promise me?"

Kean nodded. "Okay."

"And don't worry about me. If you get the chance to run, you run. Understood."

Kean nodded again, tears glistening.

The door opened, and hands grabbed Damon, dragging him from the car to the ground. He heard scuffles, and the driver threw Kean beside him.

"Hello, boys."

Damon glanced up at the voice. *Oh, fuck.*

7

FREDDIE

reddie tried not to feel annoyed that Damon had not replied to his last message. Instead, it had been left as delivered for the last six hours. Damon was busy, but too busy to look at his phone? What were they doing?

"Your Highness?"

Freddie glanced up at Brett and blinked. "Sorry." He shook his head and put away his phone.

Brett didn't look pissed off at him, which was surprising because this was probably the fourth or fifth time he'd had to gain Freddie's attention during the hour-long update Freddie had asked for. "We still don't know where the vases came from. The information the hotel gave the police led to a dead-end company. No paper trails. Nothing."

"And the people who were hurt, how are they now?"

"They're all fine. Back home and at work like it never happened."

Freddie exhaled. "Maximum amount of fear with few casualties. Was that the entire point? To make people scared?"

Brett held out his hands. "We can only assume. The amount of explosives in each vase wouldn't take a building down, even if they put all of it together. It basically made a lot of noise."

A knock sounded, and Freddie called for them to enter. Christian came in with his dog, Oreo. Despite only having had her for a couple of months, Oreo was already well-trained. She stayed at Christian's side until he waved his hand and then bounded over to Freddie and Brett. Freddie scooted to the edge of his seat, uncaring about any dog hairs that might get on his suit—it wasn't like he didn't have twenty others in his wardrobe if he needed them—and fussed over the little Labrador. Although little was relative. She was already twice the size from when Christian got her.

"Afternoon," Brett said. "I thought you were staying close to Oscar today?"

Christian sighed and settled next to Freddie. "I was, but Hilary ordered me to leave because Oscar kept slipping into little mode."

Freddie frowned, scratching Oreo's ear. "Does he need it?"

"Not at the moment. He's been sinking into it easier and more often lately, possibly because of everything going on. I'm wondering if it's because I'm there. I mentioned that to Hilary, and she told me to leave to see if it made a difference. She said she'd call if it didn't."

"Let me know if there's anything I can do."

Christian raised his eyebrows. "I think you're doing enough, aren't you?"

Freddie clenched his jaw. "It's not enough."

"It never will be. At least, that's what it'll feel like," Brett said. "Until we get a break, it'll never feel like we're doing enough to keep people safe. To keep *you* safe."

"You don't need to worry about me. We all need to concentrate on those who are in the fallout areas." Freddie sighed. "Those people caught in the aftermath of it all."

"That's not our fault," Christian said.

"Maybe not, but will they see it that way?" Freddie met Christian's gaze, seeing the answer in his eyes. "Anyway, is Oscar excited about tomorrow?"

Christian's eyes lit up. "He is. That could also be part of the reason he's close to being Ozzie. I can't wait to see his face when he wakes up to his presents. I persuaded Wally to join us for breakfast in the morning as an additional surprise."

Freddie grinned. "I bet he'll love that. It's been a while since he's seen Wally, hasn't it?"

Christian nodded. "Yeah. Donovan took him and the kids to the Caribbean for a month. They only got back on Saturday."

"Well, remember, you can't keep him to yourself all day. We have plans for him, too," Brett said.

"And us," Freddie added. "He's going to be spoilt rotten."

They laughed, and Freddie checked his phone again when Brett left them, shaking his head.

"What's wrong?" Christian asked.

"Nothing."

"There's definitely something."

"Damon's not answering his messages." Freddie sighed and rested his head on the back of the sofa.

"I know something happened between you and Damon, but for him to stay away for so long is unlike him."

"It is, but it's the job that's taken him away this time, not because of what happened. I'm sure that would've done something."

"What happened?"

Freddie hesitated, but everyone knew each other's business, mostly anyway. "We crossed the friendship line, and I don't know if we can get it back."

"You slept with him?"

Freddie shook his head. "We played. For the first time ever. But..." Images flashed in Freddie's mind, and he couldn't regret sharing that with his best friend.

"But what?"

Freddie froze and then said the one thing that scared him the most. "I want more, but I didn't think I was gay."

"You know what we do. It doesn't matter what label you think you have; you can be whatever you want to be. Maybe you only like Damon. I know you've played with men before, as most of us have. How did you feel about them?"

"Nothing. Like it was a job."

Christian stared at him. "What does Damon want?"

"I don't know. But it can't happen, Chris. What do you think the public would think of having an heir with a male partner?"

"Who gives a damn?"

Freddie glared at him. "You know better than that."

Christian sighed. "Talk to your father. He'll be able to give you the best course of action and do it before Damon comes back. That way, if you decide to go ahead, you can start from the moment he's here."

"I don't know."

Christian pushed to his feet. "Regardless, you need to do something."

"He's due back tomorrow night if everything goes according to plan. Otherwise, it will be Wednesday lunchtime."

"Are you working tonight?"

Freddie was grateful for the change of subject. "Yes. Unfortunately, so are Lottie and Arthur."

Christian winced at his siblings' names. "Stay away from them, and they'll stay away from you, maybe."

"I want them to try something. The mood I'm in, I'll kick them out of the club faster than anyone can complain."

Christian laughed. "I'd pay to see that."

"What are you talking about? You'd be helping."

They laughed, and some of the ache in his chest eased. He wished he could see Damon and figure out if what he was feeling was reciprocated. But even if it was, did they have a chance?

"I've heard nothing from him in three days!" Freddie paced his suite with Douglas, Mav, George and Christian watching.

"He's been busy, Freddie," Douglas said. "It's not exactly a minor job he's been given."

"He said he'd be back by today. We're heading out in less than half an hour, and he's still not here!"

"Let's go to the event. I'm sure he'll turn up with an excuse." Christian clapped Freddie's shoulder, squeezing.

"I still don't like the idea of you being there," George said.

"We can't have the same people going to the events. We have to mix it up. Freddie didn't go to your event, George, so it's his turn," Christian said.

"Doesn't mean I have to like it."

"We're supporting Mary. It's been a while since she did an event like this, and to then be the focus of a potential threat is not pleasant." Freddie sighed. "I don't like anyone attending events at the moment, but we have to. We can't let Aunt Charlotte make us go into hiding. She's won half the battle if that happens."

"Why do you still call her 'Aunt?' She's not much of one," George asked.

Freddie shrugged. "Habit."

"Well, stop. It's creepy." George pouted, staring at his phone.

"Aren't you a bundle of joy?" Freddie said.

George glared at him. "Back at you."

Freddie allowed that, although chatting had helped him to forget about the one person who could usually talk him down and make him ready to attend these events. It was like he was missing something without Damon by his side. He hadn't taken Christian's advice about speaking to his father. Andrew was the last person he wanted to explain his situation to at that moment. There wasn't anything he could do to help because, despite what his family thought, the public would not be as supportive as they thought they would. It would be too big of a change for them to adjust to. At least, that was what he thought.

"Come on. Let's go. I'll keep an eye on him. There's plenty of security and lots of protocols in place," Christian said.

George winced, and Freddie frowned. "What's really wrong, George?"

"I'm worried. Go. I'll be fine."

Christian led him to the door, but Freddie couldn't get rid of the itch that told him something wasn't right. He couldn't figure out what it was, and he ignored it as best he could.

Mary was the ambassador for this specific charity, but it was one they all loved—The Children's Helper Elves. It raised money to help families with children who have long-term caring needs, providing financial aid for costly equipment and medication.

The event was busy, more when word spread that Freddie was there. Their guards, Brett, Locke and Owen, stuck to them like glue, except when they greeted the people they walked near, receiving handshakes and smiles from them until Freddie begged for a breather. The guards escorted him and Christian into a slightly less packed hallway, and Freddie leaned against the wall, banging his head back and staring at the ceiling.

"I don't remember these events being this stressful," he commented, wishing Damon was with him. He could always make him laugh at the most inopportune moments.

Christian rested beside him. "It's the stress of not knowing if something's going to happen. Every interaction is fraught with potential."

"I wish he'd message me," Freddie murmured.

"Tomorrow, we'll speak to Uncle Andrew. He might know something. They probably got delayed with the audit."

"But why wouldn't he message to say so? Even if he's mad at me, he wouldn't leave me hanging about something like this."

Christian faced him, keeping his voice low. "Maybe he needs time to sort where his head's at. Same as you." He paused. "I assume you didn't speak to your father?" Freddie said nothing, which was an answer in itself. "Yeah, didn't think so."

"I'm scared, Chris," he whispered, checking around to make sure no one was close enough to hear. "I'm not my father. I'm not perfect like he is. I'll never measure up to what he's given this country."

"You don't need to, Freddie. You need to be *you*. If you try to be your father, of course, you'll fail because you're not him. Lean into *your* strengths, *your* vision, *your* version of perfection." Christian stepped in front of him, making Freddie look at him, even when his stomach was rolling. "Don't forget, he changed the rules of the club because of your comments."

"Ah, I see you're the one to blame for the new, so-called improvements to the rules, are you?"

The brittle voice of their aunt shattered their quiet conversation, and the guards surrounded them when Charlotte stopped several feet away. He could only describe her dress as a Victorian-era knock-off, but with an unhealthy amount of black, as if she was in mourning. Someone had coiled her hair onto her head, leaving her slim neck exposed, and Freddie had an unbecoming urge to grab a sword and bring back the death penalty—executioner style.

She rolled her eyes and shook her head. "As if I'd do anything at such an event like this."

"What do you want?" Freddie asked. "Should you even be here?"

She placed her hand on her chest and gasped theatrically. "No one would dare ask me to leave when I've donated such a large sum of my personal accounts to this worthy cause, surely?"

Freddie gritted his teeth and stared at her. If it had been a movie, fire would stream from his eyeballs and incinerate her on the spot. He pushed aside his fantastical thoughts and focused on the person who made their lives hell.

"I'm sure people would understand if you had a prior

engagement that makes it impossible for you to stay for too long," he said.

She linked her fingers and rested them in front of her. "Well, it so happens...I don't." She lifted her chin, the corner of her mouth curling.

"How's Juliet's pregnancy?" Christian asked, stepping to the side of the guard. "I hear it's been a *long* pregnancy."

Charlotte's eyes narrowed. "It's going well."

"Really? When is she due? Because there's been some conflicting information. I distinctly remember you being excited about the due date of 20 November." He tapped his chin. "But that date's been and gone, and surprise! No baby." Christian glanced over his shoulder at Freddie. "Didn't you say that Charles had told Patrick she was due on 10 March?"

"That's right. Aww. Maybe he's not good at maths." Freddie put his bottom lip out.

Charlotte gave a tight smile, but Freddie noticed her fingers turning white. "The baby will have a wonderful family when it arrives."

"Minus Charles," Freddie said. "Being in prison as he is."

Charlotte smirked. "Oh, didn't you know? The police released him on Monday."

Freddie's heart skipped a beat, and his lungs forgot how to work. *What the hell?* He shared a glance with Christian. "Isn't that wonderful news?" he said, noticing a couple entering the hallway behind his aunt.

Charlotte peered over her shoulder and sighed. "Well,

it was lovely catching up with you both. I hope to see you soon." She smiled. "Some of you sooner than others," she added and swished her skirt, whirling around and away from them.

The pit in Freddie's stomach increased. Something had to be done. They had to have missed something that pointed to her. They had to. And what the hell with releasing Charles?

"Uncle Andrew, Charlotte was here." Freddie glanced at Christian when he started talking, realising he was on the phone. "No, nothing's happened. Just her with her bitter remarks. She brought up some not-so-wonderful news. Charles is out." Christian stared at the wall, listening to what Freddie's father said. They couldn't take the chance of putting it on speaker in an unknown place like this. "Okay. We will." He ended the call. "Uncle Andrew wants us home. Mary, too."

"I second that," Brett said. "There's no telling what she did while she was here."

Freddie's stomach burned hotter, and if he clenched his jaw any harder, he would break it. "This has to end," he gritted out, storming towards the exit with his bodyguards scrambling to cover him.

"Your Highness, slow down," Brett said. "Don't get yourself killed because you're angry."

Freddie pivoted and faced him. "Angry? Angry doesn't even cover what I am right at this moment, Brett. I don't even think rage would be a good enough descriptor."

Owen rested a hand on his arm. "Even so, Your Highness, we need you protected to help take her down," he murmured.

Freddie stared at his bodyguard, breathing through the boiling pit in his stomach. After a few deep breaths, he nodded.

"Delta, it's time to go," Brett said, pressing against his ear. "Edinburgh and Cardiff are heading home."

Christian settled beside him in the car when they finally escaped from the event some twenty minutes later. They didn't see Charlotte again, luckily, because Freddie didn't know if he would've been able to refrain from choking her. He'd never had as many dark thoughts as he had when she was the topic of conversation. She'd spawned Charles, who was more brawn than brain. She had to have made a mistake somewhere.

"She'll get what's coming to her," Christian said. "Karma is a bitch like that."

"If I get my hands on her, karma won't have the chance."

"You'd have to wait in line."

Freddie glared at his cousin. "I'm the heir to the throne. I don't wait," he said haughtily, managing not to laugh, despite the seriousness of the situation.

"Well, if you're going with that train of thought, your father gets the first punch."

Freddie snapped his mouth closed and pouted. "You're mean."

Christian laughed, causing Freddie to join in, releasing some of the tension in his body. "I didn't say you couldn't do it."

"Maybe I could sweet talk Father into letting me go first. Sort of like torturing heir in training?" He snorted and set Christian off again.

It was nice to push aside the cloak of nastiness that Charlotte left over them. He hadn't wanted to take it back to Windsor, and what would've usually been Damon's job had been done brilliantly by Christian.

"Thank you," he said when they'd stopped laughing.

Christian tapped Freddie's chin. "Always."

Freddie checked his phone, the message to Damon still showing as delivered but no reply. "What are you doing, Damon?" he murmured.

8

CHRISTIAN

Christian had tried his hardest to distract Freddie from worrying about Damon, and it seemed to have worked for now. He had no qualms that it would last longer than a few hours if he was lucky, but it had helped some. Having Charlotte attend the event hadn't helped matters, and everyone was stressed and pissed off, especially him. He'd had enough of her, and they needed to shut this down once and for all.

They dropped Freddie home first, and Brett drove Christian to Oscar. He needed to hold Oscar and be reminded of how precious life was. It was hard to do when Charlotte made him want to kill her. It wasn't often he felt that way, but with her, it was easy. Oscar could soothe his soul in a way no one else could.

His little had waited up for him, and Christian banded his arms around him the moment he closed the front door.

"Hey, sweetheart," he murmured.

"Are you okay?"

Christian sighed. "I've been better." He pulled back and cupped Oscar's cheeks, dropping a kiss on his lips. "Let me make some hot chocolate, and I can tell you about it." He led Oscar towards the kitchen.

Despite not wanting to give his boyfriend more things to worry about, he refused to leave him in the dark. If something happened while Christian wasn't with him, he wanted Oscar to have every piece of information possible in his arsenal to ensure he stayed alive. If that meant giving him difficult and sad news, then he would.

They settled onto the stools at the breakfast table, thigh to thigh, and Christian explained what had happened with Charlotte at the event. Oscar squirmed with the need to withdraw into his little space, but he didn't, and Christian was proud of him.

"Charles is out already?" Oscar whispered.

"Yes. I can't believe no one knew. I'll have to ask Uncle Andrew to check with Commissioner Thomas about it. Usually, he's the first person to call about things like this." Christian slid an arm around Oscar's shoulders. "It'll be fine. We're well protected." He said the words, but he hated he had doubts.

"How's Freddie?"

Christian blew out a breath. "Not great. Messed up that Damon's not responding to his messages. You were right about them." He grinned. "When they finally admit it to themselves, I think we'll all see the fireworks."

Oscar's cheeks flushed. "I think it's quite adorable how

they don't even realise. They may as well be in a relationship already with how they are with each other."

"I'm sure we can be kind and point that out soon." Christian chuckled and pressed a kiss to Oscar's temple. "Damon needs to answer Freddie soon, or Freddie will go searching for him. Appointments be damned."

"To be a fly on the wall if that happens."

"You want to be a voyeur, do you?" Christian murmured, trailing his lips along Oscar's jaw.

"Oh!" Oscar closed his eyes and tilted his head to give Christian better access. "I never thought of it like that."

Christian nipped at his earlobe. "You want to watch someone? See their cock disappear inside another person while I do the same to you?"

"Um... Oh, um... What?"

Christian grazed his teeth back along Oscar's jaw to his mouth. "I'm sure that can be arranged." He kissed him, and Oscar opened immediately, tangling their tongues and helping them to forget their problems, even if for a short time.

Tomorrow would come soon enough, and with it, answers they probably didn't want.

9

DAMON

"How have you enjoyed the accommodations these past two days?"

The moment the sneering voice started talking, Damon wanted to punch the person it came from, though that was highly unlikely with his arms shackled above his head. Charles stepped closer, and Damon lifted his pounding head to glare at him. It was all he had the energy for.

"Tut, tut, tut. So impolite."

Damon coughed to clear his parched throat, hissing when his chest ached. "You've made an error being here in person, Charles."

Charles laughed, the sound echoing around the cavernous area bisected by steel bars that created cages—or prison cells. "No one knows where you are. No one knows where I am—except for a few select people. No one has any clue this place even exists." Charles waved his hands around them.

"Where's Kean?" Damon coughed again, spitting a wad of blood on the floor.

Charles laughed. "Enjoying some alone time in a different part of this place."

Damon had no idea what state Kean was in. Charles had ordered the driver to take Kean, and another guy had grabbed Damon. The last vision he had of the man was of his terrified expression. If Charles had done to Kean what they'd done to him—god help Charles when Damon got his hands on him.

Another cough wracked his body, and a shiver followed in its wake. He had a feeling he had an infection from one of the many cuts he'd been given. Nothing to end his life, but plenty to hurt him. From what he could tell, he had bruised, possibly broken ribs; black eyes, one of which was almost closed; a bruised jaw; and bruises and cuts all over his body. Charles had ordered him to be stripped naked and hung up by his wrists, the soles of his feet barely touching the floor.

"Anyway, back to business. Tell me what you found from your 'audits.'" Charles made air quotes with his fingers.

It was the same question he'd asked every time he visited. And Damon gave the same answer, everything he could except about those three companies. He had no idea if Kean had given up the information, but Damon refused to cave. If they realised he'd found them, it might make things worse for everyone. Damon had no evidence to back that up other than his instincts, and that was all he had at the moment.

"It's almost as if you're repeating a speech prepared by George," Charles huffed. "Surely you found something?"

"The managers of those businesses were crap at keeping records in any kind of order. But they kept records. I found nothing, which is what we had hoped for. But with your line of questioning, I guess it means I've been looking in the right direction and getting a little too close."

Charles gritted his teeth. Damon couldn't see it, but he could hear the grinding. "I don't believe you."

Damon coughed again. "That's your prerogative."

Charles kicked at Damon's legs, sending him spinning before Damon could gain traction with his feet again. He hissed at the pain streaking through him, but he refused to make any other acknowledgement.

"Get him down," Charles ordered.

Two men came towards him, and Damon tried to brace himself on his feet to stay upright when his weight returned, but the moment they uncuffed his wrists, he fell to his hands and knees, swallowing a groan. Hands gripped his hair and dragged him vertically, his knees still resting on the floor.

"Say cheese," Charles said, and a blinding flash of light briefly lit the room. "I'm sure this will go over well with your 'friends' when they receive it." Charles chuckled.

"You're going to hell, Charles," Damon croaked.

"No, not me. I've seen the way you look at Frederick. You're one of the people we're working to eradicate from this family."

Damon coughed. "Aww, you called me family."

Charles kicked him in the chest. The man holding his hair could not stop Damon's backward momentum and took a chunk of his hair when Damon was ripped from his hands. Damon curled in on himself, trying to protect his most vulnerable parts in case Charles continued his assault.

"There is no way you're family. No matter how you look at your best friend, he won't take the risk of alienating the population."

Damon laughed, which turned into more coughing. "You're hoping, anyway."

"He values the public too much to take the risk," Charles argued.

Damon ignored the spike arrowing through his chest at the words that he had told himself too many times to count. Hearing Charles agree was something he didn't want. "Does he? What about Douglas and George? They're in relationships with men."

"They'll never be king," Charles spat. "Thank god."

"Charles." Damon used his shaking hands to push himself to sitting, resting back against the cold, bare brick wall. "If you want an outlet for the feelings you have towards men, all you need to do is slake it at the club." He coughed, holding his ribs. "You don't need to take me prisoner and strip me naked to get your rocks off." He was baiting him, but he couldn't resist. He doubted anyone would find them, and if he could annoy the hell out of Charles before he left his world, he would.

Charles stepped forward but paused when an unfamiliar voice said, "Your Highness? It's time."

Freddie's cousin stared at Damon for several long minutes, his face highlighting all the things he wanted to do to Damon—and not the pleasurable kind, not that he wanted that from Charles.

"We're not finished, but you'll wish we were." He faced the man who'd held Damon still. "Lock him to the wall." Charles left without another glance at Damon.

Damon braced himself for being dragged, but the man reached for a long length of shackles and wrapped them around Damon's already bruised and weeping wrists, locking them in place. Then he locked the cell and disappeared.

Air left Damon's lungs when he let his body relax. He hurt everywhere, though surprisingly, Charles had avoided his groin. He wasn't sure he wanted to know why that was, but he'd call it a win for now. He rested his head back against the wall and closed his not-so-blackened eye. He wished he'd replied to Freddie's last message. He'd received it before they'd climbed into the car, and he'd wanted to check in with Kean before replying. He never got the chance.

Would Freddie be worried about him? Would they be searching for him? Or did he think Damon needed space and wouldn't come looking?

It was some consolation that Kean was sure to be missed. Even if no one looked for Damon, someone would try to find Kean.

A rattling noise drew his attention, and he tensed again, lifting his head to see what he could through one eye. The noise came closer, but he couldn't figure out what it was until a metal trolley with a TV on top came into view, pushed by the driver who'd brought them here.

"Hello, again."

"What did you do with Kevin?"

The man grinned, his glacier-coloured eyes dancing. "I told you, he's taking a well-deserved rest."

"Is he still alive?"

The man said nothing, just smiled. "His Highness has something to show you." He switched the TV on and pressed a couple of buttons on a remote. The screen showed the front of a building with an empty podium and microphones.

"It's a pleasant building," Damon said.

"Patience."

Damon coughed and tried to swallow against his dry throat. He'd not been given any water since he'd been woken by it being sprayed on him that morning. He wanted nothing more than to fall asleep, but he couldn't do it yet. He had to make sure everyone was safe, and if that meant he had to take whatever torture or punishment Charles dealt, he would.

Noise rose from the TV, and Damon refocused. He frowned when Charlotte stood at the podium with a sad expression.

"Thank you for coming." She paused, looking down for a second before staring into the cameras again. "It is with a heavy heart and a weary soul that I stand before you today. Your king...is not who he pretends to be. It is breaking my heart to stand here and tell you the awful transgressions he's responsible for because he is my *brother*. I can't explain how painful it is to have to go to this extreme measure to ensure the safety of our population.

"King Andrew might have won your hearts with speeches and actions, but behind closed doors, he's...not someone you want to run your country. Despite my brother's convincing speech about unity and inclusion and baring his soul about his bisexuality, he's a liar. Andrew is not bisexual. He's not a family man. He's not a good husband.

"King Andrew is a monster. A man who orchestrated a bomb that took the life of his own wife. A man who ordered an assassination attempt on his own family during Christmas. A man responsible for so-called accidents, explosions and much more that have wreaked havoc on our family these past few years. I can no longer stay quiet, even if I have to put a target on my own back to ensure the safety of this country. Please, take care. Be wary of his words in the coming days because they will try to undermine my courage in speaking out. Make up your own mind. Thank you."

She stepped away from the podium amidst a roar of words from those around her. She disappeared from view, and the TV went dark.

"That should give your family something to distract

them instead of looking for you," the driver said. He winked and pushed the trolley back out of view.

Damon was at a loss for words. He couldn't believe Charlotte had put all that on Andrew's shoulders. Making it seem like it was all Andrew's doing and not her own. It was a smart move on their part, the driver had said. Everyone would be running around, trying to do damage control for Andrew's reputation, rather than searching for two inconsequential people. What Damon didn't understand was why? Why was it important that no one found him and Kean? Did they have more information than they realised? If they did, so did Neil, Christian's boss. They automatically uploaded every piece of information they received to an address Christian had given them to make sure they had copies of the reports. They wouldn't see it in time to save them, but they had it and would hopefully find something in it to put Charlotte and her followers down for good.

Damon moved slowly to the corner to give him the best place to rest without falling. Luckily, the chain let him go that far. He let the wall support him on two sides, dropping his head back. He ignored the cold air and brought Freddie's face to the front of his mind. The only regret he had was that he'd never felt Freddie's lips against his own. He'd had the joy of having Freddie's arm around him several times, but nothing beat after their scene two weeks ago when Freddie wrapped him in his arms and held him tightly. Damon hadn't wanted it to end.

What was he doing now? Did he have his family's

support? If something happened to Damon, it would be another thing that Freddie would blame himself for, and Damon didn't want that. He'd be sad, but he'd forget after a while and have the space to find someone to replace him. The idea hurt, but it was for the best. He inhaled as best he could and exhaled again. He didn't know how long he had if they left his infection untreated.

As he drifted towards a sleep he didn't want to give into, Damon wondered how they would answer Charlotte's accusations. She seemed to have covered a lot of ground with her speech, covering each eventuality. Except for the club. She hadn't mentioned anything about that, and it would've been a good way of ruining his reputation. Why hadn't she brought that into the equation? Did she have plans to use the club against them?

The next thing he knew, voices woke him, and he winced when he lifted his head, trying to see who was coming. He tensed when the driver threw Kean into the cell next to Damon and locked the door.

"Enjoy the company." He walked off, leaving them alone.

"Are you okay?" Damon asked, slowly moving closer to the cell bars, stopping when his chains restrained him from going any further.

Kean nodded, gripping the cell bars, his face black and blue with some dried blood on the side of his eye. He still had his trousers on, but his shirt was missing. "I'm okay. You're not."

"I'm fighting fit." Damon grinned, ruining his words with a round of wracking coughs.

"How are you even still alive?" Kean asked.

"I've had enough training to keep me alive for a bit longer."

"Training?"

Damon nodded. "I'm a secret bodyguard. Freddie's, to be precise. Few people know." He held his stomach, coughing again.

"Including Freddie, I'm guessing." Damon didn't answer. "Where are we? Do you know?"

Damon shook his head. "No idea. And from what I've seen, no one is going to come looking yet."

Kean's expression made Damon wish he'd tempered his answer. "What happened?"

"Charlotte's gone vocal—about *Andrew's* reign of terror."

"What? Who would believe that crap?"

Damon snorted and groaned. "You'd be surprised. Plenty of people out there want to see the end of the monarchy. This is another nail in the coffin."

"Are we going to get out of here?" Kean asked.

Damon couldn't reassure him. "I don't know. I'm sorry."

Kean sniffed and shook his head. "You've nothing to be sorry for. I wish…"

"Yeah. Me, too."

They were quiet for a bit, only Damon's laboured breathing breaking the silence, until Kean said, "Why are they focusing on you?"

"What do you mean?"

"I've barely received any torture from them, but you…"

Damon tried for a smile and felt his lip split again. "It's probably because they think I have more information than you do. I've been doing these audits for longer than you have." He coughed and leaned back again. "I think we have something we don't realise we have. From what Charles implied, they think we've found something. But if we have, I've no idea what it is."

He closed his eyes, his energy depleting once more. He slid to his side on the floor, not having the strength to take himself back to his corner, and fell into darkness.

Someone rudely awakened him when someone threw freezing cold water over him. He spluttered and coughed, the pain from his body's automatic movements making his head swim.

"Leave him alone!" Kean shouted.

"Careful, or you'll be the next recipient," Charles threatened.

"Kean! Stop!" Damon coughed, trying to clear his airways. "It's fine." He pushed himself to sitting. "Back again so soon? You must love my scintillating company," he said to Charles.

"I'd rather drink my own piss than be here with you. Although causing you pain is quite fun. I wish they'd allow this type of play at the club. It'd make things much more interesting." Charles grinned, and Damon's stomach turned.

"It'd cost too much in clean up to provide this," Damon said. "The cost of body bags alone would be astronomical if you were in charge."

"True." Charles chuckled. "Well, I'll have to make do

with my wife. She takes it beautifully." He winked. "Although..." He glanced at Kean. "I have a fairly blank canvas I could work on."

"Not going to happen," Damon said, using the wall to stand on shaky legs.

Charles wandered closer. "Oh, yeah? And who's going to stop me?"

"Me," he said. He needed Charles a little closer.

Charles obliged. "Really? And what do you think you can—" His words were cut off when Damon throat-punched him and placed a foot behind Charles's, sending him sprawling on the floor. Charles coughed, scrambling back from Damon. He hadn't done much damage, but Charles would find it extremely uncomfortable to talk for the next few days.

Men came running at Charles's squawk, and Damon slid down the wall to the floor. Guns pointed at him, and hands lifted him to his feet again. They removed the cuffs and replaced them with the shackles hanging from the ceiling again. He didn't care where he was, provided they stayed away from Kean. He didn't know if he'd be able to hold on if they started on him while Damon watched.

Luckily, once Damon was hanging by his wrists again, everyone cleared out. Charles said nothing, but his glare was enough to show Damon had a limited time left, and the slice of his hand against his neck was the icing on the cake. Somehow, he had to figure out how to get Kean out of this mess. He might be the only other one holding the key to figuring out what they knew that they didn't realise they knew.

He shook his head, his thoughts no longer making much sense.

"Damon?"

"I'm good. Stay out of trouble, 'k?"

"Okay."

Unconsciousness found him once more.

10

FREDDIE

"What the hell is going on?" Freddie said several hours after Charlotte's speech had gone viral on all channels and the internet. "Charlotte's speech, Charles being released, Damon missing. What else is going to happen?"

"Has anyone heard from Kean?" Mav asked.

Freddie stared at him. "Why would that matter?"

Mav raised his eyebrows but ignored the tone Freddie wouldn't usually take with him. "Kean went with Damon. You didn't know that?" Freddie shook his head. "Your father wanted Kean to learn about the businesses to help him with his studies."

"How come I didn't know about that?"

"Did you need to?" Christian asked, the voice of reason.

"I'm fed up with the secrets around here!" Freddie's breath heaved. "Why can't everyone tell me what the hell is going on?" He continued his pacing, threading his hands through his hair. "Has anyone heard from Kean?"

"I'm asking," Mav said, fingers flying over his tablet. He lifted his head and met Freddie's gaze. "No one's heard from Kean, either."

Freddie froze. "I thought he was mad at me," he whispered. The ache in his chest deepened. "Where the hell are they?" He glanced at Christian, who was already on the phone. He dropped into a chair, lowering his face to his hands. Damon had to be okay. He had to be.

His phone beeped, and he yanked it from his pocket, hope lighting his chest, only to be snuffed out when it was a number he didn't recognise. Still, he opened it, the slight flicker of a chance that Damon had used a different phone to message him. He stared at the image and stopped breathing. His heartbeat continued, thrashing in his ear at a rate that would've been alarming if he hadn't been solely focused on the picture. Eventually, he had to breathe but hyperventilated.

"Freddie!"

Hands grabbed him, thrusting his head between his legs, but Freddie fought them, not wanting to take his eyes off the phone.

"Get that phone off him!" Christian said.

Nails bit at his skin, a hand prying the phone from his fingers. When the image disappeared, spots swam in front of him, and he closed his eyes, but the picture was burnt behind his eyelids.

A broken and bruised Damon on his knees.

"We'll find them. We'll find them. We'll find them all."

Christian's voice was a lifeline, and it centred Freddie. He pushed everything down, locked it away and sat upright, dislodging those holding onto him. He stood and headed for the door.

"Freddie!"

He didn't stop, storming down the corridors to his father's office. He ignored Randall when he entered and walked straight into the inner room, barely noticing the others in the room. He stopped in front of his father, who stood and grasped Freddie's biceps.

"What's wrong?"

Freddie couldn't unclench his jaw enough to speak, but Christian spoke for him.

"Damon is…not good."

Andrew let go of Freddie and reached for something, his pained exhale advertising when he'd seen what they had sent. He glanced at Freddie. "What do we know?"

Freddie swallowed hard. "I haven't had a reply from him since Sunday evening. I sent a message on Monday morning, which was seen but not replied to. I've heard nothing since."

"And Kean?"

"No one's heard from him," Mav answered.

Andrew's jaw clenched, his eyes briefly falling closed. "Randall, get on the phone with the last company Damon was supposed to be visiting. Find out whether or not they turned up. Christian, check with Neil and see what the last information that was uploaded. Mav, check everyone's social media in case they posted anything. Kieren, get security footage from the hotel and the route they were supposed to take to the company."

People disappeared as Andrew sent orders to them until it was him, Douglas, George and the three people who had been with his father when they'd entered.

"Sit, Freddie," Andrew said.

"I'm fine." He clenched and released his fists. "Why...?" He shook his head. He couldn't concentrate enough for his thoughts to make sense. All he could see was the image of his best friend. "They need to go," he said.

"Who?"

Freddie glared at his father. "Charlotte. Charles. And anyone else caught in it. I don't give a damn, but they've gone too far now. Coming after you. Going after Kean and Dam..." He swallowed, breathing through his nose. "This has to stop."

"I don't know what else we can do." Andrew sank onto the sofa, and Aunt Victoria covered his hand. "We have everyone trying to get information or tracking things down. The rest of them are trying to contain the issues cropping up from Charlotte's speech."

"Someone has to know something."

"They know plenty. They're not willing to share," Uncle William said from where he paced at the back of the room.

Freddie frowned. *Some* people might be willing to share for the right incentive. An idea formed, and he explained his thoughts.

An hour later, he stood in an empty, windowless room,

waiting for his first interviewee. He didn't hold out much hope, but if they each gave enough, he might be able to piece something together. Maybe.

The door opened, and he stepped to the back of the room like he'd been told to until the prisoner could be secured to the immovable table in the centre of the room.

When the door closed, leaving the two men alone, the prisoner grinned. "Well, well. The prodigal son. To what do I owe the pleasure?"

"The pleasure depends on your answers, but I'm offering you a chance to get out of here."

Looking into Talon's eyes, Freddie's stomach churned with the glee visible.

"Ooh, lucky me. What do you want?"

"Tell me everything about Charles, Charlotte, anyone else involved that you know about."

"Why would I do that? From what I hear, things are pretty exciting right now."

Freddie leaned on the back of the chair and let Talon see exactly how he was feeling at that moment, and Talon blanched. "They may be exciting, but there's only going to be one winner. And I promise you, it won't be them."

Talon worked his jaw, his gaze never leaving Freddie's. "All my interactions were with Charles. We met at the club, and one day, he approached me, mentioning that I seemed to be holding back. Initially, I denied it, thinking he was a plant trying to catch me out. But he persevered and, eventually, showed me how it felt to be free of constraints." Talon smiled, his gaze going distant.

"Kendal wasn't the only one?"

Talon smirked. "Of course not." Freddie clenched his fingers on the chair but said nothing. "When Charles called asking for something, I couldn't not give him it when he'd showed me the error of my ways."

"Umar."

"Well done." His smile turned into a grimace. "Unfortunately, you messed up *my* plans, but Harvey already had his orders. Regardless of what happened to me, Harvey would continue."

Freddie felt sick. "Who else?"

"Huh?"

"Who else did you hurt? I want names." Talon hesitated. "Freedom comes with a price," he reminded him. Talon gave him the names of several subs Freddie recognised from being members of the club, and Freddie locked his anger down. "What else do you know?"

Talon shrugged. "Not a whole lot. Charles barely spoke to me, except in the club. He mentioned nothing about anyone else."

"What about locations or dates?"

Talon frowned and shook his head. "Nothing. All Charles cared about was making Douglas pay."

"Pay for what?"

Talon gazed at him as if he was stupid. "Being gay. What else?"

"Anything else to tell me?"

"Don't think so." Talon leaned back. "When am I leaving?"

Freddie nodded towards the door, and a police officer came in. Talon grinned, holding out his hands for them to unfasten the cuffs. "I hereby charge you with grievous bodily harm against..." The officer read off the names Talon had given Freddie. "As confirmed by your own statement. You will remain in custody until further notice."

What Talon didn't know was that those charges would stick because they already had one statement from a woman Talon had admitted to hurting. Freddie hadn't gone into this with any inclination to let the man free, regardless of what he said.

"You fucking asshole!" Talon spat, pulling against the hold the guards now had on him. "You'll get what's coming to you!"

Freddie blew out a breath and waited for the next prisoner to be brought in. He had no idea if any of them had any information that could help them, but he had to try. Damon had been with his captor for too long already. He shook his head, pushing the thought aside.

He went through the same process with Harvey, though he had even less to say than Talon did. He hadn't known it was Charles who had requested the attempt on Patrick. He said it had been arranged through an unknown number, and because of what had happened with Talon, Harvey was more than happy to hurt them. He was mighty put out that Charles had reneged on the deal that Harvey would have been protected. Freddie, however, wasn't surprised.

His third prisoner was willing to sing with no coercion. Vincent may have been a one-time drug dealer who owned most of Slough, but now he had "nothing to lose," according to him. Freddie wasn't sure he saw the correlation, but he wasn't turning his back on potential information. Unfortunately, Vincent had nothing new to add to what he'd already given the police in the first place.

While Freddie waited for his last visitor, he called Christian. "Have you heard anything else?"

"The security footage came through. Damon and Kean were seen getting into the car that Uncle Andrew had assigned to them, but once they left the hotel parking area, they entered a blind spot. We haven't been able to locate which direction they went in yet. Also," Christian paused.

"What?"

"Kevin's body has been found."

"Their driver?" Freddie closed his eyes. "Who the hell was driving the car?"

"We don't know."

Freddie dropped his head, gripping his phone as if it was his lifeline. "Did Neil find anything?"

"Gia received their last upload, which was Sunday evening. She's going through it as we speak."

"Do you really think they found something from that last audit?"

Christian sighed. "I don't know. But something must've spooked them for them to take action. Why now?"

"I don't know, and I wish to god I did." A knock sounded. "I have to go."

"Any luck?" Christian asked.

"Not yet."

"Speak to you later."

Freddie ended the call and waved for the guards to bring him in. When the guards left again, he crossed his arms over his chest. "Tobias, how nice of you to join me." Tobias stared at him. "When you were questioned, you said the only reason you turned against your king was because of money. Is that true?"

Tobias exhaled. "It was true then, and it's true now. I'm a simple man, Your Highness. I don't need much, but money makes the world go around."

"Why now? You were with my father for two years."

"I was bored. Plus, the odds were in their favour. I either put myself in with them and come out on top, or I would've hung with the rest of you. It was nothing against you personally."

Heat burned inside Freddie, but he kept it contained. "How were you contacted?"

"Via burner phone, mostly. Once, a message was left on my car."

Freddie frowned. "You never mentioned that before."

Tobias shrugged. "Didn't seem relevant."

"Where was your car at the time?"

"Windsor."

"And you didn't think it was relevant that someone had left you a message from within a place that had strict security measures?"

"I couldn't have been the only person on the inside." He shrugged again. "I barely thought about it."

"Were you told of any locations that might be of value to us?"

Tobias shook his head. "The only thing I was told about was Sandringham."

"You're no use to me if you have no information," Freddie snapped.

"I never said I didn't have any information," Tobias said.

Freddie tilted his head. "And what might that be?"

"I overheard a phone conversation someone was having when Your Majesty visited Kensington Palace last November."

Freddie waited for him to continue and prompted him when he didn't. "And?"

"They were saying something about Portley. I'd never heard the name before, and it stuck with me. I'm not completely sure, but I think the voice belonged to Charles."

"And you wouldn't be saying this just to get Charles into trouble, would you?"

"I know other things that would get him into trouble, but nothing that relates to the issues you're having now." Tobias chuckled, and Freddie's temper flared again.

"Why did you not provide any of this information to the police?"

Tobias stared at him. "I signed an NDA, remember? I can tell you because you're part of it all, but no one else. Or does my being arrested mean I can spill the beans now?" He smirked.

"Your NDA still stands. Tell me everything you know."

By the time Freddie left the prison, exhaustion had claimed him. He allowed Owen to bundle him into the car and stared out of the window for the journey home. They had enough information to lock Charles away for many years on assault and battery charges, mainly towards his wife, but everything else was hearsay. But Portley seemed relevant. The name hadn't sounded familiar to Freddie, but maybe Christian could cross-reference it. He'd ask him when he got back, needing the time in the car to decompress. He pulled his phone out and clicked on the image that already haunted his nightmares, and he hadn't even slept since he'd received it.

Before he could view it, a hand covered the screen. "It won't help," Owen said.

Freddie dropped his hand. "I need to see him."

"Then find a different picture. One of him whole and happy."

Freddie nodded and pressed the home button before he could see the broken version of his best friend. Instead, he found a photo that had been taken several weeks before. Before they'd crossed the line and potentially ruined their friendship. Damon's smile radiated out from the screen, and Freddie couldn't help but smile back. He flicked to another photo, one Douglas had taken at the barbecue they'd had with the bodyguards. Damon had been looking at Freddie, and something in his eyes had tears filling Freddie's.

Freddie was on the edge, realising Damon meant more to him than even best friends, but he wasn't sure it could happen. Would Damon be too traumatised by everything that had happened to him? Would he even want Freddie near him after causing his kidnapping?

He shoved the phone back in his pocket and refocused outside the window, watching the scenery blur past them. Would Damon ever see the outside world again?

He bit his lip all the way home and climbed from the car with a heavy sigh. He didn't stop by his rooms; he went straight to his father's office, which was the unofficial hub of their investigation.

"Any news?" he asked the moment he passed the threshold.

"Not really," Christian said, rising from his chair. "You?"

"Potentially. Has any of you come across the name Portley in your research?"

"Portley sounds familiar," Gia said through the speakerphone. "Hold on. Let me find it. Yes!" Furious typing sounded, but Gia's voice overrode it. "Portley was a location mentioned in the BG Construction company records. It's in Kent. From what I can see from the map, there doesn't seem to be anything there."

"But that doesn't mean that there isn't," Neil said, interrupting Gia. "I'll try and get some fresh photos of the area, but it might take a while."

"If something or someone is there, we can't wait," Freddie said. He turned to his father. "Can we send someone to check it out?"

Andrew shared a glance with William. "If we're going to check it out, we might as well go all out and send people who can rescue and arrest anyone who might be there. We wouldn't want to wait for backup in case they see our man."

"I'm going with them," Freddie said.

"Absolutely not!" his father said.

Freddie stopped in front of his father, letting him see everything he hadn't wanted to show before. "I can't lose him, Father. If he's there, I need to be there, too." He swallowed and inhaled, ready to bare the truth. "I think he's more than my best friend," he whispered.

He expected his father to be shocked, but Andrew smiled and cupped Freddie's face. "I know, son. I know." He sighed. "You can go. But! You must listen to everything they tell you and do what you're told. I want you both back alive. Understood?"

"Understood," he whispered.

"Get your ass into something suitable to wear while we finalise details."

"Yes, sir."

Freddie raced from the office, running down the corridors to his suite, hearing footsteps following him. He didn't look behind him. Instead, he continued until he flung open his door. He began stripping the moment he was inside, dropping his coat and his jacket where he was.

"Freddie!" George called.

Freddie stopped but continued unfastening his shirt. "What?"

"Don't get dead."

Freddie grinned, a feeling of invincibility coming over him. He'd kept up with some of his training from the Air Force, so he wasn't too concerned, and though his back still twinged now and then, he wouldn't let it stop him. "I won't."

"Bring him back to us."

"I plan to."

"And get your head out of your ass."

"I plan to do that, too."

He dressed quickly, choosing dark, thick clothing, and then headed back out of his room. Douglas now stood with George. Freddie hugged them both.

"No matter what happens, take care of everyone," he said to them.

"Don't go saying stuff like that," Douglas said. "I don't want to hear the 'if I die' speech."

"I don't need to because you know it all." Freddie hugged them again, grinned and raced through the corridors to where some of the security team waited. "Let's do this. Let's bring them home."

11

GEORGE

George stared at the door Freddie had raced through and rubbed a hand over his chest. Arms came around him, and Douglas rested his head on George's shoulder.

"He'll be fine. He has plenty of people going with him. Plus, he has anger on his side. I bet anyone who comes up against him will wish they hadn't," Douglas said.

His words helped a little, but it didn't stop George from feeling like everything was hanging in the balance. If things went wrong, it could go disastrously wrong. If Freddie died—and how he hated having to think that— they'd be distraught. If Damon died, Freddie would die inside, which was just as bad.

"He'll be fine," George repeated, saying the words over and over in his head might help. "I'm going to find Timothy and Eddie."

"Okay. Call me if you need anything." Douglas tipped

George's chin with his finger and disappeared, probably to find Mav.

George exhaled and strode down the hallways to his suite, needing to find his men. He didn't need to imagine what Freddie was going through because he'd been in a similar situation when Timothy had been attacked the previous year. It had destroyed him to see the man in the hospital, hooked up to monitors, but he had survived. As would Damon. He had to.

"Has he gone?" Eddie asked, rushing over and into George's arms.

George closed his eyes and breathed in his boyfriend's scent. "Yes. It's a waiting game now."

"He has plenty of well-trained people with him," Timothy said from beside them. "He'll be home—*they'll* be home before you know it."

"I hope so."

His men led him to the bedroom and settled him between them, pulling the cover over them. They weren't initiating sex, just comforting him, which he appreciated. Despite enjoying the blissful blankness of an orgasm, he couldn't do it while he worried.

Instead, his men talked about their day, even though most of it had been said earlier in the afternoon, but George listened, letting his mind stay in the present instead of where Freddie had gone. He asked questions, though he couldn't have said what they were until his stomach growled. They climbed from the bed, and Eddie sat with George on the sofa while Timothy placed a food order with the kitchen. He doubted anyone would be eating in the dining room that night, if they were eating at all.

George stared blankly at the TV for a few minutes, wishing for news, but couldn't sit still any longer. He paced to the window and peered into the darkness, wrapping his arms around himself. Had they reached the place yet? Were there people fighting against them, trying to kill them? Would they succeed?

A blanket came around his shoulders, jerking him from his thoughts. "Dinner's here," Timothy said.

"I don't know if I can eat, after all," George murmured.

"We'll help. One bite at a time, and you'll be strong when Freddie and Damon need you."

"I hope they don't need me."

Timothy tightened his hold on him, and George rested his head against his chest. "I hope the same, but let's plan for a little help, even if it's only bringing them a change of clothes."

George nodded. "Okay."

Timothy guided him to the sofa next to Eddie, then sat beside him, boxing him in. George kept the blanket around his shoulders and took the plate Eddie offered, leaning his head briefly on Eddie's shoulder in thanks. The food was a selection of buffet-style food, and he popped a grape in his mouth. Timothy and Eddie made conversation around him, and although he didn't talk, his body relaxed, and he continued to eat. One bite at a time, as Timothy had said.

He had to believe Freddie and Damon would be all right. They had to be.

12

DAMON

Damon knew the moment the sun set because he heard the generators kick in. Wherever they were, it was somewhere with not much electricity because the generators ran all night. Sounds were amplified with his current lack of sight, but there wasn't much in the way of noise, except for the generators and his and Kean's breathing or movements. Another shiver flowed through his body, and he held his breath until it stopped, not wanting to let Kean know how bad it was getting.

He had no energy at all. He could barely get himself upright whenever their captors came into the room now. The weakness was a telltale sign of the infection winning its war against his body. Sweat coated his forehead, and where his ribs had cried out in pain before, there was now a numbness seeping through him. He didn't want it to win yet. He had to look out for Kean. There was still a chance he could get free, but Damon couldn't concentrate enough to figure out a plan.

It would be easy to fall asleep and stay there, coating himself in the warmth of his memories while his body succumbed to his injuries, but every time he thought about it, Freddie's face flashed before him. Freddie wouldn't want him to give up; therefore, every time, Damon forced himself awake again. He'd accepted that he wouldn't live through this, but he'd love to take someone else with him. Hopefully, Charles, if fate was feeling kind to him, but he'd take anyone as a win.

"Damon?"

Kean's voice drew his attention. "Yeah?" he whispered.

"What's that?"

Damon opened his mouth to ask what he was talking about when he heard shouting. He gripped the wall, pulling himself to a seated position and cocking his head.

"It sounds like someone's upset them." Damon huffed a laugh. "I'd love to see—" A loud bang cut off his words, and Damon watched to see who had slammed through the prison door.

The driver.

Holding a gun.

Crap.

The man unlocked Damon's cell and strode for him.

"No! Leave him alone!" Kean shouted, gripping the cell bars.

"Kean, remember what I said." *Don't worry about me. If you get the chance to run, you run.*

"No. I can't."

"Yes, you can."

Kean sniffed. "Okay."

He could hear the sadness in Kean's voice, but he concentrated on the asshole with nothing left to lose in his eyes. Kind of like Damon. The man grabbed Damon's hair, the lack of pain was another point in favour of him kneeling at death's door, and yanked him to his feet. He wrapped an arm around Damon's chest, holding him in front of him, resting the gun at Damon's temple.

"Damon!" Kean murmured, tears clogging his voice.

"It's okay," he soothed.

Footsteps clattered down the hallway, and two men in tactical gear with guns stopped in the opening to the cell.

"You won't get out of here alive," one soldier said.

"I don't need to. I need to take him with me," the driver snarled, shaking Damon. "I die, my finger still pulls the trigger."

"Not if we shoot your hand," the second soldier said, and Damon frowned. That voice.

"None of you are that good of a shot." The driver laughed. "No, if I'm going, so is he. And it will devastate your precious prince. Exactly as we want him."

Why would they want Freddie upset? It wouldn't stop him from doing his job. His thoughts wouldn't link together enough for him to figure it out. His legs trembled, and for a split second, he wondered, coherently enough, if he could use that against the man holding him. Slowly, he took more of his own weight on his feet, trying not to do too much at once and advertise what he was doing.

The first soldier was talking when Damon tuned into the conversation again.

"—help us, we can help you. I'm sure you don't want to go down with this lot. I guarantee whoever was here is now in custody, and they'll be singing soon enough, blaming everyone but themselves. Why not get in there first?"

The driver laughed, and it vibrated through to Damon's back. "As if. The moment I let him go, you'll shoot me."

"No, we need you alive," the first soldier said.

"I wish we didn't," the second said, and Damon frowned again. Who was that? He brushed aside the thought. They needed to end the standoff.

Damon didn't know if he could get the soldiers' attention, but he waved his fingers near his thigh, pointed at himself and then at the floor, and flashed five fingers. The first soldier dropped his head, and Damon assumed he understood. He spread five fingers, counting down, and when he got to none, he let his knees buckle. The driver grunted, trying to keep Damon in front of him, but a sharp triple rap of a gun sounded when Damon hit the floor.

"Damon! Damon!"

Hands gripped him, cupping his face, gently turning it until the most beautiful sight filled Damon's vision. He reached a shaky hand up and touched the man's cheek.

"My angel...looks like my...best friend," Damon murmured between laboured breaths. "Tell him...I love him." He sighed.

His hand fell away, and his angel disappeared.

13

FREDDIE

"*D*amon! No! Fuck! Damon! Stay with me!"

Freddie tapped Damon's cheek, trying to get him back with him. His teammate, who happened to be Owen, pushed Freddie aside, growling at him, "I need to do CPR," when Freddie refused. Freddie fell back onto his ass against the bars.

"He has to be okay."

Freddie turned his blurry vision to Kean, who knelt at the bars with tears trickling down his cheeks. Freddie couldn't say anything and returned his focus to his best friend. Owen blew into Damon's mouth and started compressions on his chest as more people filed into the cell area. Freddie's instincts kicked in, and he grabbed his gun, aiming for the entrance, and the men paused. It took him a second for the shouting and his brain to kick into gear.

"Freddie! It's us. Let us help." Brett's voice.

Freddie lowered the gun to the floor and turned back to Damon when Owen sighed and stopped working on him.

His heart skipped a beat. No! He couldn't…

"He's back. I need fluid and antibiotics! Now!"

Freddie couldn't move, staring at the man lying naked and completely still on the floor. He was barely recognisable, and Freddie couldn't see an inch of skin that hadn't bruised except for his groin.

Men worked around him, fitting Damon with an IV and putting him on a board to transport him to the vehicles. They draped a cover over him, and two men lifted the board. Freddie's eyes followed as they strode for the entrance.

"Your Highness, we need to go," Brett said. Freddie blinked at him and frowned. "We need to go," Brett repeated.

He glanced at the entrance again, and Damon was gone. Freddie scrambled to his feet and raced for the door. He couldn't leave Damon alone. He exited into the dusk-coloured night, the chill seeping through his clothes while he ran for the helicopter they were loading Damon onto, not letting his anxiety get the better of him. Laughter sounded, and he paused, glancing over his shoulder. Charles knelt on the ground in handcuffs, with a gun pointed at him, but a grin spread across his face. Freddie's focus narrowed on the man, and he stormed towards him, leaning into his face and gripping his chin.

"If you think your time in prison before was easy, brace yourself for what's waiting for you this time."

Charles didn't lose his smirk. "I'll be out before you know it."

Freddie grinned, and Charles lost some of his smile. "We have evidence of you being here, Charles. Each soldier carries a camera, recording everything we did tonight. Plus," he paused, moving closer, "you tried to kill the man I love. If you think you're getting away with that, you *don't know me at all*." Freddie let him go and turned away.

"I told Mother you'd follow in their footsteps. Good luck."

Freddie stopped and gritted his teeth, staring at Owen, who nodded at him. He whistled and twirled his finger, and the soldiers gave Freddie their backs, including Owen. Freddie spun and kicked out his leg, booting Charles in the jaw. He watched the man go down, and no one helped him back up.

"That's assault!" Charles spat.

"I didn't see anything apart from you falling and hitting your head," Owen said, turning back around. "You're clumsy. I'd be surprised if you made it to prison without hurting yourself further."

Freddie glared at another person they'd arrested when they'd arrived. Elizabeth. It would devastate Christian that his sister was there, even though there was no love lost between them. She was still family, as fucked up as they were.

"You'd do well to tell them everything," he said. "Why go down by yourself?"

Elizabeth raised her chin, but he could see it trembling. She gave a small nod but said nothing. She should be scared.

Freddie inhaled and headed for the helicopter Damon was in, climbing in to sit beside him and putting the head-phones on. He wanted to hold his hand, but his fingers were swollen, and he couldn't bring himself to cause him any more pain. Instead, he focused on watching his face as they rose from the ground. He catalogued every inch of it, every bruise, every cut, every smudge of dirt.

"Do you want to wash his face?"

Freddie blinked at Owen, who he hadn't realised had slipped in beside him. "I don't—" He coughed, clearing his throat. "I don't want to hurt him."

"You won't. He's not in any pain at the moment. Clean him up, and we can put some gauze on those cuts."

Freddie nodded absently, taking the sterile wipes and liquid. He wet a wipe and brushed it gently across Damon's forehead, removing the dirt and dried blood. Each clean bit of skin made Freddie's heart hurt more. How had Damon survived? His entire face was a mass of blue, black and purple. Red, too, if he included the cuts.

When he finished, he covered his mouth with his hand and stared at his best friend. Would Damon come out of this in one piece? He had to. Freddie couldn't deal with any other outcome. The moment he'd heard Damon say he loved him, it was as if the last piece of the jigsaw had slotted into place. Freddie had known exactly why no woman had interested him for such a long time. But how long had he been in love with his best friend? How much time had he wasted being afraid of what other people thought rather than following his heart? He loved serving his country, but he would give it up in an instant if it meant he could have Damon by his side for the rest of his life.

Damon had to get through this. There was no other option.

"We're five minutes out," the pilot informed them through the headphones.

"What damage do you think he has?" Freddie asked the medic, who'd been looking after his best friend.

The medic sighed. "It's hard to tell for definite without a more detailed examination, but I'd say he had several bruised, possibly broken ribs and a couple of broken fingers. Obviously, I can't see internally, but the rest seem to be bruises and shallow cuts. His body should heal, assuming the infection doesn't get any worse. Don't quote me on that."

Freddie nodded. His body would heal, but what about his mental state?

When they landed, guards were there to escort them into the hospital, and Freddie stayed close to Damon.

"We need to take him for x-rays and scans. You need to wait here, Your Highness," one nurse said.

Freddie bit back an argument and nodded. "Take care of him."

She smiled. "He'll be back soon, and you can sit with him."

"Thank you."

He watched until Damon disappeared and then slid

down the wall when his legs refused to keep him upright. Owen grabbed hold of him and lifted him.

"Not here, Your Highness."

Keeping hold of Freddie's elbow, Owen escorted him into a private room and closed the door behind them. Freddie sank into a chair and put his head in his hands. He wasn't sure how long he could keep it all bottled up. The rage, the bitterness, the happiness, the sadness, the pain and everything else he couldn't name. It was all swirling inside him, waiting to explode out of him.

"I can't..." He shook his head and stood, aiming for the door, but Owen blocked his way.

"No. You need to stay here for now."

Freddie met his gaze, and he was sure anger swarmed in his own. Owen nodded and held up a hand. He stepped to the side of the door and opened it a crack, talking to whoever was outside, and then he closed it again and faced Freddie.

"Okay. Let's go."

Freddie frowned. "You said—"

"You want to fight, Your Highness, and there's no target. Come on. Hit me."

Freddie stepped back, shaking his head. "No."

"What? You're weak without backup? You don't have the balls to take people head-on without someone holding onto your coattails?"

Owen was baiting him, but damn if he didn't find the chinks in his armour. "Stop."

Owen gained on him. "You didn't even know Damon was missing until he'd been with them for three days."

"I thought he was mad at me." Freddie gritted his teeth.

"He was suffering while you were having fun with your family." Freddie said nothing. "They stripped him naked and beat him, and god knows what else." Flames burned in Freddie's stomach. "He wasn't given food or water." His breathing increased. "And still, he was stronger than you were."

Freddie didn't even realise he'd hit Owen until the throbbing in his hand began, and by that point, he was done. He shoved and wrestled with his guard, knocking things over and crashing into equipment until Owen took him to the ground, Owen's arms wrapped fully around Freddie while he struggled. Owen wouldn't budge, and Freddie couldn't get free.

"Let it go," Owen said, grunting with the effort it took to hold Freddie. "Let it go. Let it go," he whispered repeatedly.

Freddie couldn't breathe. Every time he tried to inhale, his lungs burned, his sides ached, and his throat felt raw. His entire face hurt. But the place that pained him the most was his heart. How could he have not known something was wrong? How could he have left Damon in their clutches? What kind of friend was he?

A voice startled him. It was deep but pain-filled. "Those were all the accusations I threw at myself when my little sister was kidnapped," Owen said, not releasing his hold on Freddie, but now it was more comforting than restraining. "She was fourteen; I was seventeen. She went to stay with a friend after an argument with our parents."

He sighed, shaky as it was. "We assumed her friend's parents would let us know if there were any problems. We'd all gone through the situation before, and her friend's parents were happy to let her stay, often without a single phone conversation for days." Owen sniffed. "We never knew she hadn't arrived because her friend wasn't expecting her. It was three days before we realised something was wrong. By that point, she'd already been through hell."

Freddie tightened his grip on Owen as much as he could. "I'm sorry."

"We were too late for Amy, but we got there in time for Damon. You are *not* to blame for what happened. It took me many years in therapy to realise that. The only person to blame is the person or people who did this."

Freddie's eyes burned, and he swallowed, tears overflowing. "I don't know if I can do this right now."

"Yes, you can," Owen said, leaning closer to him. "I heard what you said to Charles." Freddie stiffened. "Damon has always been yours, but now, you are his. Be what he needs now, and he'll return the favour when he's able. Trust in *his* words."

Tell him…I love him.

Freddie breathed deeply for several long minutes, and then Owen helped him to a sitting position. Freddie faced him. "Thank you, Owen. For everything."

Owen gave a small smile. "You're welcome." He rubbed his jaw. "You have a mighty fine right hook, by the way."

"Oh, shit, sorry." Freddie winced at the red, swollen

area on Owen's jaw and glanced at his hand, opening and closing his fist. He hissed. "I'm out of practice."

Owen chuckled, and Freddie joined in before wiping his face and standing. He held out his hand to his guard and yanked him up, keeping hold of his hand when they were both upright.

"I mean it. Thank you. Few others would've let me take a swing at them."

Owen snorted. "I'm sure I deserved it for one reason or another." He paused. "You need an outlet. Something to get rid of that rage. It clouds your judgement and enables you to miss things, to make mistakes. If you need it, we can spar. Say the word."

Freddie nodded, and they let go. "How do I look?"

Owen glanced him over. "Like you've taken on an asshole and won?"

Freddie laughed and shook his head. "Damn right we did. Now to get rid of the other ones." He sighed when a knock came and rubbed at his face, though why he bothered, he didn't know. There was no getting rid of the evidence of his tears.

Owen went to the door and opened it a crack, listened and nodded. "Damon's in his room now. You can sit with him unless you want to freshen up first?"

"I don't have anything to change into."

"Christian has something for you. He's outside."

Freddie exhaled and clapped his hands on his thighs. "May as well get changed. I don't know how long they'll let me stay with him, but there's a higher chance if I'm clean."

Owen nodded. "Shall I let Christian in?"

Freddie hesitated. "Not yet."

Owen grabbed the change of clothes and closed the door again, handing them to Freddie. "There's a bathroom through there." He pointed to a door Freddie hadn't even noticed.

"I'll be quick."

"Take what time you need."

Freddie closed himself in the bathroom and dropped the clothes onto a chair. He rested his hands on the sink and stared at his reflection. Smudges of dirt streaked his face with tear tracks clearing a path through it. His eyes were bloodshot and swollen. Nothing but rest would make him look any better, but he would do his best. He stripped down to his boxers and set the water running, using hand soap to clean up as best he could. At least the dirt and tears had disappeared, but the redness... He sighed. He dried off with some paper towels and dressed in the trousers and shirt Christian had brought for him. He scrunched the old clothes into a ball and held them away from his clean outfit while he exited the bathroom.

"Let me take those," Owen said, grabbing the bundle.

"Let's rock and roll," Freddie said, pretending the nerves and fear weren't circling him once again.

"Yes, Your Highness."

"Will you ever call me Freddie?" he asked.

Owen grinned. "Highly unlikely, Your Highness." He opened the door a crack and checked before widening it.

Locke was the first person he saw, and she nodded at him. "Your Highness."

Christian was next because he barrelled into him and hugged him so hard that Freddie could barely breathe, but he returned it fiercely. "Glad you're back."

"Is everyone back at Windsor?"

Christian nodded. "Uncle Andrew wouldn't allow anyone else to leave, just in case."

"Good. No point in putting more people in danger than necessary. Speaking of which, thank you for the clothes but go home. Oscar will worry otherwise."

Christian shook his head, but Freddie insisted. "Okay, but you need to call everyone and keep us updated. We're all staying at Windsor for now."

"Is that wise?"

Christian shrugged. "Can't be any worse than what happened at Sandringham."

Freddie conceded his point, hugged him again and sent him on his way after hugging and thanking Brett first. He'd make sure to thank them again properly, but he needed to see Damon now.

Owen led the way to the room they had put Damon in, pausing at the door. "Remember, he might look worse because of all the bandages and machines, but he's fine."

Freddie braced himself and slid into the room, withholding his gasp when Damon's bruised body came into view. He hadn't forgotten what he looked like—god, he didn't think he ever would get that image out of his mind —but it all seemed real again. So much hurt waged on such a small target. And he didn't mean small in stature. He slid into the chair waiting at the side of his bed and took in the additions. Three of his fingers were braced together on his left hand. He had a cast on his right ankle and foot. His chest was bandaged. The gauze Freddie had put on his face in the helicopter had been replaced with fresh ones.

He stared at the broken body of his best friend and felt the tears threatening again. How had he survived such torture? Most civilians wouldn't have coped with it, but Damon looked like he'd gone through hell and walked free. How was Kean faring?

Freddie glanced over his shoulder, but Owen stood guard outside of the door instead of inside like Freddie had thought he would. He returned his gaze to Damon, watching the rise and fall of his chest and counting the beeps of the machine. Unable to withhold touching him any longer, he gently rested his hand over the top of Damon's less injured one, sighing when the warmth bled into him. He'd been scared Damon would be cold to the touch, but he'd always been warm-blooded.

He scooted his chair closer, resting his elbow on the bed, his chin in his palm and his other hand covering Damon's hand, and waited.

14

DAMON

amon woke feeling overly warm and pushed at the covers, gasping when pain shot through him. He tried to open his eyes but could only see blurry shapes and too bright lights. An irritating beeping sat beside his head, and he turned his head away from it, groaning when his face hurt.

He remembered seeing an angel who looked like Freddie and then floating away from the pain. He thought he'd died. But the dull ache covering his entire body said something different.

"Damon? It's Freddie. How are you feeling?"

Opening his mouth to answer, he found his mouth too dry and, instead, smacked his lips together. Something prodded at his mouth, and he automatically opened for it, sucking when he felt a straw. The cool water calmed the desert in his mouth and throat, and it hurt to swallow. He pushed at the straw with his tongue, and it disappeared.

He tried to talk again.

"Like I've been to hell and back," he croaked.

"You're not wrong," Freddie said, but there was something else in his tone.

"What's the damage?"

Freddie stayed quiet, and Damon opened his eye again, trying to focus on him, but it was pointless. He couldn't make anything out.

"Come on, Freddie. Am I destined to look like..." He trailed off, unable to think of someone or something black and blue. "Never mind. I can't think."

Freddie coughed. "Um, you're, er, extremely bruised." That something was still in his voice. "Your ribs weren't broken, thankfully. Your fingers, however, are. You've shallow..." Freddie exhaled and cleared his throat again. "You've shallow cuts everywhere, and you might have a concussion, but we'll have to wait and see with that one."

"Not a bad list. Sounds like Charles went easy. I should take offence—" He stopped when Freddie interrupted him.

"Easy! You think he went easy? Bloody hell, Damon!"

Damon heard the scrape of a chair and the rustling of clothes. "Don't leave!" he shouted, his heart rate increasing. A hand slid on top of his, and he exhaled.

"I won't. I was pacing." Freddie's hand rested on top of his head. "I don't know where I can touch you without hurting you." He sounded wrecked, and Damon turned his hand up to link fingers. It ached, but he didn't care. He needed Freddie with him.

"Anywhere. Anytime."

Freddie snorted. "Stop being an ass. If I hurt you, I'll never forgive myself."

Damon wished he could see Freddie's face because his words could be taken in a different context. He didn't want to get into it at that moment. "This wasn't your fault, Freddie," he said instead. "This would've happened to anyone who did the audits. It happened to be me." He gasped. "How's Kean?"

Freddie's thumb stroked his hair. "He's okay. Not as bruised as you, but he'll be hurting for a while."

"Is someone with him?"

"His parents. They don't want to leave his side, understandably. But I think Kean is getting fed up with them being there."

"When it's time for him to leave, call Kendal and see if there's any chance they can look after him for a few days while he recuperates. I think it would be good for them both."

"That's random," Freddie said after a minute. "Any reason why?"

"They've both been through trauma, and if I...trust my instincts, they might find something...they didn't expect." His brain started pulling him down. "Sleepy. Don't leave."

"I'll be right here."

Damon swore Freddie's lips pressed against his forehead, but sleep tugged at him.

He woke on a painful inhale and groaned, his hand pressing against his ribs. Taking stock of his body, he ached everywhere. He tried opening his eyes, and he winced at the lights, dim though they were, but he could open both eyes and make out more details than the last time he'd opened them. Mainly Freddie, who sat in the chair with his head pillowed on his arm on Damon's bed. His back was going to kill him when he woke.

He wanted to touch him and run his fingers through his hair, but Freddie needed to sleep. Damon wished he knew what time it was or even what day, but he supposed it didn't matter. He stared at Freddie, the stress lines usually there when he was awake absent in his slumber. Stress was only a little of what bugged Freddie. The moment he woke, he'd start blaming himself again, and Damon didn't want that. The only people who were to blame were Charlotte and Charles.

Had they apprehended Charles? What about the driver? He'd been shot, but had it been fatal? He had many questions, but none urgent enough to wake his best friend. Therapy was in his future because he could feel the niggling, annoying images wanting to batter at his brain, but he pushed them back for now. He'd deal with them later. If he could focus on Freddie, everything else didn't matter.

A soft knock came, and the door opened, Andrew sliding inside. Damon lifted his good hand to his lips, making the universal sign asking him to be quiet, and Andrew nodded, coming closer.

"What are you doing here?" Damon whispered. "It might not be safe."

"I needed to see you both with my own eyes," Andrew whispered back, glancing at Freddie. "You've given too much to this. I'm sorry."

Damon smiled and shook his head, then wished he hadn't. "You don't need to be sorry. As I told Freddie, we know who is to blame for this."

Freddie snuffled, and they paused while he sighed, settling down again.

"Doesn't stop me feeling sorry."

"Have you seen Kean?"

Andrew nodded. "He's banged up, but he's okay. I managed to get his parents to go home, at least for a few hours. He can rest in peace."

Damon smiled. "He'll be grateful for that." He swallowed against his dry throat, and Andrew noticed, bringing a cup and a straw to his mouth. Damon drank gratefully, and when he finished, said, "What time is it?"

Andrew checked his watch. "It's three-thirty in the morning. On Saturday morning. You've been here for over twenty-four hours already."

Damon raised his eyebrows. "Damn, whatever they gave me is good stuff."

Andrew chuckled. "The best. I need to go. Rest up and take care of yourself."

"I'll take care of us both," Damon said, tilting his head to Freddie.

"You take care of each other. You have a lot to work out."

Damon frowned, but Andrew pressed his lips to Damon's forehead and tiptoed across the room before Damon could ask for an explanation. What did they have to work out? Damon rested back when he realised there was some information he needed to relay to everyone. Not much, but Charles had let a few things slip, and although he only had his own ears as proof, it was information that might help them figure out what their plan was.

Other than killing them all.

Freddie snorted and woke himself up, lifting his head and wincing. He rubbed the back of his neck and sat upright, his hand moving to his back.

"You'll need another massage," Damon murmured, his mind going somewhere he had no intention of following with his body any time soon.

Freddie started and sent an amazing smile his way. "You're awake! I thought you were going to sleep through the weekend."

Damon slipped his hand into Freddie's. "No way. I'd miss your company."

Freddie stared at their joined hands. "I thought I'd lost you."

"I'm right here, and I'm not going anywhere."

Freddie lifted their hands and pressed the back of Damon's hand to his cheek, closing his eyes. Tears were close to the surface for Freddie, and he asked a question instead. "What happened?"

"Well..." Freddie cleared his throat, lowering their hands again. "I kicked Charles in the face."

Damon stared at him before bursting out laughing and groaning when his ribs screamed at him. He panted through the need to laugh and through the pain.

"I would've given money to see that."

"Ah, unfortunately, it wasn't caught on camera."

Damon grinned at him. "You seem put out about that."

"I am! My finest moment wasn't videoed." Freddie shrugged. "Owen didn't want evidence of it."

"I'm glad. No point borrowing trouble." Damon yawned. "No! I'm not sleeping again."

Freddie laughed. "Your body needs it."

"Don't care. Tell me what else happened? How did you know where we were?"

Freddie stared at the bed for a few long moments before tears trickled down his cheeks. "I didn't even know you were missing for three days," he whispered. "I thought you weren't talking to me when you didn't reply to the message. That you were mad at me." He shook his head, dislodging more tears. "It wasn't until Charlotte's speech that we realised something was wrong. I'm sorry." He brought his wet gaze to Damon's, and Damon ignored his pain and reached for him, dragging him close and wrapping him in his arms.

"You don't need to be sorry. I keep telling you that."

"I should've known! You never ignore me, even when we disagree," he murmured in Damon's ear.

Damon closed his eyes, enjoying the closeness. "This was different, wasn't it? You weren't to know I wouldn't ignore you after the way I left things." He pulled back, cupping Freddie's cheek. "I should be sorry, not you."

Freddie shook his head. "No. You had every right." He stared at Damon, something changing in his eyes when he leaned forward, pushing Damon's aching body back into the bed. Damon let out an exhale of relief, and the corner of Freddie's mouth curved, but Freddie didn't move back.

He rested his hands on either side of Damon, keeping the minute distance between them.

"What?" Damon said after Freddie kept staring.

"How did I miss it?" Freddie whispered.

Damon frowned. "Miss what?"

Freddie stopped breathing. "How did I miss that I..." He swallowed hard. "That I'm in love with you?" he whispered.

Tears filled Damon's eyes, and his breath caught as he stared at Freddie, hoping he'd heard the right words. "What?" he breathed.

"It took me too long, and I'm sorry. I wasn't sure I had the strength to stand up to everyone, but this made me realise I had something more important I could lose. *You*."

"Am I still asleep?"

Freddie smiled and shook his head. "No. I love you, Damon. If you think you could love me back—"

Damon stopped his words by grabbing the back of Freddie's head and pressing their mouths together. It hurt, but he didn't care. It was their first kiss, and he couldn't wait any longer. It was a press of their lips together, but Damon's head spun. Freddie pulled back, stroking his hair.

"Hey, stay with me, Damon. Breathe for me. Calm down. Come on, you can do it."

Damon inhaled, a wave of oxygen filling his lungs and easing the dizziness.

"That's it. Get those monitors under control."

Monitors? Then he heard the beeping going wild, and Damon chuckled.

"You'll get me kicked out if I stress you out too much."

"No one would dare," Damon murmured, closing his eyes and enjoying the petting. "Did you mean it?"

"Damon, look at me." He did, and Freddie stared right back. "I love you."

Tears escaped the corners of his eyes, and he whispered, "I love you, too."

Freddie's mouth gaped. "You do?"

Damon nodded. "For a while now. I didn't—don't—want to jeopardise anything. I know how much your position means to you."

"If they can't—"

"No. We'll figure it out. Let's not borrow trouble while I'm still in hospital." He yawned again. "No, damnit!"

Freddie dropped a chaste kiss on Damon's lips before pulling back, and Damon immediately felt bereft. "Sleep. I'll be right here."

Freddie had said the magic words, and sleep claimed him once more.

The next time he regained consciousness, he asked to see Kean. It had been two days since they'd been rescued, but Damon had been asleep for most of it. Freddie refused to let him get out of bed, saying Kean was already up and about and didn't mind coming to visit. Damon wasn't happy, but he lost the argument. He was extremely happy to see Kean, though.

"Come here," Damon said, opening his arms. "I won't break."

Kean sniffled and leaned down to hug him. "I can see that. No matter what they did, you didn't break."

Damon studied him when he pulled back. "How are you holding up?" he asked when Freddie had left them alone to talk.

"Surprisingly well, considering." Kean stared at his hands. "I expected to have nightmares, but so far, I've been okay. It could be that I'm exhausted."

"You're not the only one." Damon chuckled. "I keep falling asleep on people. Don't take offence if it happens with you."

Kean grinned. "I won't. Did you tell him?"

Damon smiled. "He loves me."

"I'm glad, but that's not what I meant."

Damon lowered his gaze. "Not yet."

"You think that's going to be harder than telling him you love him?"

"Definitely."

They were quiet for a moment, and then Kean chuckled. "It's probably better to tell him now when he can't beat you up for it."

Damon tried for a smile. "But I can't follow him if he leaves."

Kean sighed. "True." He glanced over his shoulder. "Do you honestly think he'll be mad about it?"

"Not about being a bodyguard, no. He'll be mad that I did it without telling him. I've kept too many secrets from him over the last few months, but this goes back years. If anything, he'll be more upset about *how long* I've kept it a secret than the actual secret itself."

"Rip the plaster off?" Kean suggested.

"Maybe." Damon cleared his throat. "When are you getting out of here?"

"They said I can go tonight. I'm waiting for my ride."

Damon covered Kean's hands. "If you need anything at all, let me know, okay? I'm a phone call away. Day or night."

Kean nodded. "Thanks. Same for you."

A knock came, and Freddie poked his head through the door. "Kean, they're here."

Kean stood. "Freddie, can you ask them to come in? Mum and Dad wanted to speak to you," he finished at Damon.

Freddie coughed. "It's not your parents."

Kean frowned. "Then, who…" He trailed off when Kendal entered the room, giving a small wave.

"Hey. I hope you don't mind. I thought you might prefer somewhere quieter than home," Kendal said, wringing their hands. A blush flushed their cheeks.

Kean glanced at Damon, who nodded and smiled, and Kean faced Kendal. "Are you sure? I don't want to be in your way."

"You won't be. It'll be nice to have some company. The house can get quiet…" They trailed off and jangled their keys.

"Thank you. I appreciate it." Kean turned back to Damon and raised his eyebrows. Damon hid his smile as best he could. "You are a menace, even bedridden."

Damon couldn't help smiling at that. "What else can I do for fun?"

Kean leaned down and hugged him again. "Thank you," he whispered. "I know you took the brunt of their… actions. I know you antagonised them to keep them away from me."

Damon cupped Kean's nape. "And I'd do it again in a heartbeat. Now," he nodded towards Kendal, "go see if you can get a happy ending."

Kean snorted and pulled back. "Yeah, like that's going to happen."

"You never know."

They said goodbye, and Freddie saw them out before returning. "Everything okay?"

"All good."

"Are you going to elaborate on why I had to call Kendal and make them lie about why they were here?" he asked, sitting beside Damon on the bed and holding his hand.

Damon grinned. "You wouldn't believe me if I told you."

"I believe everything you say." Damon raised his eyebrows. "Okay, maybe not, but you can try."

"It's not my secret to tell, but I will say that this will give him the answers he needs if he takes up the opportunity."

Freddie stared at the door. "He's in love with Kendal?" Damon said nothing, and Freddie sighed. "Fine. How are you feeling?"

"Fed up. I want to get out of this bed."

"One more day. The doctors want to take another

couple of tests before you leave to make sure your head is how it should be and that your fingers are doing okay. You'll be hobbling along for a few days, but everything else should sort itself out soon enough."

"Have you heard any more about Charles and Elizabeth?" Freddie had already broken the news that the driver didn't survive.

Freddie shook his head. "Last I heard, they'd been arrested without bail. The video feed was conclusive enough to send them straight to prison without passing go."

"A Monopoly reference. You must be feeling good." Damon grinned. "You need to sleep in a bed, Freddie. Go home and get a good night's sleep. You can come back first thing in the morning to annoy me."

Freddie shook his head. "I don't want to leave you."

"I know, but I'm going to need your help tomorrow." He aimed for Freddie's helpful personality. "Get some sleep, and you'll have enough energy for me." Damon winked, and Freddie flushed.

"Fine, but I'm leaving two guards behind."

"Okay. Whatever you think is best."

Freddie sighed. "So much has happened in the last week that I feel like I can't find my feet."

Damon squeezed his hand. "Everything is coming back to earth. Us included. We'll figure it all out. But get some sleep first. Tomorrow will be a busy day."

"Yes, sir."

Damon winced and shook his head. "Nah, doesn't

sound right. Suits you much better. Can't wait to play with you again."

"When you're well enough, we can rectify that."

"Glad to hear it."

Freddie stood and let go of his hand but leaned over him, pausing a millimetre from Damon's lips. "I can't wait to see where we go with this," he whispered.

"All the way," Damon replied, and Freddie closed the distance.

The kiss was soft, a mere brushing of their lips, and Damon wanted more. When Freddie moved to pull back, Damon grabbed the back of his head, stopping him.

"Kiss me like you mean it."

"I don't want to hurt you."

"I don't care. I want to feel you for the hours you're not here," Damon murmured.

Freddie paused for so long Damon didn't think he would, but then Freddie lowered his head again. It started out like their earlier shared kisses, but when Damon became frustrated, Freddie licked at his lips, and Damon opened for him. They tilted their heads to get closer, deeper, and Freddie licked inside his mouth, tangling their tongues. Damon pulled Freddie closer, deepening their kiss further despite the sharp bites of pain through his jaw and cheek. Damon's head spun, and he needed air, but he refused to pull away. He didn't want it to end.

But end, it did, and Damon whimpered even while air rushed into his lungs.

"Good enough?" Freddie asked, breathing heavily.

"No. I think we need to try again," Damon slurred, eyes still closed.

Freddie chuckled. "Tomorrow. Sleep. I love you."

"I love you."

Damon watched Freddie exit the room and then closed his eyes. If they were the kisses he'd get every day from now on, he'd never leave Freddie's side.

15

FREDDIE

reddie didn't want to leave Damon, but he had to admit he was tired. Plus, he wanted to get things ready for Damon when he left the hospital the following day. If he had his way, Damon would stay with him at Windsor, but it was Damon's decision. Damon's parents weren't happy with Freddie at that moment. Understandably. Freddie wasn't happy with himself, either.

Owen and Locke escorted him to the car.

"How is he?" Owen asked on the way home.

"He seems upbeat. I don't know if that's good or not."

Owen nodded. "Once he gets settled somewhere other than hospital, you'll be able to figure out a lot more."

Freddie stared out of the window, the streetlights flashing by and making him blink. "Let's hope so."

Twelve hours later, he was back at the hospital, helping Damon into clothes fit for public scrutiny. Journalists had somehow found out he was in hospital—probably Charlotte's doing—and were waiting at the exits. Freddie had brought Damon a hoodie, and he could hide his face if he wanted to.

"No," Damon said when he mentioned it. "I'm not hiding. If Charlotte brought attention to this, so can we."

"I haven't asked Father if—"

"I have. I spoke to him this morning. He's happy for us to start fighting back."

Freddie frowned. "Why didn't he tell me?"

"You were already on your way here. We have a meeting with him when we get back."

"So, what? You want to accuse Charlotte of all her wrongdoings?"

Damon shook his head and settled on the bed so Freddie could put his socks and shoes on. "I want to accuse *Charles*. I want to show everyone what he did. Well, some of what he did. It's the start of the rebuttal campaign."

"Father's already started." He slipped trainers on Damon's feet.

"He has, but this is us backing him up with evidence. Me."

Freddie stood and tapped his fingers against his thigh. "I don't like you being in the limelight."

Damon snorted. "I think that ship has sailed. I've been your best friend for almost forty years, and now, I'm your…" He shrugged. "Whatever we are."

"Boyfriend," Freddie said, ducking to catch Damon's eyes. "You're my boyfriend. I thought you, of all people, would be able to say that. I thought *I* might be the one to struggle with it."

Damon chuckled. "Me, too. I wasn't sure if you wanted to advertise it all yet."

"Maybe not advertise it, but I won't deny it if anyone asks. But we need to speak to Father first."

"I know. This is the first step of many." Damon stared at him. "Side by side, hopefully."

"Guaranteed."

Freddie dropped a kiss on his lips and helped him to stand, exhaling through the twinge in his own back. His movements had become easier, but his ribs were still painful if he moved wrong, Damon had told him. Damon settled into the wheelchair, and Freddie grabbed the handles. Owen held the door open for them, and Locke and a new guard, Hudson, waited in the hallway to escort them to the waiting vehicle at the main entrance. They didn't see the point in trying to make a stealthy exit when there were photographers at every one of them.

"Are you sure about this?" Freddie asked again when they got closer to the already flashing camera lights.

"Yes."

Freddie had known Damon was strong, but to see the resolve in his expression was a little unnerving. Locke and Hudson stood in front of them when they exited the hospital to the sounds of shouting. The "guests" were kept back by police, but it didn't stop the questions from being thrown their way.

"Prince Frederick! Who did this?"

"Do you know who did this?"

"Have they been arrested?"

"Are you going to take care of Damon?"

Freddie stopped the wheelchair and helped Damon to stand, putting an arm around his back and holding under his elbow with his other hand while trying to ignore the journalists like he usually did. He stepped forward, expecting Damon to come with him, but Damon stood still. He glanced at his best friend, saw the resolve and inwardly sighed. Hopefully, he stuck to whatever he and Freddie's father had agreed upon. The reporters quietened as if they knew he was going to say something.

Damon lifted his head. "The people responsible for my injuries have been arrested. However, they are pawns in a plot much bigger than anyone could understand. We managed to cut these people off, but there are more hiding. Some are in plain sight. King Andrew has done *nothing* wrong. *Nothing.*"

"Who did this to you!" a reporter shouted.

Damon's jaw clenched. "Prince Charles did this, and they have him in custody."

The noise intensified, and the journalists shouted more questions and nudged each other to get closer. Freddie glanced at Locke and shook his head.

"Enough," he said to Damon. He forcibly helped Damon more towards the car that waited for them.

By the time they were all sitting in the car, Damon's face was streaked with pain, and Freddie cursed. He pulled Damon against him, allowing him to lean his back against Freddie's front. Hopefully, it would help reduce the pain until Freddie could get him settled into bed again.

They journeyed in silence, and Freddie was sure Damon had fallen asleep. Freddie stared at his profile, tracing the bruises and wished he could have time alone with Charles again. It wouldn't take Freddie long to make him look like Damon had done.

Damon was right. They had only taken part of the group away. A major part, but still only a part. As for the property, there was the connection to BG Construction. And that connection to the audits Damon had been doing. For Charles to have risked taking Damon and Kean, they must've found some information, even if they didn't know what it was. Neil and Gia were still going through what they had uploaded, but so far, nothing had jumped out at them.

Freddie frowned and stared at the floor of the car, his mind whirling.

"Your Highness? Are you okay?" Owen asked.

Freddie held up a finger while he followed his train of thought. Maybe it wasn't one piece of information they had. Maybe it was lots of pieces of information that, when they were all put together, created a complete picture.

"They found the last piece of the puzzle," he murmured.

"Your Highness?" Owen leaned forward.

Freddie glanced up. "How close are we?"

"Two minutes out."

"Can you arrange for a meeting with everyone the moment we get back? I think I have something."

He had no idea if it was the right something, and someone else could've had the same idea and had been working on it, but maybe they hadn't. They'd all been gathering information over the past two years since Charlotte started her vendetta, but part of their problem could be that they've not been putting all the pieces together.

"We need to finish the jigsaw," Freddie said once everyone had arrived in his suite.

He'd wanted Damon to lie down in bed, but he refused, and Freddie had some household staff members bring in a more comfortable sofa to create a makeshift bed for him instead. Damon had grumbled, but Freddie had told him it was that or bed.

"What do you mean?" Christian said, perched on the arm of an armchair where Oscar sat.

Freddie paced while he spoke. "We've been thinking that all these events were individual attacks, but what if they are dominoes?"

"Dominoes?" Andrew said.

"Yes!" Freddie raked his fingers through his hair. "Every time something happened, we reacted, changing the way we did things, moving staff around, cancelling events, etcetera. What if that is what they want us to do? I've been trying to figure out why they chose now, of all times to go after Damon and Kean. Damon has been auditing for months. If they were worried, surely they would've stopped him earlier?" He paused, staring at his father. "But what if they only tried to stop once he found the missing pieces of the puzzle."

"What missing pieces?" William asked.

"Well, that I don't know. But if we think about the potential start of these attacks—the helicopter crash." His heart raced. He hated going back to the memories, but he needed to be strong like Damon was. He flicked his gaze to Damon, seeing the pain in his eyes. The pain *for* Freddie because he was the only one who knew everything.

"That was three years ago. What makes you think that was the beginning?" Douglas asked, his arm around Mav, who worked furiously on his tablet.

Freddie crossed his arms over his chest. "Two days before…Charles had confronted me about playing with men at the club. He told me I shouldn't be doing it. It was unnatural, and he didn't want me getting hurt because of it." He locked gazes with his father. "I brushed him off, giving the usual response we give when members don't like what they've seen. Charles threatened to 'show me' how wrong I was and that I wasn't as invincible as everyone thought I was."

Andrew stood, staring at him. "Why didn't you tell me?"

"At the time, I didn't connect the two. It was only later, after speaking with Damon about it, that I realised he could've followed through with his threat. But then nothing else happened."

"And you think that was what? The catalyst?" William asked.

"I don't know for definite. But it seems likely that it was the first show of force."

Christian stepped closer. "What was the point of that piece of the puzzle?"

"Showing how vulnerable we are," Damon said. "Security was tightened up further after that if you remember."

"They're trying to discredit you," Kieren interrupted.

Everyone turned to stare at him, and Kieren shuffled. Patrick stepped closer. "Discredit us?"

Kieren nodded. "Making it seem like Freddie couldn't fly the helicopter. That Douglas couldn't be trusted when he was arrested. That you can't choose the right people to keep you safe when the fire happened and the...bomb. They're trying to weaken your foundation with the country."

"To make us look incompetent," Andrew murmured. "Why not bring the club into it? That would turn people against us in one article, I'm sure."

Freddie shook his head. "It's where they do business."

"What?" Andrew stared at him.

"When I visited Talon at the prison, he mentioned Charles had approached him at the club. At first, I thought it was because they were similar in personality, and Charles needed someone to take the fall. But then Tobias said something that has been bugging me. He said he couldn't provide the police with any of the information because he signed an NDA." Freddie stared around the room. "What happens at the club has to be kept quiet."

"Including conversations about treason." Andrew covered his mouth with his hand. "They've used our own rules against us."

"Every person who works closely with us is given a membership to the club and an NDA to sign. They could've approached anyone, and how many of those can we trust to have said no?" Douglas said.

"How far does this go?" Andrew said, dropping into the chair behind him.

"But if Charlotte has been dealing with gay men for years," Andrew glanced at Henry and gave him a small smile, "why escalate three years ago? What happened to set her on the plan to remove us and take over? That's what I can't understand. There must be a catalyst."

Freddie shrugged. "I don't know. But I think we have all the pieces of the puzzle now. We need to find out where they go to see the entire plan."

Andrew sighed and stood. "Okay. Let's leave it there. It's a lot to think about, but everyone needs to rest." He stared at Damon, and Freddie chuckled when his best friend pouted. "Don't look at me like that, young man. If I don't look after you, I'll have your parents breathing down my neck."

The reminder of his parents had Damon looking away. Andrew didn't miss the reaction and glanced at Freddie, who shook his head. He didn't want his father to mention it. Damon's parents had wanted to visit him in the hospital but had cursed Freddie for being the cause, and Damon had told them to stay away. They had no idea of the relationship their son and Freddie now had.

Freddie had planned to announce it to everyone but decided against it. Instead, he leaned on the back of the sofa Damon lay on and dropped a kiss on his lips. He didn't care who saw.

"Oh, fucking hell, yes! Did you finally get your head out of your ass?" George shouted.

Freddie grinned and held up his middle finger towards

his brother. Laughter sounded, but Freddie only had eyes for Damon.

"Will you let me get you into bed now?"

"Only if you're there with me," Damon replied.

"I'm not sure if that's a good idea. If I roll, I'll hurt you."

Damon smirked. "And if you don't touch me, I'll hurt you."

Freddie laughed and exhaled quietly as he stood, resting his hands on the sofa to reduce the spasm in his back. He tried not to let it show, but Damon had always been far too astute.

"Your back?" Freddie didn't reply. "I can give you a massage?"

"Let's concentrate on getting you better first. My back can wait." Freddie rounded the sofa and pulled the cover aside, helping Damon sit upright.

"Stop trying to take my weight, idiot. You'll make your back worse."

"I'm fine."

Damon glared at him. "Do I have to shout for a guard? Because I will."

Freddie held his hands up. "I'm trying to help."

Damon manoeuvred himself to standing with a little trouble, but he did it. "You can help by kissing me when we're all snuggled up in bed."

Freddie walked beside Damon, heading for the bedroom and kneeling to help him remove his shoes and socks. They worked carefully to remove the shirt, and Damon settled back to allow Freddie to slide the trousers down, leaving him in his boxers, which Damon grumbled about.

"I don't wear boxers, Freddie. You know that."

Freddie sighed. "We had this argument in the hospital. Do you really want the tighter briefs on while you're bruised?"

"It keeps everything in place!"

Freddie glared at him. "Does that matter at the moment?"

Damon exhaled. "Fine. Get in here with me."

"Bossy, bossy. I've got work to do." Freddie stripped to his boxers, belying his words. Despite his words being true, he couldn't resist spending some time holding Damon, even if it was barely lunchtime.

He slid in beside his best friend and pulled the covers over them carefully. He wasn't sure how to lie, so he didn't hurt Damon.

"Hold my hand and put your head against my shoulder. That shouldn't hurt."

Freddie frowned, still unsure, but did what he'd asked. The unique scent of Damon invaded his lungs, and Freddie inhaled through his nose, wanting more of it. He closed his eyes, battling back tears.

"What's wrong?" Damon whispered.

"I can't believe I almost lost you."

Damon squeezed his hand. "Well, you didn't. I can still annoy you for years to come."

Freddie sniffed and swallowed the lump in his throat. "Glad to hear it. Now, rest."

"Stay with me."

"Always," Freddie whispered.

He watched the rise and fall of Damon's chest, like he'd done in the hospital, while he slipped into slumber. It wasn't the first time they'd shared this bed, but it was the first time with meaning. He had no clue what the future would hold, but he would abdicate the throne if the public didn't support his choice of partner. After coming close to losing Damon, he couldn't go through that again. But that meant there was a serious conversation he needed to have with his father. Who would take over if none of them was accepted? Aunt Victoria was the first in line that had a relationship the country would accept. Would she be willing to take over? Would Mary, if Victoria said no? It was a convoluted path, but one they needed to figure out before anything more was said to the public.

He couldn't give Damon up. That was clearer than anything else. After realising what he'd been feeling all this time, he cursed the time he'd wasted. They could've been together for several years already if, as George politely put it, Freddie had got his head out of his ass.

Now that he had, and though their future was uncertain, he would spend it with Damon.

16

DAMON

Three days later, Damon could walk without support, assuming he was careful—and he rested every so often. He'd visited the security room a couple of times when Freddie had been dealing with his duties, though being away from him was more difficult than Damon had expected, and he'd sat down with Timothy, who appeared to be the resident therapist these days. It became apparent that he wasn't doing such a good job of hiding his protective streak when Freddie called him out that afternoon.

"That's the second time today you've moved in front of me when there was a knock at the door. What's going on?" he asked quietly when George and Douglas settled onto the sofa.

"It's nothing. Feeling cautious, I suppose." Damon shuffled towards the sofa, but George calling his name stopped him. He glanced at him, and George stared back. Damon sighed, winced and sat. "Fine."

Freddie sat beside him. "What's fine?" He glanced between Damon and George. "What's going on?" he asked again.

Damon faced Freddie, knowing he was going to get mad. "I've been training to be a bodyguard."

Freddie frowned. "What? When?"

"For three years." Freddie's jaw clenched, and he narrowed his eyes but didn't say a word. "I'm a secret bodyguard, if you will. Someone trained to fly under the radar and be like everyone else unless needed."

"And who are you protecting?" Freddie's voice was low, and Damon heard the undercurrent of anger. Damon didn't reply. He just stared at him. Freddie huffed. "Me." He stood, stalking to the door, but didn't leave. "More secrets, Damon? Anything else about *my* life you think *I* should know?"

Damon grimaced but took the hit. He wasn't wrong. "I promise this is everything now."

"You promise. Really? Because from where I'm standing, you've been lying to me for three years! Doesn't anyone think I deserve the right to know who's putting their body between me and a potential bullet?" He glanced at George. "And as for you... Why didn't you tell me?"

"It wasn't my place."

"How come he told you?"

George stood and flung his arms wide. "Because he saved my fucking life, Freddie! If it wasn't for him being trained, we would've been in trouble when Isaac went down. He protected me and got me to safety."

Freddie lost some of the tension in his body, but his jaw was still tight. "I have work to do." He left the suite, slamming the door behind him, and Damon flinched and hissed when his body ached at his sudden movement.

"That went well," Douglas said. "Why didn't you tell him before now?"

Damon leaned back, resting a hand against his ribs. "They thought he wouldn't let me protect him."

"They were right. He won't allow it because you mean too much to him." Douglas sighed. "If he had to choose between himself and you, he'd choose you every time."

"Another reason we didn't tell him."

George leaned forward. "Who's this 'we' you keep saying?"

Damon worked his jaw. "Your father, Brett and…others."

"The security team, you mean," Douglas said, shaking his head. "They all know better. Especially Father."

George stared at Damon. "Did they make him keep it secret, too?"

Damon didn't pretend to misunderstand what George had figured out. "Yes. Kieren wasn't allowed to tell anyone. Not even Patrick."

"Oh, dear." Douglas groaned. "This is going to blow up spectacularly."

A knock came, and Damon tensed, rising, but Douglas waved him off and opened the door. He spoke quietly to whoever was there and then closed the door again. Leaning back, he stared at Damon for a long moment.

"Your parents are here."

Damon sank into the sofa and closed his eyes. It was inevitable, but he'd hoped he had more time. Before he could respond, the door flew open—and Douglas went flying—and Freddie stormed in and over to Damon.

"No more lies!" he demanded, leaning down and caging him in with his arms. Damon nodded, putting his hand over his heart. Freddie sighed and pecked a kiss on his lips. "I was told your parents are here. I wasn't sure you wanted to speak to them alone."

Damon's heart skipped a beat, and he breathed through his nose to stop the threat of tears at Freddie's consideration. He shouldn't be surprised. Freddie was protective of his family and friends. He had thought he would be too angry, but Damon was glad he was there.

"Please."

Freddie knew what he meant and sat beside him. "They're waiting in the receiving room. We'll go to them. I don't want their anger to taint this suite for us."

"They're angry?" Damon asked, letting Freddie help him stand.

"Do you think they won't be? They don't exactly like me."

George snorted, and Freddie glared at him.

"It's not you they don't like. It's the situation," Damon said.

They headed for the door. "We'll see you later," Freddie said to his brothers.

Damon wanted to snuggle into Freddie as they walked, but he'd found it hurt more to lean to the side instead of staying upright, and he consoled himself by holding his hand. They didn't rush, neither in the mood to receive his parents' wrath.

"They're probably wanting to see how I am because I've not seen them since the hospital," Damon murmured.

"Uh-huh. And my name's Pinocchio."

Damon snorted and held a hand to his ribs. "I'm sure you like me suffering. That's why you keep telling jokes."

Freddie stopped and gently pushed him back against the wall, cupping his cheek with one hand. "I never enjoy seeing you in pain, no matter the cause." His gaze devoured Damon. "I'd take everything from you if I could."

"And that's why I didn't tell you about the bodyguard thing. You wouldn't listen to me if you thought I was putting myself in danger to save you. And I *needed* you to listen if that happened. Saying it as your best friend had a higher chance of success than saying it as a bodyguard."

Freddie closed his eyes and inhaled. "You're right. It still doesn't make the lies and secrets okay."

"I know, and I'm sorry. I really did think I was doing the right thing."

"We need to be a team. Right here, right now."

"We've always been a team," Damon said.

Freddie shook his head. "Not truly. Not with the secrets. But now we can." He rested their foreheads together. "We can work together completely now, and I will do my best to listen if our safety is compromised."

"*Our* safety?"

"Yes. Our safety. If you're with me as my boyfriend, you'll be in a similar amount of danger as I am. We work together to get ourselves out of it. Agreed?"

Damon nodded. "Agreed." Freddie touched their lips together, not taking things any further, much to Damon's dismay. "I can't wait until I'm better. You're such a tease."

Freddie grinned. "I try."

They continued to the receiving room, stopping outside to stare at each other. "Are we telling them the whole truth?" Damon asked.

"About us? Yes. About everything else? I don't think we have much choice. They're involved now, even if they didn't want to be."

Damon frowned. "What do you mean?"

"Us together has pointed a target on their back." Freddie hesitated. "I'd understand if you want to reconsider."

"Reconsider what?"

"Us."

Damon pulled his hand away and pressed his finger into Freddie's chest. "No. A million times no. No take-backs. You're stuck with me."

Freddie's mouth twitched, and Damon kissed him harder and deeper than they had done before. It hurt, but he didn't want Freddie to misunderstand him. He pulled away, gasping.

"I didn't think I'd ever have this with you."

Freddie brushed his thumb over Damon's cheek. "Me

either. It took me a while to realise where my feelings were going, but you're right. No takebacks."

"Say it again," Damon breathed.

"I love you."

Damon chuckled. "I meant the 'you're right' bit, but I'll take that instead." He lifted his head. "I love you."

They shared another gentler kiss, then faced the door, threading their fingers together again.

"Ready?" Freddie asked.

"No, but let's go."

Freddie opened the door and let Damon go first, and he did, but he refused to let his hand go, eyes darting around the room to check there were no surprises. He needed to borrow strength from him. The strength from their relationship because he knew exactly what his parents' reactions were going to be at their news—the same as when they'd found out he was in love with Freddie. At the same time they'd found out he'd started training. It was what had triggered their biggest argument and sent Damon straight into Andrew's office for a new job, which led to the auditing job, which led to his current condition. In their eyes, the royal family was a curse, and they didn't want Damon anywhere near them.

Luckily, they had no choice. It was Damon's life, and one he was happy to live, whether or not he was with Freddie.

The minute his mother saw their joined hands, she put a hand to her mouth and cried out, "No!" His father put an arm around her shoulders, but his face was a stone mask.

"Mr and Mrs Winchester, I'm—"

"No!" His mother shouted. "You don't get to say anything in this situation. You're the reason he's in this condition in the first place!"

"Sarah," his father said.

"No, Jerome. Enough is enough." She stared at Damon. "Why can't you see what this is doing to you?"

"What it's doing to me?" Damon said, stepping forward and letting go of Freddie. "You mean, how it's making me the person I want to be? How I'm helping people like I've always wanted to do? How I'm with the most incredible man on the planet?" Damon shook his head. "What parent wouldn't want that for their child?"

"I wouldn't!" Sarah shouted. "I want you safe! I want you to live a long life! I don't want it cut short," her voice broke, "because you're with them when a bomb goes off!"

Damon reached a hand back for Freddie, knowing that would've hurt him. When his warm hand slid into his, Damon squeezed. "That was unkind."

Sarah's watery eyes met his, and though her chin trembled, she raised her head. "It's the truth."

"Maybe, but you have no right to come into his home and raise your voice at him. *You* taught me better than that." He swallowed. "I will not stand for your verbal abuse towards my boyfriend. Ever. And if you can't accept my choices, then you need to leave." He stared at them for a second longer, then turned to Freddie. "It's time to go."

"Damon, no!" his mother called, reaching for him.

Unfortunately, she tugged on his shoulder, and he cried out, pain streaking through his ribs. Freddie caught him and held him carefully while Damon panted through the fire against his boyfriend's shirt. He loved saying that, even thinking it, and it helped him to smile.

"Are you okay?" Freddie murmured against his temple.

"Yeah." He swallowed, exhaled again and lifted his head. "Thanks."

"You're always welcome. I think it's time for more paracetamol." Freddie dropped a kiss on his lips, then his eyes widened, and he glanced over Damon's shoulder.

Damon kept hold of Freddie but shuffled around to see his parents. His mother sat on the sofa in his father's arms, her tear-stained face staring at him.

"I'm sorry. I never meant to hurt you," she said. "I'm scared."

He understood she meant more than hurting his ribs, and he nodded. "We all are." He glanced at Freddie. "Let's sit."

Freddie helped him to the sofa opposite his parents and settled beside him, allowing Damon to lean against him in a similar position to how his mother sat. Damon rubbed a hand over his jaw, and Freddie's fingers tapped a silent rapport on his thigh.

"I know you don't want to hear from me, but there are a lot of things happening right now." Freddie broke the silence. "We've kept many things quiet until this happened." He waved at Damon. "Damon's right. We're all scared because everyone knows what happens when someone's cornered. They strike out. We only have a guess as to when or where or who. And now that Charles is in prison, things are even more unsteady."

"Who is doing it?"

"Charlotte," Damon admitted.

"Princess Charlotte? The Princess Royal?" his father said, disbelief clear in his voice and expression.

"Yes," Freddie confirmed. "She's been waging a war behind the scenes for years. Apparently, she's stopped waiting and is now taking action."

"But her speech—"

"Was misdirection," Damon said. "She wanted everyone's attention on Andrew so they wouldn't see what she was doing."

"Which was?"

Damon stared at his hands. "Trying to get information from me."

"What information? What could you possibly know to warrant this?" his mother asked, waving her hand at his injuries.

Damon sighed. "I've been working with Andrew and others to figure out what the hell is going on. I think we got close. Too close. They were trying to find out what I knew."

"And what did you know?"

"Too much, yet not enough."

Sarah rubbed her eyes. "That doesn't make sense."

"We have a lot of information, pieces of a puzzle, and we think we have all those pieces now, but we need to put it all together now. It's tricky."

Jerome blew out a breath. "There's no way we can persuade you to leave this behind, is there?"

Damon chuckled and glanced at Freddie. "No, Dad. Never."

His father rubbed his hand on his mother's arm. "We need to let him go, sweetheart. He needs to do what he thinks is right."

Sarah's tears overflowed, and Damon rose with Freddie's help and knelt in front of her. "I promise I will be as safe as can be. I'll take all possible precautions. I'm trained. I can't make a promise to survive because no one can, but I will do everything in my power to make sure it happens."

He put his arms around his mother, who gently hugged him back. "I love you, Damon. And I'm sorry."

He didn't say anything, not sure their behaviour was okay, but he allowed them the comfort of his silence. After several long minutes, Damon's body ached too much for him to stay in that position, and he pulled away. He rose, leaning heavily on Freddie.

"We have to go. We have work to do," Damon said.

"You're always welcome here," Freddie added.

Damon was grateful for the words, but he had a feeling they wouldn't be seeing much of his parents from then on. They might surprise him, but they were more likely to bury their heads in the sand and pretend it wasn't happening than stay and face the music. Their being there in the first place had been a surprise. He'd expected them to wait until he went home.

The guards guided his parents towards the exit, and Damon and Freddie went in the opposite direction.

"Are you okay?" Freddie asked.

"Yes, and no." Damon gathered his thoughts. "I don't think we have to worry about their interference anymore. I doubt they'll be back. But at least I feel better having seen them. One less thing to worry about."

"I'm sorry."

Damon squeezed his hand and smiled. "Thanks."

"What work do we have to do?" Freddie asked. "I thought you were supposed to be resting."

"Well, before this happened," he thumbed over his shoulder, "I would've waggled my eyebrows at you, but after that, I need some paracetamol and to look over the records from the companies. We're missing something."

"You need to rest."

Damon shook his head. "I need this to end. We need this to end."

"Agreed, but I have a better idea for today." Damon raised his eyebrows. "Let's get everyone together. Have a break from everything Charlotte-related."

"But—"

"But nothing. It will still be there tomorrow."

Damon sighed, wincing. "Fine."

Freddie pulled him to a stop and slid his arms carefully around him. Damon snuggled into his chest, ignoring the ache in his body. "I have to speak with Father. I want you to get settled in, and I'll call everyone to meet us there whenever they can. Everyone needs a reset, myself included." He chuckled. "And you know how often I say things like that."

Damon smiled. "Never."

"Exactly. I mean business."

"Or rather, you *don't* mean business."

Freddie pulled back, grinning. "Hudson, can you make sure he takes his paracetamol when he gets back? I'll only be gone half an hour or so."

"Yes, Your Highness."

Damon frowned. "I can do it myself, you know."

Freddie dropped a kiss on his nose. "I know you can, but I also know you'd prefer not to have them. This way, I know you'll take them."

"I don't know if it's a good thing that you know me so well."

Freddie's face lit up. "It's a great thing." He leaned down, lowering his voice. "I know things about you that you probably wished I didn't. And I can't wait to use every ounce of that knowledge when you're feeling better."

Heat bubbled inside him, and Damon sighed. "Are you sure we can't do that now?"

"No." Freddie chuckled. "Go. I'll see you soon."

Damon kissed him and let him go, though he wished he could stay with him all the time. Was that the love talking or his worry? It hadn't gone unnoticed by himself that he was hyperaware of their surroundings all the time. Even when Freddie seduced him with his words, Damon still knew where everyone was. His training had kicked into overdrive, it seemed. Would it stay that way forever or until he healed from the trauma this had caused, physically, emotionally and mentally?

The questions followed him into his doze after taking his tablets and waiting for Freddie to return. The new sofa was a lot comfier than the old one, that was definite.

17

FREDDIE

reddie called George, watching Damon disappear with his new bodyguard. "Hey, I thought you'd be happy to know we need a get-together. Everyone needs to meet in my suite."

"Why, what's happened?"

"Nothing. We need a break, George. I'm declaring one. Call the Thirsty Thirteen and arrange for food and drink. I have to visit Father first." He headed for his father's office.

George whooped through the phone, and Freddie grinned, feeling lighter than he had in a long time. "I'll get right on it."

"One thing. If you go to my suite, be careful going in without knocking. Damon might be asleep."

"Okay, we'll be quiet."

Freddie snorted. "Yeah, like you can do that."

"I can!" George huffed. "I can try, at least."

Freddie reached the office. "Right, I'll see you in a bit."

He ended the call and entered the room, seeing Randall behind his desk. "Hey, Randall. Is Father busy?"

Randall stood and bowed his head. "He doesn't have any meetings or phone calls scheduled, if that's what you mean? As for busy..." Randall smiled.

Freddie chuckled. "Understood." He knocked on the door and waited until he was called in before opening it. "Father."

"Freddie!" Andrew rounded the desk and hugged him. "I wasn't expecting to see you today."

"I wanted to discuss a few things if you have a minute?"

"Of course. Have a seat. Do you want a drink?" Andrew headed for the little table.

"Tea would be great, please."

His father asked about Damon while he made the drinks, and then they lapsed into silence until Andrew sat opposite him. "What did you want to talk about?"

"Have I made the wrong decision being with Damon?" He blurted out a question he hadn't voiced before.

Andrew raised his eyebrows. "Do you love him?"

"Yes."

"Then I don't see why it would be the wrong decision."

Freddie sighed. "It seems cut and dried, but it's not, is it? There are many other considerations other than my feelings."

"Like what?"

"The public. What are they going to think about having a gay heir? It's going to make everyone a much larger target, even if Charlotte wasn't involved. I keep trying to think of the pros and cons of it—"

"Let me stop you there. There are no pros and cons to this topic. I don't care what the public thinks about your relationship. They can start a mutiny if they want. All I care about is if you're happy. Your mother…" He swallowed and inhaled. "Your mother would have had something more substantial to say, but I don't give a damn about the repercussions, Freddie. Your happiness is more important than keeping a crown. If they get rid of the monarchy, so be it. It'll be a pleasant change of retirement options."

Freddie's eyes filled, and he looked down at his cup, trying to hold back his tears. He'd been emotionally wrung out lately.

"It's because of everything that happened," Andrew replied, and Freddie realised he'd said it aloud. "You need time to decompress."

Freddie chuckled. "That's what I said to George a few minutes ago. I've called a Thirsty Thirteen meeting. Food, drinks, friends and family. You're welcome to join us."

Andrew smiled. "Maybe in a bit. I have some work to finish."

Freddie tapped his fingers on his cup. "Damon's parents visited."

"I heard. How did that go?"

"Not great." Freddie snorted. "Damon thinks they're going to cut ties completely."

"Well, that's stupid." Andrew shook his head. "Means I have one more son in the family."

Freddie stared at his father and swallowed his emotions. "You're amazing. Do you know that?"

Andrew shook his head. "I'm not. I'm a decent human being."

"I hope that if my time comes, I can make you proud."

"You already do, Freddie. Don't try to be anyone but yourself. That way lies bumpy roads." Freddie nodded. "There is one thing I need to talk to you about. All of you, really, but you can be my sounding board."

"Everything okay?"

"Not really. Charlotte has been a thorn in my crown for far too long now. Her speech has made things a thousand times worse. Everyone is working to rebut everything she said, but without proof that it was Charlotte and not us, we can't answer their questions." Andrew sighed. "I want to go public with everything. And I mean *everything*. I know I spoke about our orientations before after your mother...after everything that happened with George, but I think we need to bare our souls."

"In what way?"

"Every way. Reiterate our orientations, tell them what we've been through and what Charlotte has been doing. Give them the proof we *do* have to make their own decisions. By hiding, I think we've done ourselves a disservice, and it's coming back to bite us."

Freddie blew out a breath. "That's a lot."

"I know. What do you think the others will say about it?"

"I don't think they'll mind."

"Can you see any problems we might encounter that I might not have thought of?"

Freddie stayed quiet for a moment, working on the scenarios he could think of. "The only one I can think of is Charlotte herself. We don't know what evidence she had or can fabricate. She's the loose flag flapping in the wind. There's no telling what she's capable of."

Andrew snorted. "I think we know exactly what she's capable of after what happened to Damon."

Freddie's chest ached, remembering those terrifying seconds when he thought Damon was dead. His father hadn't had their luck. He'd lost his wife.

"I don't see why any of them would disagree, but I'll bring it up with them when I get back."

"No, enjoy your afternoon and evening. We can talk again tomorrow."

Freddie studied his father, seeing the stress lines between his eyebrows, the extra lines on his face that appeared almost overnight. Or had they been there for a while and Freddie hadn't seen them?

"Why don't you come and join us? We're getting everyone together. I'm hoping we can lure Kean from Kendal's house as well. Maybe if Quinn came, Kendal would, too. Why not invite everyone? You could ask Uncle William and everyone."

"How about a we'll see, then?"

Freddie narrowed his eyes. "Don't think you can get away with that. When we were growing up, the 'we'll see' was always a no while making us think it was a maybe."

Andrew laughed, his eyes crinkling, and Freddie was

glad to have lightened the mood. "All right. Yes, I'll come. I'll invite some others, but we won't stay too long. Will that work?"

"Perfect." Freddie stood, taking his cup over to the table. "I might invite the security team, too."

"If you're going to invite them, you might need to move the location to somewhere bigger."

Freddie frowned. "Good point. I'll let you know where we are when we decide what we're doing."

"Okay. Now, go. Have fun with your beau." Andrew hugged him and clasped his nape. "You're doing great, Freddie. I'm proud of you. Never forget that."

"Thank you, Father."

He exited the office and stopped by Randall's desk. "Is there anything on the agenda today for the security team?"

Randall stood. "Not that I'm aware of, Your Highness."

"Can I arrange for the receiving room to have a few more tables and chairs added in? We're having a party, Randall. And everyone's invited. Including you."

That flustered the man, and he made his excuses for his attendance. "Wouldn't the ballroom be a better option?"

"It's too…" Freddie waved his hand, unable to think of a good word.

"Uptight?" Randall said.

"Exactly."

Randall smiled and said they would adapt the receiving room within the hour. Freddie thanked him and headed for his suite, excited to be able to do something for everyone. Going out to events was hazardous to their health, but having an impromptu party there should be fine. He hoped.

He entered his suite to find most of the usual group already there. Christian, Oscar and Robert were missing, but he assumed they would be there once Robert and Oscar finished work. He smiled at Damon, whose face lit up when he saw Freddie, warming his heart, but spied the man he needed. He held up a finger to Damon.

"Kieren, can you call Brett and invite all the security team to the receiving room, please?" He clapped his hands, getting everyone's attention. "We're moving this party to the receiving room!"

"Why?" George called.

"Because this suite can't hold everyone I've invited!" He focused on Henry and strode towards him. "Can you call Kean and invite him and Kendal, and ask Kendal to invite Quinn and his partner?"

Henry nodded. "You're really going all out."

"We need this."

Freddie squeezed his shoulder and headed for Damon, leaning over the back of the sofa and sliding his arms around Damon's chest with gentle pressure.

"Hey, you." Damon smiled up at him. "You've been busy."

Freddie's cheeks heated. "It kind of got out of control. I started inviting everyone. I've invited Father, and he's invited Uncle William and Aunt Victoria and everyone. I've asked Kieren to invite the security team and Henry to call Kean, Kendal and Quinn." He grinned. "Maybe too much, but there we go. Everyone's been working hard..."

Damon covered his hands. "It's a great idea."

It took them a little while, but eventually, everyone was relocated to the receiving room he and Damon had been in earlier, although now it was full of chairs and tables. They'd be fine if no one wanted to dance, though they might be able to swing that, too.

More and more people turned up, and Freddie glanced around, realising how big their 'group' had become. He didn't want to mention it to George, but they'd need a different name to cover them all. However, thirteen was what they had ended up with in the nucleus, and that was a good number, even if some people were superstitious about it.

"Penny for them," Damon whispered.

Freddie smiled at him. "I'm thinking about how close we've all grown. It makes it seem silly that we kept the security team at arm's length all these years. I think working together has made us a force to be reckoned with."

"I agree. Even if they do allow you to take stupid risks, like arming up to save your boyfriend." Damon smirked.

"Even if." Freddie chuckled. His gaze stopped on his father, talking to Kean and Kendal. He had his arm around Kean's shoulders and a hand covering Kendal's hand and was talking to them. "Wonder what that's about," he murmured.

Damon cleared his throat, and Freddie peered at him. "I'm not sure."

"Hmm. You know something."

Damon sighed. "I do, but I can't tell you." He grabbed

at Freddie's shirt. "It's not a secret, just a confidential conversation of a personal nature that I can't reveal. Please don't go."

Freddie kissed his temple. "I'm not. Colour me intrigued and a little worried." He stared back at the trio. His heart pounded, and his brain tumbled over that one word—trio. "Does it involve those three being closer than they are?" he whispered, unsure what his feelings were on the subject.

"How the hell… Never mind. Yes, and no. They're not together if that's what's worrying you."

"I wouldn't say I was worried. Confused and concerned, maybe."

"Why concerned?"

Freddie tapped his fingers on his thigh. "After my conversation with my father this afternoon, I had the feeling he was struggling with things, but I'm now wondering if he's struggling with his feelings more than anything."

"I can imagine something like this would be a strain on his mental health."

"I can't get into it here, but later I'll explain what we talked about. It's making me see the conversation in a different light. He's considering making an announcement, but I don't know if this had something to do with the decision."

Damon leaned his head on Freddie's shoulder, stealing his attention. Freddie kissed his head. "It might be good for you to talk to him about it. He might feel like he doesn't have anyone he can talk to."

"What about Uncle William or Aunt Victoria?" Freddie asked.

"They're not his children." Damon leaned back, meeting his gaze. "If he's considering a new relationship, he might think you won't want him to because of your mother's memory."

"That's rubbish." Freddie shook his head.

"And that's what he might need to hear from his son."

Freddie sighed. "Do you really think he wants to talk to me about his sex life?"

Damon chuckled. "Probably not, but it wouldn't hurt to tell him you're okay with it, anyway."

Was he okay with it? He watched his father interact with Kean and Kendal, and he searched deep down and realised he wanted his father to be happy, too. Starting a new relationship wouldn't change how he felt about his late wife, but he might be able to drag a few more happy moments from his remaining years. That was something Freddie didn't want to think about. For one reason, when his father died, it would make Freddie the king. For another reason, if he was in a relationship with them, what would happen? There was a significant age gap.

They spent the afternoon and evening in good company, and Freddie finally said goodnight when Damon yawned for the tenth time in ten minutes. He asked Douglas and George to meet with him the following day and led Damon back to their suite. He was glad they'd changed locations because it meant he could get Damon to bed without the noise disturbing him.

He helped him into the shower, gliding his hands over

Damon's body to make sure he was clean. And maybe for other reasons, too. He couldn't wait until Damon was fully fit again and he could get his hands on him properly. Dreaming about their one scene together was the only thing keeping him going without sending him crazy with lust.

"Freddie," Damon murmured, leaning his head back on Freddie's shoulder.

"Yes, sweetheart."

"Make me come."

"Your ribs—"

"Please, Sir! I need you."

Freddie stared at Damon's cock, red and swollen with need. He wrapped his hand around it, feeling Damon twitch at the contact. He tightened his hold and stroked to the head, twisting his wrist slightly on his downward stroke.

"Oh, yes!" Damon's nails gouged into Freddie's forearms, and his chest heaved. He was going to hurt himself. Freddie let go. "No!"

"Back against the wall."

Damon did, and Freddie dropped to his knees, staring up at his boyfriend with a small smile at Damon's openmouthed shock. It was understandable, given that Freddie had not sucked anyone's cock. Ever. He was looking forward to it, except that he didn't want to be bad at it.

Damon didn't move, frozen in place, and Freddie had to coax him to breathe. The moment he exhaled, Freddie sucked the tip of him into his mouth and curled his tongue around it. Damon inhaled shakily and slapped his hands against the tiles. Freddie held the base of his cock and widened his mouth, taking Damon a little deeper. He wouldn't be able to deep-throat him. Not yet, anyway. He focused on using his hand in tandem with his mouth and his tongue to drive Damon to the edge. It needed to be fast because Freddie refused to hurt Damon further. It was going to be bad enough when Damon came. His ribs would undoubtedly scream at him. But Freddie couldn't deny such a plea.

Up, down, up, swipe, down. He put his arm across Damon's hips when he began thrusting, knowing it would send pain through him, and Freddie wanted mostly pleasure for him for this experience.

Damon tensed, and Freddie held the tip of his cock in his mouth and tongued the underside while his hand continued to stroke the length.

"I'm… I'm…" Damon exhaled heavily, his eyes drifted shut, and he pulsed his release into Freddie's mouth.

Freddie continued his ministrations until Damon's trembling changed to those relating to sensitivity rather than pleasure. He pulled off and stood, his back aching a little, but nothing rest wouldn't help with.

"Fuck, Sir. I can't wait to get you inside me." Damon's speech was slurred, and Freddie chuckled.

"Soon." He switched off the shower. "Time for bed."

Freddie quickly dried Damon off and led him to the bed. They both slid between the sheets, and Damon lay on his back—the best position for his ribs. It meant Freddie got to cuddle up to him instead of the other way around. He didn't get to do that too often, being the

Dominant in all his scenes. It was a pleasant change of pace.

He rested his head against Damon's shoulder and slid his arm over his hips, trying to avoid any area that might hurt.

"Thank you," Damon mumbled, and he was already asleep before Freddie could respond.

Their route might not be easy, but he would find a way for them to live the best lives they could. His mind went to his father and the potential trio. The primary concern he'd mentioned to Damon was the age gap. Not because he had a problem with it but because it forced them to face his father's mortality. Andrew was sixty-six years old, and though he didn't know how old Kendal was, Kean was the same age as Henry, making him thirty-one. Although it pained him to think about, his father might not be around when Kean and Kendal get to his father's current age. He would listen to Damon and bring it up with his father, making him aware that he didn't have a problem with it. It might help with the speech Andrew mentioned making.

No matter what happened, he'd have his father's back, like his father had his. It was the least he could do. And none of them would forget his mother, who would whole-heartedly agree to the union if she'd been able to tell them.

18

DAMON

The following day, they were all called to a meeting in Andrew's office. Damon wondered if it had something to do with the conversation Freddie had with his father. Although Freddie had said he would explain, they'd been busy from the moment they'd awakened and he hadn't had time. But Freddie gave him a quick rundown while they strode through the hallways.

When they were all sitting, Andrew steepled his hands in front of his chin. "I would like to make a speech in response to Charlotte's accusations, but how I think it would work best, you might not be happy with. I want to go through it all with you now so you can voice your opinions before we confirm the final speech."

"I'm sure whatever you have to say will be fine, Father," Douglas said.

Andrew smiled at him. "Thank you, but this is different. It's not my life or the royal life that I want to talk about. It's all of you. It's everything that's happened to us since Charlotte started. I want to go public with everything."

"And by everything, you mean...*everything?*" Freddie asked.

"Yes. Complete honesty with the public."

"Is that wise?" George leaned forward, and Timothy rubbed his hand up and down George's back.

Andrew sighed. "I don't think it can make things any worse than Charlotte's accusations have made it."

"But there are plenty of people who don't believe her. Who side with us," Patrick said.

"True. But there are many who don't. Charlotte's words have set in motion those people, and threats are as volatile from them as from Charlotte herself."

Freddie shook his head. "As if we didn't have enough to contend with."

"You're going to paint a target on your back if you do this," Kieren said.

Andrew nodded. "More than likely. But I truly believe this is the only recourse we have. We could stay quiet, but the public would see us hiding. It's been long enough that rumours are already flying. I have to face the accusations sooner rather than later."

Damon's heart pounded. There were too many variables. "What are you wanting to say about us? I mean, I understand answering the accusations, but what difference does bringing the princes into it make?"

Andrew crossed his legs and linked his fingers. "I want to talk to them about your relationships. I want them to see you as people first and foremost."

"But won't that bring out the haters even more?" Freddie asked. "I can imagine a lot of them won't be happy about having three gay heirs."

"That's part of the reason I think it would be a good idea, showing them you're still the same people you always were and that your orientation doesn't change that." Andrew leaned forward. "I have faith the public will accept us all."

Damon wasn't sure, and he could see similar expressions on the other occupants. Andrew meant well, but he had a lot more faith in the public than anyone else did. Was it misplaced faith? Did Andrew know something they didn't?

"If you think this is the best idea, then I'll support you. You've never steered us wrong," Douglas said.

The rest of them followed suit, except for Freddie and him. Damon covered Freddie's hand, squeezing. His best friend stared at him for a long moment, and his mouth curved slightly. "I don't have a problem with it, but I insist we talk with security before we agree to go ahead. This is a difficult situation, and I won't have anyone's safety put at risk."

Andrew glanced around the room at each of them. "Thank you." He sighed. "I know this is a lot to ask, and I wish it wasn't necessary, but I believe we have no choice. Charlotte has put us in a position where we need to appeal to the public's knowledge of us, to our past activities and behaviours. I don't know what else to do."

George stood. "I'll help with the speech if you want."

"I'd like that." Andrew smiled. "Your mother told me of your skill, and I'd be honoured to have your help."

George grinned. "You've had my help for years, Father. You just didn't know it."

Andrew stared at him, then laughed out loud. "You're the one helping Randall with the speeches?" George nodded. "Well, I'll be damned. I thought you were doing them for other people."

"Now, why would I let other people have my work and not the people who mean the most to me?" George hugged Andrew and whispered something in his ear, causing Andrew to tighten his grip.

"Let's visit the security team and break the news to them," Freddie said.

"I'll get Randall to let them know we're on our way so we don't get a gun in our faces like Kieren did when he showed up unannounced," Patrick said with a grin.

They chuckled and dispersed, Damon sticking close to Freddie. He threaded their fingers and rubbed a hand against his biceps. "Are you okay?"

Freddie exhaled. "I have no idea. On one hand, I can see what Father is saying about making the public remember our past actions and that we're the same people, but I can't help but feel like we're standing in front of a target."

Damon leaned his head against Freddie's shoulder, trying to give what comfort he could. Freddie was right.

Many people within the commonwealth would not feel kindly towards them, no matter what their past could show. Prejudices were rampant and hard to extinguish.

He paused. Was that what she wanted? Was everything they were considering following the road she wanted them to explore? Did she want other people to take the risk of assassinating them or removing them from the throne so she would have the chance to rise and claim what's not hers?

"Damon?"

He blinked and stared at Freddie, rubbing a hand over his jaw and scratching his stubble. "Are we doing exactly what she wants us to?"

Freddie stepped closer. "What do you mean?"

"She's setting us up for potentially millions of people to go against us, and we're going to potentially alienate whoever else is left? Is this what she wants?" He shook his head. "I'm not making sense." He sighed. "Andrew said himself. He can't see any other path through this. Maybe that's what she's hoping for. By backing us into a corner, we might make the move she wants us to, and she won't have to worry about taking us out. The public will do that for her."

"You're right." Andrew stepped back into the office. "But I still don't see what choice we have. If we keep quiet, we're as good as over, anyway."

His expression was one of profound sadness, and Damon's heart clenched. Was this how his rule ended? How the family was removed from power forever?

When they settled in the security meeting room,

Andrew explained the situation to each bodyguard, and Damon watched their expressions grow grimmer with every word. When Andrew finished, Brett said, "Is this wise?" echoing George's words from earlier.

"We don't have much choice." And once again, Damon's instincts said that was what Charlotte wanted, but he couldn't see another way either.

Brett sighed. "I don't like it." He stared at Andrew, who stared back. "But...there would be a few conditions I'd have to insist upon."

"Like?"

"Give us a few days to get the security arranged. Your safety is paramount. Also, don't tell anyone outside of this room." He glanced at Andrew again. "Except Randall, of course. Lastly, none of the princes is allowed to attend."

"We need to show our support, or they won't believe a word he says," Douglas said.

Brett stared off to the side for a moment. "We can have you attend virtually. Have a screen behind His Majesty showing you standing in support. You don't have to physically be there."

"I will be." Damon's heart skipped a beat when Freddie spoke. He should've known. "The two highest royals always attend events like these. We can't change that."

"I disagree. Anyone who knows you'll both be there has the opportunity to take out—like you said—the two highest royals at the same time."

"But you said we shouldn't tell anyone. That would mean the risk is considerably lower. And if you don't mention my attendance to the media whenever this gets announced, I will be a surprise," Freddie argued.

"Or you'll be an added bonus." Brett stared him down, but Freddie didn't budge. "I think I need to retire," he mumbled, rubbing his face. "Fine. But not a word about this until we've decided all the finicky details. Understood?"

"Yes, sir!" Freddie and Andrew said at the same time.

Brett rolled his eyes. "Any other news to break to me?"

"No. When do you think we can do this? Time is of the essence," Andrew said.

"Can you give us until Monday? That's four days."

Andrew nodded. "Sure. Mav, would you be willing to contact the media on Monday morning to let them know the speech will be at midday?"

"Of course. I'll get Winter to help." Winter was an acquaintance of Mav's that helped him when he lost his job—thanks to Douglas—but she'd remained a contact they occasionally asked to help them with their media reach.

"Don't give them more than an hour's notice. They'll all drop everything to get there regardless of what plans they had. I guarantee it," Brett said.

Three days later, they were all hyped up despite everything being ready for the announcement that was going out at eleven the following morning. Freddie couldn't sit still, pacing the room like a caged tiger. Damon was at his wit's end with him. It didn't matter what he did to distract him. It lasted all of a few minutes, and then Freddie was back pacing again.

Damon slapped his thighs and stood carefully. "We're going to the club."

Freddie shook his head. "I'm not in the mood."

"Don't care. We're going." Damon headed for the door. He paused with a hand on the handle and glanced over his shoulder. "Do you really want me to find someone else to play with?"

Freddie narrowed his eyes at him. "You wouldn't."

"We both need a release of this tension, Freddie. Tomorrow is going to happen regardless of what we do. Why not spend this evening seeing if you can play my body as perfectly as Patrick plays his piano?" He raised his eyebrow, then opened the door and walked out.

He'd only taken two steps across the threshold before Freddie grabbed his hand and settled into step beside him. Damon hid his smile.

"You're not well enough." Freddie squeezed his hand.

"I can easily lay back and let you work on me. Isn't that what I need?"

Freddie snorted. "If what I do to you is restful, I'm doing it wrong."

"I never said it was restful. I said I could lie back and let you work on me. There's a difference."

"Exactly. I don't think you're exactly up for what I do."

Damon pulled them to a stop before Windsor's doors. "I can take whatever you give me because it's you. You know me. You'll understand every twitch I make and will change your plans to accommodate." He lowered his voice. "I know *you*. You wouldn't hurt me without my consent, and even then, I'd have to plead with you. Trust in us. We know each other inside and out."

Freddie's eyes darkened, and he wrapped his arm around Damon's back gently. "Not quite, but I'm looking forward to finding out the 'inside' bit and soon."

Damon touched the tip of his tongue to his lip and closed his eyes. He wanted that so much and damned his injuries to hell and back twice before he could open his eyes again. The heat was barely banked in Freddie's gaze, but he was completely in control. He didn't think anyone had more control than his best friend did, and that was saying something. Freddie had been trained by the best to *be* the best, and Damon would be the one in receipt of it all. He couldn't wait until he was fighting fit again. To have all that power unleashed on *him*. A shiver went through him, and Freddie smirked.

"Time to go," he whispered.

Clarice had kindly let them know that most of the Thirsty Thirteen were already there, either working or playing. Damon didn't want anyone intruding on their playtime. Without even discussing it, they changed and headed straight for the medical room. Freddie needed to decompress before the speech, and even if he spent all night, Damon would do whatever it took to make it happen.

Freddie closed the door behind them, and they both darkened the windows to keep those people outside from watching. Damon had caught a few curious gazes while they were heading for the room, and it wouldn't take long before the gossip spread about them. He didn't care, and he was sure Freddie didn't, either, especially with the entire country about to know about them when Andrew made his speech.

Damon pushed the thoughts aside, concentrating on Freddie, who, although he wasn't pacing, was still tense.

"Where would you like me, Sir?" he murmured.

Freddie glanced to the side and watched him from the corner of his eye. "In the bathroom. Naked. It's time to get clean."

Damon inhaled through his nose. "Yes, Sir." He entered the bathroom, which was a wet room with a shower, bath and toilet. There were two small drains to remove the water from the shower and one large drain to remove...other stuff. It was spotless and sterile, as he would expect from a hospital environment.

He stripped slowly to not exacerbate his ribs, folding his clothes and putting them on the shelf by the door, and knelt in the centre of the room. He stared at the floor, but his gaze was high enough that he could see when Freddie crossed the threshold.

"Well done. You can be such an obedient sub when you want to be," Freddie said. "What's your safe word?"

"Cheesecake, Sir."

Damon didn't move his head, but he was aware of where Freddie was, even when he was busy behind him. The shower started, and Damon's breathing increased, knowing what was coming. He'd done this to himself but never had this done *to* him before, but that didn't mean he didn't want it. It was a tad humiliating, but that made it all the more enticing. Goosebumps rose along his skin, and he watched the rise and fall of his forearm hair.

"Straddle the toilet bowl," Freddie said, his voice husky. "Face away from me and lean forward."

The one thing about this toilet was how it had been adapted to help with enemas. It didn't have a tank at the back of it, like most normal toilets. This one had a larger bowl and a cushioned back that could be adjusted to different angles. Damon straddled the bowl and faced the cushion, leaning forward and resting his arms on the back.

"That doesn't hurt your ribs, does it?"

"No, Sir."

"Good. Are you ready to be cleaned?" Freddie asked, and the sound of him pulling on gloves had Damon shivering.

Damon inhaled. "Yes, Sir."

"Spread yourself for me."

Damon reached behind him and palmed his ass cheeks, pulling them apart. With the toilet bowl being larger, Freddie was able to reach beneath Damon's ass without any obstacles in his way. Freddie rested something against Damon's entrance and paused.

"This is going to take several refills before I am finished. Each time I tell you, I want you to clench and retain the water I've put in you. Understood?"

"Yes, Sir."

"If at any point, your injuries hurt, you will tell me *immediately.*"

Damn him for thinking of that. "Yes, Sir."

Freddie pushed the nozzle inside him, and Damon bore

down. It felt like a small dildo, and Damon had no problem taking it.

"That's it. Now for the water."

The sensation of warm water on his insides was always weird at first, but the spray must've had some nodules or something on it because he could feel it along his entire channel.

"Okay, retain for me."

Damon did his best, clenching his insides as Freddie removed the device. He closed his eyes and concentrated on tensing his muscles to keep the water inside him.

"And keep going while I insert again. You're doing well."

Damon's chest loosened at the praise. He wanted to do well. He didn't want to let Freddie down. The nozzle pressed against him again, and because Damon was clenching to keep the water in, it was more difficult to slide in, though not by much. Freddie didn't warn him when the water would start that time, and Damon relaxed a little while he filled his ass. His lower stomach was becoming full, and he wasn't sure how much Freddie wanted him to take. Damon had only ever done one fill to himself at a time—he'd fill, retain for a few minutes, release, then refill again. This was something he'd never experienced, and he relished being able to share it with Freddie despite his best friend seeing him in this position.

"Retain," Freddie ordered, and Damon clenched again.

This time when he fully removed the nozzle, a squirt released before he could hold it back, making a humiliating noise. His cheeks heated, and he closed his eyes. His forehead was already resting against the cushion, so at least Freddie couldn't see his embarrassment.

"Colour?"

"Green, Sir."

"Glad to hear it. Do you think you can take another?"

Damon took stock of his body. "Yes, Sir."

Please, please, please, he chanted in his head.

19

FREDDIE

Seeing Damon in such a humiliating position sent a thread of pride through Freddie. He had given enemas to club members before, but this one was more important than all of those put together. They were preparing him for this moment. Having Damon naked, holding himself open while Freddie pumped him full of water, was arousing. And trusting. And Freddie wouldn't take that for granted.

"Well done. Keep going for me," he said, inserting the squeeze bulb nozzle into Damon's channel. Some of the fluid escaped as he slid it deep enough to do its job, but a little was nothing to worry about. He squeezed the silicone ball, pushing the water through to the nozzle inside Damon and, therefore, into Damon's ass. "That's it. Almost done."

Damon squirmed, his head rolling on the backrest of the toilet. Freddie finished emptying the bulb. "Right, retain again." Damon clenched, and Freddie pulled the instrument free, receiving another squeak of noise in reaction.

He could've chosen several enema options, but he'd wanted Damon to experience the penetration several times to see his reaction to it. Freddie put the equipment to one side, ready to be cleaned, and slid a hand to Damon's lower stomach. It was slightly distended, which is what he wanted.

"Colour?" Freddie removed his gloves.

"Green, Sir." Damon's voice wobbled, and Freddie stood beside him, running his fingers through Damon's hair and pushing it out of the way to see his expression. Damon's eyes were closed, but he licked his lips, and his breathing was elevated.

"Would you like a reward for being such a wonderful sub?" he asked, scratching at Damon's scalp.

Damon sighed, and his eyes fluttered open. "If..." He swallowed. "If you think I deserve one, Sir."

"I definitely think you do." Freddie's fingers went to the zip of his leather trousers, and he pulled his cock free —easy to do when he'd gone commando. "You can take your hands away from your ass, but keep clenching. Rest your cheek on the edge of the backrest. You're the right height for me," he murmured, aiming his cock at Damon's luscious lips. "Just the tip." Damon opened his mouth, and the first lick around the head had Freddie's eyes rolling back in his head. It was the first time he'd felt Damon's mouth, and it was worth the wait.

He heard a puff of air being expelled, and he pulled his

cock free. "Keep retaining. A little longer." He pushed back in, and Damon's tongue licked and laved his slit and head. Damon lifted his head, but Freddie put his hand in his hair, pulling him back to rest. "Don't strain yourself."

He allowed Damon to take him higher, then pulled back slowly. "Perfection." Damon whimpered, and Freddie dropped a kiss on his lips. "More soon."

He stepped back behind Damon. "Spread yourself again." Damon did. "And let go."

Damon exhaled, and the moment he relaxed, water began dribbling from his hole. It took a few minutes for it to stop, and Freddie praised him through every moment. The trust Damon had placed in him was insurmountable.

"Colour?" he asked, using a cloth to clean him up.

"Green, Sir," Damon breathed.

Freddie washed his hands and stood beside Damon again. Damon opened his mouth, and Freddie chuckled. "Eager, are you?"

"Yes, Sir."

"How did that feel?"

"I felt full. More than I ever had before. It was amazing." Damon scrunched his nose. "Not a fan of the latter part."

Freddie ran his fingers through Damon's hair again. "I want you to stroke yourself. See if you can make us both come at the same time, but you can only use your mouth on me. If you come before me, you'll be punished when your injuries have healed. If I come before you, you don't get to come. Understand?"

"Yes, Sir."

He could see the determination on Damon's face, and Freddie hid his smile. "Go ahead." He stepped closer, and Damon sucked him down. It was an excellent position for Damon because the backrest of the toilet supported his upper torso, and he was at the right height that he didn't need to move much. His ass was probably aching from being sat on the porcelain of the toilet.

He could see Damon's arm moving and leaned to the side to watch his hand working his cock while his mouth and tongue teased Freddie mercilessly. He pushed aside the horrible thought of how he'd become good at blow jobs, instead focusing on how Damon was here with him and no one else.

A particularly strong suck sent a streak of fire down his spine. He was getting close. Was Damon going to come first, or could he get them both to the finish line? He had faith in him, especially when he focused on Freddie's nerves, which made Freddie smile because what he had planned after this was exciting.

He groaned, Damon's mouth working harder and stronger, and Freddie steadied himself on the wall and locked his knees. "Yes, that's it. Almost, D. Almost." He wanted to grab the back of Damon's head and hold him against him while he gagged on his cock, but he refused to hurt him. "Fuck, yes."

His entire body tensed as he went over the edge, his head dropping back even as he leaned into the wall. His brain went on hiatus during the pleasure overload, and when he came back to himself, Damon rested contentedly against the backrest, eyes closed. Freddie glanced underneath and saw the remains of his release.

"Such a good sub." Damon hummed, and Freddie smiled. "Sit upright for me. How are your ribs?"

Damon winced a little but smiled. "They feel okay. Maybe a little sore from being in the same position for so long."

"Well, we're heading back to the room for your final procedure for tonight. You'll be able to rest on your back and get comfortable." He helped Damon to stand and manoeuvre himself off the toilet, steadying him when they entered the main room. "Have a seat while I get the table ready."

Damon did, and Freddie put the examination table in the correct position for what he needed. He brought the leg rests up to make Damon comfortable and pulled a paper sheet across it all.

"Okay. I'm ready for you now. Climb onto the examination table, please." Damon did, but Freddie didn't miss the grimace he gave. "Colour?" he asked, putting the screen between them and the door.

"Green, Sir."

"How's your pain level on a scale of one to ten right now?"

Damon exhaled. "Maybe a four, Sir."

"The next exam will be a lot more relaxing for you. All you have to do is lie there." Freddie pulled on some gloves and found the equipment he needed, making sure Damon could see everything he was putting on the tray. Carrying it to the trolley next to Damon, he set it down and rolled it to Damon's side. "Let's get your legs in the leg rests to make it a little more comfortable for you." He helped, not wanting Damon to put too much pressure on his ribs. It was a fine line between making him uncomfortable for scene reasons and hurting him because Freddie was careless.

"Sir?"

Freddie stared at him. "Yes?"

"Can you tell me what's going to happen, please, Sir?"

Freddie smiled at him. "You're going to have one of those piercings you always wanted."

Damon's eyes widened, but they lit up. The Thirsty Thirteen had discussed piercings a few weeks ago, and the moment Freddie had heard how many Damon wanted, he'd wanted to be the one to do them for him.

"I thought it was a good time to do it. Do you still want it?" The answer was visible on his face but Freddie was glad of the confirmation.

"Yes, Sir."

"We're starting with something small, to begin with." Freddie settled on a stool to one side of him and sterilised one of Damon's nipples. He picked up the metal forceps and clamped them on the nub. Grabbing the piercing needle, he said, "Deep breath for me."

When Damon exhaled, Freddie pierced the skin. He removed the clamp, and barely ten seconds after the initial piercing, he slid the barbell into place, removed the needle and secured the bead on the end. He cleaned around it, then rolled the trolley to the other side of Damon's body.

"Again," he said when the clamp was in place on the

other nipple. Damon inhaled and exhaled, and Freddie repeated the process on that side. Once he finished, he cleaned both nipples again and then removed his gloves. "Colour?" Freddie asked.

Damon exhaled a couple of times. "Green, Sir. Thank you."

Freddie pushed the trolley aside, washed his hands and stopped by Damon's side. He leaned down and rested his fingers in his hair. "You're welcome." He brushed his lips across Damon's. "Now it's time for a nap."

He helped Damon from the table and to the bed, snuggling him under the covers while he fetched drinks for them, then he climbed in beside him, having removed his clothes first. Damon moved into his side but kept his chest away for obvious reasons. He would be tender for a few days, but Freddie would help him keep it clean and free from infection. He held the straw to Damon's mouth, and he drank and drank until over half had gone.

"Well done," Freddie murmured, placing the drink on the bedside table. He rubbed a hand up and down Damon's back, pressing kisses to his forehead and temple. "How are you feeling?"

Damon hummed, and Freddie grinned. "Good. Great even. A little sore, too."

"Do you mean from the piercing or your ribs?"

"A little of both. My ribs probably hurt more, but not enough to stop me from doing anything. An ache, really."

Freddie chuckled. "You don't have to sell it to me. I trust you to tell me the truth."

"I will." Damon yawned. "Do you know what time it is?"

"No, and I don't care. Go to sleep."

"Yes, Sir."

Freddie held him, his breaths calming into those of sleep, and then continued to hold him as the minutes went by. He stared at the ceiling, everything that was happening coming back to haunt him. Tomorrow was a monumental day for them as a family and as the royal family. It could all come crashing down around them when his father finished his speech. In a little over ten minutes of talking, their entire lives could change. Andrew said he didn't mind them being removed from royalty, but it would be a travesty because his father had done nothing but good things for the country. He'd given his entire life to the public, and for their opinion not to matter to him at all would make him inhuman.

Damon moved in his sleep, and Freddie countered it, making sure he wouldn't inadvertently touch his chest. Freddie had decided on the piercing for several reasons. The main one was that he hated the idea of someone else doing it for Damon. Protective? Maybe. Possessive? Definitely. He couldn't help it. He refused to hurt Damon more than he already had.

Damon snuffled and woke with a quick exhale. Had he had a bad dream?

"Are you okay?" Freddie murmured.

"I am now."

Damon still had nightmares about what happened to him, but not regularly. Hopefully, soon, they'd leave him in peace. Freddie wanted to distract him, so he rolled over him, making sure to keep their chests apart, and Damon opened his legs without Freddie asking. He thrust his hips, nudging his already-hard cock against Damon's, and Damon's eyes widened, his pupils dilating.

Freddie dropped to his forearms, keeping their lower bodies together, and kissed him. He couldn't get enough of him. His tongue snaked between Damon's lips and tangled with Damon's tongue, increasing the depth and heat of the kiss. He kept moving his hips, rolling his dick against Damon's, needing more from him despite everything he'd already given Freddie, but Freddie would never let him regret it. All of Freddie belonged to Damon, and he needed to prove it.

"Give it to me, D. I want you to come for me," Freddie ordered after he'd torn his mouth away.

"Everything. You have everything," Damon said, arching his back to bring their groins harder against each other.

Freddie lowered his hand, wrapping it around both their cocks, and watched their heads thrust through the grip. "That's it, baby. Take what you need."

Damon gripped Freddie's shoulders, his nails biting into his skin, his eyelids fluttering closed, his hips worked in tandem with Freddie's. Whenever their heads bumped past each other, it sent a shiver of pleasure through him, and before long, the tingle flowed down his spine. He kissed Damon again, biting his bottom lip and pulling it away from him before letting go and soothing it with his tongue.

"Come on, D. I want to see your come all over you, and then mine will follow. Do you want that? Do you want my invisible mark on you? It's different from the piercings. Those you can see every time you look in the mirror. But this? Covering you in my come, making you mine." He lowered his head, whispering in Damon's ear. "Will they smell me on you? Will they know?"

Damon whined and came all over his stomach. The sight sent Freddie over the edge, and he had to lean over Damon while he regained his breath.

"Holy shit," Damon murmured before his arms went lax, falling to the bed.

Freddie chuckled and lifted his head to answer, but Damon was asleep again. He could tell because the small crease between his eyebrows was gone whenever he slept. He carefully rose, grabbed a warm cloth to clean Damon up, and climbed back in beside him. Holding him, he smiled and closed his eyes.

A knock sounded, and Freddie startled awake. It meant they were out of time. Freddie didn't want to move, but they had no choice. Although he could flash his prince card and get out of it, he wouldn't. He hated it when others did that, so he wouldn't do it himself.

"Damon," he murmured against his forehead. "We have to go."

Damon exhaled and nuzzled into Freddie's chest. "Tired," he mumbled.

Freddie smiled. "I know, but I'll get you home and to bed as quickly as I can. How about that?"

"With you?"

"I wouldn't have it any other way."

It took a few more nudges, but finally, Damon climbed out of bed. Freddie helped him to dress, and they exited the room to an almost empty club. There were a few stragglers, like themselves, who were coming from the rooms, but other than the monitors, it was quiet. The music had stopped, and there were no sounds of play. It was an eerie sensation to be there when nothing was happening because it felt empty. When they exited into the conversation room, they found the Thirsty Thirteen, minus Patrick and George, who were finishing their monitoring duties.

"Hey, did you have a good night?" Douglas asked, standing to hug Freddie.

"Just what the doctor ordered," he deadpanned. They all knew of his proclivities.

They laughed, and Damon flushed before complaining, "I need more sleep."

Freddie squeezed his hand. "Say good night to George and Paddy for us, please. We're heading out."

"Will do," Christian said with a nod.

Freddie led Damon to the changing room, helping him to undress and redress before doing the same for himself. Damon was almost falling asleep standing by the time they were heading for the car after signing themselves out. He fell asleep against Freddie for the journey to Windsor, and Freddie had to coax him awake again when they arrived. A sleepy Damon was a grumpy Damon, but Freddie persuaded him to wake up enough to get back to his suite.

He locked the doors behind them and led Damon to

the bedroom, stripping him off and snuggling him under the covers. He was sure Damon was asleep before he'd even pulled the covers over him.

Freddie stared at him, the love he felt overwhelming him. Would Damon stay with him if Freddie lost everything? The moment he thought it, he mentally slapped himself. Damon didn't care about his money. He never had. If anything, Damon would probably prefer it because they wouldn't be in the public eye as much. He might even get his parents back if that happened.

Freddie sighed and left the room, wanting to check a few things on his phone before he went to sleep. If he could sleep. He didn't know whether to hope for their removal or pray for them to be retained. There were pros and cons for each. It was no longer in their hands. Father was making his speech in the morning, and after that, it was the public who would make the final decision about their role within the royal family.

He'd spent his entire life being taught how to be a prince. Did he even know how to be a normal person? Would the public's scrutiny continue if they threw them out? Were they destined to be dogged at every corner regardless of the outcome? Probably.

He settled onto the sofa and scrolled through his phone, soon losing himself in the tasks he needed to complete. Tomorrow was another day.

20

DAMON

They all stood in the room behind where the journalists waited, and Damon had second thoughts. No, not second. Probably the fiftieth by now. He wasn't convinced that this was the right route, but he had to agree that it would show their humanity. Freddie and Andrew were talking off to the side, and by the expression on Freddie's face, he wasn't happy. Instead of joining them and easing Freddie, he wandered over to Simon, the head of security for Andrew's personal guards.

"Hey, how's it all going?"

Simon sent a small smile his way. "Everything's in place. The screen is working. Security is in place." He sighed. "Nothing else we can do to make sure this goes well. Let's hope everyone is behaving."

Damon clasped his hand on Simon's shoulder. "We'll be fine."

"Do you have your gun?" Simon stared at him. Damon nodded. "And who are you to concentrate on?"

It was Damon's turn to sigh. "Freddie."

Simon nodded. "Locke, Owen and Hudson will be with you. The rest of us will focus on His Majesty and the respective royal members in attendance."

They'd already gone through this, but Damon could understand they were on edge. Running through plans over and over was part of the way they dealt with the high-stress job.

"Understood."

"Simon?" a voice came through the radio.

Simon lifted it to his mouth. "Go ahead, Brett."

"Mav says everything's ready to go. He and Winter have confirmed everyone they contacted is in place, and security has closed the doors and is not letting anyone else inside," Brett said.

"Understood. We'll give them five minutes to settle before we let the royals into the room."

Simon glanced at him and nodded towards Freddie and Andrew, and Damon nodded back. He strode over to them.

"Sorry to interrupt. We've got five minutes until they take us inside," Damon said.

"Thanks, Damon." Andrew reached for Freddie's forearm and squeezed. "I know you're worried, but no matter what we do now, we're going to have backlash, as I've mentioned. We're backed into a corner, and it doesn't matter how we respond. Some people won't be happy about it."

Freddie exhaled. "I know. Doesn't mean I have to like it."

Andrew chuckled. "If you agreed with every decision I made, my son, you wouldn't be who you are."

Damon hid a smile at the words, knowing exactly what Andrew meant. They often argued about certain aspects, never fully agreeing, even when the decisions had been made. But their support of each other never wavered, even if they disagreed. It was a beautiful relationship.

"It's time, Your Majesty," Simon said from beside him.

"Thank you, Simon." Andrew sighed. "Let's do this." He hugged Freddie. "I love you."

"I love you, Father. Don't get dead," Freddie said.

Andrew laughed. "I'm sure you're picking up more and more of George's language every day."

Freddie grinned, but it didn't reach his eyes. "Is that a bad thing?"

"There are worse ideas."

They headed to the door, and Andrew nodded for Simon to open the doors. Simon went first, then Andrew, then Freddie and Damon, with bodyguards surrounding them. The weight of Damon's gun at his lower back was comforting amongst the packed room. There must've been around fifty journalists with a similar number of photographers. No wonder everyone was squirrely.

Andrew stepped up to the podium, putting his papers down before greeting the occupants. "Thank you for coming today. There are a lot of rumours flying around that I will address today. First and foremost, I would like to draw attention to the support I have from my family, both in this room," he waved his hand towards him, Freddie and Kean on one side, and William and his children on the other, "and those unable to be with us in person." He pointed above his head where the screen showed Victoria and her husband, Douglas, Mav, George, Timothy, Eddie, Patrick, Kieren, Henry, Robert, Christian and Oscar standing together.

"I have their permission to give the information I will provide, have no doubt about that." He sighed. "You all know about the speech my sister, Charlotte, gave almost two weeks ago. From what I've heard, some of you believe every word, and some of you don't. Everyone is entitled to their opinion, but I request one thing. Hear *our* side of the story and then decide for yourself. I have been your king for twenty years, and before that, I was your prince since birth. Everything I have done has been with the country's well-being at the centre. If you don't believe anything else, please believe that.

"Charlotte's accusations hurt. There's no denying that. Hearing my sister accuse me of such atrocities has been as heart-breaking as realising *she* was the cause of them, not me. We have plenty of evidence to show who was responsible for each of the events I'm about to describe, whereas Charlotte has none." He paused, inhaling. "I'm standing before you today to tell you the truth about everything. But understand this: we are human beings. We have feelings like the rest of you. What we don't have is the ability to hide away. To keep our personal lives private. To love in quiet. All our actions are available for public scrutiny. They always have been.

But we are like you when it comes to feelings and emotions."

The room was silent apart from the occasional shuffle of movement, and Damon stared around the room, keeping an eye on everyone.

"Charlotte's opinions about the LGBTQ+ community have never been the same as ours. She vehemently denies their worth, and we have witnesses to prove physical attacks on people of a different orientation happened as much as nineteen years ago, if not more. It pains me to say that this level of disrespect has gone unnoticed by me until it was brought to my attention last year. I knew of her unkind words but hadn't realised the depravity she took part in. That is a failure on my part. One I intend to rectify.

"I mentioned in my speech last year my family is filled with people of different orientations. All of us have suffered several assassination attempts, the most recent of which was at Christmas when our Sandringham home was invaded by Charlotte's people, who tried to kill our entire family.

"Patrick was almost shot at an event last year, but he's found love with his boyfriend, Kieren, who took the bullet for him. His brother, Henry, stood before you and opened his heart about his newfound love for Robert to stop those who wanted to blackmail them. They survived a fire that was started to kill them. Christian was held under his father's reign of terror, locked up for being bisexual, then disowned, but he survived and found love with Oscar. Douglas was arrested for an assault he never committed and found Mav, who owns his heart, but he never stops fighting for those who cannot fight for themselves. George has two men by his side, one of whom was attacked and almost killed."

"It was as easy to get to you as it was to get to Timothy. You think you're invincible." The words reverberated in Damon's brain, a memory coming to the surface, one he'd forgotten about. He exhaled quietly. The driver who had held a gun to Damon's head and caused many of his injuries was dead, and now he could tell Timothy that the man who'd hurt him would never do so again.

"As for Frederick, he's survived a helicopter crash and has given his life to this country as I did before him and still do. Since my last speech, he's found the man he loves, and I couldn't be happier for them."

Freddie's fingers threaded through Damon's, and they shared a smile while rumbles of conversations went through the room.

"Damon is no stranger to Charlotte's work. He told the truth to the media after his rescue. Charles and Elizabeth were part of his kidnapping and torture but on the orders of Charlotte. Kean, who is here supporting us, was also kidnapped, but he stands here because Charlotte can't win. It's why we all stand here. No one deserves to be treated like they don't matter."

Andrew rubbed at his chest. "For the accusations that I was responsible for my wife's death, all I can say is... How dare you? Louisa was the person I chose to spend my life with. The love for your children is different. It's unconditional, but the love of a partner is one you choose. I would've never wanted Louisa to leave me, but I know the bomb wasn't meant for her." A gasp went around the room. "George was supposed to take that car to the event, but Louisa voluntarily took his place. And I know, from the deepest part of my heart, that she would've done it even if she'd known it would be her last night on earth because that is how much she loved her children."

He paused and looked down for a moment. "But even love comes at a price. A heavy one for us royals. People think they have the right to choose who we love, how we live, whether we *live or die*. And no one should have that power.

"Charlotte believes she's cleansing the world of those people who don't deserve to live, but what gives her the right to choose? Let us live how we want to live, with whom we want to live. Everyone deserves to live their life free from fear, including us.

"We will not end our investigation until Charlotte and those who follow her are found and stopped. And I hope you will support us. Thank you for listening."

Shouts rose from the journalists, but they all ignored them and headed back into the room, where Damon let out a sigh now his muscles could relax.

"I think that went well," Andrew said.

"It could've been worse, Your Majesty," Simon said with a small smile. "But can I request we leave immediately?"

"Yes, Simon. I know how much this worried you all. We can leave now."

They were all ushered into cars and returned to

Windsor without any fanfare. Freddie paused as they entered.

"I'd like to speak with Father quickly. Are you okay with that?"

Damon smiled and dropped a kiss on his lips. "Of course. I need to see Timothy. I'll meet you in the suite later?"

Freddie frowned and stepped closer, sliding his arms around Damon's waist. "Everything okay?"

Damon raised his eyebrows until he understood the undercurrent of Freddie's words. "Not as a patient, as a friend."

Freddie's body relaxed, and he smiled. "Okay. You know where I am if you need anything."

"I know."

They shared another kiss, a slightly longer one this time before they headed in different directions. Hudson followed him, and Damon stopped.

"Why are you coming with me? I thought you were with Freddie?"

Hudson shook his head slowly and swallowed hard. "I'm *your* guard, not his."

Damon opened his mouth but didn't say anything. He couldn't get Hudson to disobey orders, so he'd have to follow Damon until Damon could speak with Brett about him.

"Fine." He exhaled and continued to George's suite, knocking on the door when he arrived.

"Come in!" George shouted.

Damon entered, but Hudson stopped outside, which

Damon appreciated. "Seems like I've gained a tail," he grumbled, sitting opposite where George and Eddie were entangled.

"What?" George asked.

"Apparently, I have a guard of my own now." Damon spread his hands. "Why I need one, I do not know." He huffed. "Anyway, is Timothy here?"

Eddie nodded. "He'll be out in a minute."

"Everything okay?" George frowned over at him.

"Yeah, I need to talk to him."

"We can leave if you need some space?" George moved to get up.

Damon waved his hands. "No. It's fine. Actually, it's up to Timothy."

"What's up to me?" Timothy pulled on a jumper as he exited the bedroom.

Damon stood and wandered over to him, lowering his voice. "Whether we need privacy. I have some information about the man who attacked you."

Timothy stared at him, frozen. Then he shook himself. "It's fine. You can say whatever in front of them." He strode for the sofa, sitting beside his men.

Damon returned to his seat opposite, linking his fingers. "During the speech, I remembered something from my kidnapping. Something that pertains to your attack."

George sat upright. "There's a connection?"

Damon nodded. "While we were being driven to...that place, the driver said something. *'It was as easy to get to you as it was to get to Timothy.'* I had forgotten it until Andrew mentioned your attack."

"It was the same man?" Eddie said, gripping hold of Timothy's hand.

Damon nodded. "He's dead. It was the one who held me at the end, who Owen shot to save me. I thought you might want to know."

Timothy stared at the floor, and they let him have his silence. Then he focused on Damon and stood. Damon met him in a hug, ignoring the pain in his ribs and nipples.

"Thank you for telling me, and I'm sorry he did that to you," Timothy said.

Timothy knew a lot of what happened to Damon because he was still talking to the man in the psychologist and patient dynamic, but Damon hoped this would ease some of Timothy's wounds. It wasn't like the man didn't have his own problems, too. He received hugs from George and Eddie and gave his excuses before leaving, wanting to give them time to let the news sink in.

Hudson fell into step behind him, but Damon said, "I hate having you behind me. Can you walk beside me? At least when we're alone?"

Hudson stepped up beside him without a word and waited outside with Locke when he reached Freddie's suite. With Freddie already there, Damon immediately settled into his lap, resting his head on his shoulder, closing his eyes and trying to forget about the ache in his nipples from the position they were in.

"Are you okay?" Freddie asked quietly, rubbing his back.

"Yeah. I remembered something from my kidnapping when I was listening to your father talk. The man who held me captive when you found me? He was the man who attacked Timothy. I told Timothy he was dead. I thought it might ease his worries."

Freddie kissed his forehead. "You are such a good man, D. Always caring about other people more than yourself."

"It's the right thing to do." Damon sighed. "I see I have a bodyguard."

Freddie chuckled, the sound reverberating through his body and into Damon's. "I wondered when you'd realise."

Damon lifted his head. "Why do I need a guard?"

"Because you're the heir's boyfriend." Freddie grinned.

"But I'm trained—"

"And so is Hudson." Freddie kissed his cheek. "It's not that we don't believe in your abilities, Damon. I promise you that. After everything I've seen and heard, you're amazing. But you're also focused on me and will put your life on the line for me." Damon opened his mouth to confirm it, but Freddie put his finger over his mouth. "I get it, but I need you alive. If I lose you..." Freddie closed his eyes and swallowed hard. "I don't think I'd do as well as Father is. I need you to survive, and if that means you have a guard to keep your ass alive while you keep *my* ass alive, so be it."

Freddie rubbed his finger across Damon's lips, and Damon puckered, pressing a kiss to it. He lowered his head to Freddie's shoulder again, wriggling to get comfortable, but then climbed off him and stalked to the bedroom.

"What are you doing?" Freddie's laughter followed him.

He removed the shirt and pulled on a T-shirt, breathing easier without the pressure on him. "I need something more comfortable to wear because *someone* pierced my nipples last night," he called back, freezing when he saw Douglas and Mav sitting opposite Freddie.

Mav covered his mouth with his hand, and Douglas and Freddie burst out laughing. Damon grimaced and shook his head but took a seat next to Freddie after glaring at him.

Freddie held out his hands. "I thought you'd heard them come in."

Damon sighed and took the proffered drink. "I hadn't." He pouted and sat back, glaring at his tea. Freddie settled his hand on Damon's thigh.

"What are the initial responses?" Freddie asked, and Damon glanced up.

Mav crossed his legs, resting his tablet on his knee. "Mixed. I'd say sixty-forty in favour of supporting us."

"Could be worse," Douglas said.

"It might get worse," Freddie said. "What are the opposition comments like?"

Mav sniffed. "Some stupid ones like 'How will we have the next heir when he can't have kids?' and 'With many of them coming out as gay, maybe we should research the genetic reason for being gay.' And some not-so-nice ones like 'I knew they were all fags. Far too touchy-feely,' and 'How can we trust they can run the country like this?'"

"Any others we should note?"

Mav sighed. "I've flagged all the ones that might have some force behind them, but mostly it's people mouthing off." Mav sniffed again and fidgeted. "There are some that are calling for a petition to remove the royal family from power."

Freddie nodded. "We expected that."

"There has…" Mav glanced at Douglas, who nodded. "There has been a larger outcry about your relationship. I think it's because this was the first mention of it. We all had that when we first announced our relationships, but we need to keep an eye on it."

"What are they saying?" Damon asked.

Mav met his gaze. "It doesn't matter."

Damon put his cup down and stared at Mav. "It matters to me."

"Damon, we need to ignore them," Freddie said.

"And I will, but I still want to know."

"They're calling for Freddie to step aside as heir. For it to go to the next in line who could provide biological heirs from both parents," Mav said. "They're saying if the bloodline isn't true, it shouldn't continue."

Damon's heart skipped a beat, and his body slumped back. Basically, the public was saying that his genes weren't worth anything to the royals. To have a child, they would need to use Freddie—which was fine by Damon— but they wouldn't accept the child if the mother wasn't in the picture.

"Who would be next in line with those specifications?" he asked.

"Aunt Victoria, but she won't be having any more children; therefore, it would go to Mary," Freddie said.

Damon stared at Freddie, seeing the sadness in his eyes. He should step aside and allow Freddie to find a woman who could be a mother to his children in every sense of the word. Could he give Freddie that? Of course, he could. But were they making the right decision?

21

DOUGLAS

Douglas could see Damon's brain working, and he didn't like the expression that came over his face. Almost resolute. Damon would be willing to step aside and disappear if necessary; he was willing to bet. And that would be the worst decision ever.

There was no point in hiding the information from them because they'd find out eventually, but it didn't make it any easier to be the bearer of bad news. Or rather, for Mav to be the bearer of bad news.

"Anything else we need to know?" Freddie asked, side-eyeing Damon. The man wasn't stupid—except when it came to taking too long to acknowledge his feelings for Damon.

Mav shook his head. "That's all the data we have so far."

"Okay, thanks," Freddie said.

"Come on, Mav. Let's grab some food," Douglas said,

wanting to give Freddie and Damon some time alone. He hoped Freddie would bring up the elephant in the room, but he had a feeling he wouldn't.

"You've not long eaten!" Mav tucked his tablet under his arm.

"Since when did that stop me?"

Douglas wrapped his arm around Mav's shoulders and led him out of the room towards his suite.

"Are they going to get through this together?" Mav asked.

Douglas glanced at him, and the worry was evident in his expression. "If I know them as well as I think I do, Damon is getting ready to step back to give Freddie the 'perfect' life." He air quoted. "And Freddie is ready to tie him down, so he doesn't. I put my money on Freddie."

When they closed the door behind them, Mav dropped onto the sofa and sighed. "It's been one thing after another for your family since I started working here. I wish these people would give you a breather."

"It's never dull. Put it that way." Douglas settled beside him, teasing his fingers through Mav's hair. "We've been together almost two years now," he murmured.

Mav peered up at him, a smile curving his lips. "Seems like forever."

"It will be." Douglas dropped a kiss on his lips. "They may throw stuff in our way right now, but it won't always be like this. Things will calm down again, and we'll be able to live without looking over our shoulders every second of the day. I promise."

"It might make my life easier." Mav chuckled. "Ever

since you were the playboy prince, I've been working off my ass."

Douglas growled. "I can definitely work your ass for you." He crowded Mav until he lay back and Douglas could lean over him fully. He stared at Mav's face, the love for him building up in his chest until it could barely be contained. "I was never the playboy prince, remember? I've only ever been *your* prince."

"Exactly the way it should be," Mav murmured.

Douglas lowered himself over Mav and settled on his forearms. He joined their lips in a kiss that started slow and loving and turned carnal within seconds. There was no hiding from the data, but it wouldn't change if they took some time for themselves. Mav's hands gripped the back of his shirt, giving as good as he received until they were a tangle of limbs nearly falling off the furniture.

Douglas pulled back, panting. "I don't have to be quite so sneaky when I visit subs now. I can blatantly do it without it being a problem," he said, going back to their earlier words.

"You still have to be careful, Douglas." Mav cupped his face. "There are people out there who don't want you to know what they're doing in the supposed safety of their homes. Whenever you visit, you're putting a target not only on your back but on the sub's back, too."

He wasn't wrong, which was why Douglas continued his clandestine visits with Mav's consent. "I'm always careful. The sub's safety is my utmost concern, as you know."

"I would say I wish this was all over, but even if it was, you'd still be a pain in my ass."

Douglas laughed and dragged Mav to the bedroom. "I'll show you pain in my ass."

22

FREDDIE

Freddie could see it in Damon's eyes. He could see the indecision, the worry, and Damon was going to leave him. But Freddie had an ace up his sleeve. One he would only bring out if he had to because there was no way he was letting Damon go now he had him.

It had been two days since his father's announcement, and things had been chaotic. Freddie had met with Douglas and Mav every morning and evening to get a feel for what the public was saying, but the divide across the nation was apparent. They were still averaging a sixty-forty percentage in their favour, but in Freddie's eyes, that wasn't enough. They needed more support.

He was busy with that and with the arrangements for his event in ten days. Plus, it was Douglas's birthday the day before that. Everything that had happened that year had been a whirlwind of events and bad guys and information overload, and Freddie was ready for a break. There was none in sight. Not yet.

After finishing with Douglas and Mav, he wandered down the corridors to Damon's suite. Andrew had given Damon one many years ago when it had become apparent that his parents weren't happy with his friendship with Freddie initially. Freddie's father had always made it clear that Damon had a home here if he ever needed one. Damon had taken it to heart and spent more time there than in his own home before making it his permanent home when things with his parents became unbearable.

Freddie knocked softly on his door and entered, as he had always done. Damon had his back to him. He hunched over the table, head in his hand while holding a piece of paper up as if reading it. Freddie stepped to his side, trying to make some noise to make his presence known, so he didn't startle him.

Damon smiled at him and uncurled, grimacing as he stretched his back. "I really shouldn't sit like that. It's good for my ribs while I'm there, but the moment I move..."

Freddie moved behind him and rested his hands on Damon's shoulders. He dug his thumbs into the muscles and said, "I can return the favour now."

Damon chuckled and groaned, his head dropping forward. "You can."

"How are your ribs feeling?"

"The same as they were when you asked three hours ago." Freddie could hear the smile in his voice.

"I'm checking on you, that's all."

Damon lifted his head, tilting it to stare up at Freddie. "I know. Thank you for caring. I wish they'd heal quicker."

"Patience is a virtue and all that."

Damon glared at him. "I think I've been patient. Now, I want you to fuck me."

Freddie's breath caught, then he huffed a laugh at Damon's words. "Soon. Besides, you have something else you need to heal, too. How are you finding them?"

"Weird, but I'm managing. I'm glad I have such a fantastic doctor to change my bandages every day."

Freddie grinned. Damon stood, dislodging his hands, and turned around, sliding his arms around Freddie's neck. Freddie lowered his head and brushed his lips across Damon's.

"You're welcome." He dropped another kiss, then asked, "What are you looking at?"

Damon sighed and glanced over his shoulder. "I've been looking at timelines and the audits to see if there are any correlations." He removed his arms from around Freddie, and he immediately missed the warmth.

"Are there?"

"I'm not sure. I can see the movement of money on similar dates to some of the incidents, but they don't match exactly." Damon put his hands on his hips. "Something keeps niggling at me about the photo you received of me. Why would Charles have sent that? Surely it lessened the impact of Charlotte's speech when he did?"

Freddie stared at him. "Lessened the impact?"

Damon winced and slid his arm around Freddie's waist. "I don't mean to belittle what happened. I know it's bad. But Charlotte made that speech to get you scrambling, to get you busy…" He trailed off and stepped closer to the table. "To get you distracted…" He pushed some of the paper around, grabbed one and held it up to read. "She did it to get you off the scent of finding us. If you were distracted, you wouldn't be trying to find where we were." He held out the paper. "Charles ruined that by sending the photo because it put your focus back on us rather than what Charlotte was doing."

Freddie read through the paper, eyebrows lifting. "They were trying to hide the evidence of the money being sent to BG Construction."

"She obviously knew if you investigated deep enough that something somewhere would point towards the… place they kept us in. They removed money from the company and sent it to Jamison Investments."

"Why would that make a difference?"

"Because it could be seen as an investment rather than the money being spent on whatever they were using it for in the…place."

Freddie didn't miss the hesitation every time Damon spoke of the prison they kept him in. He refused to use the word "prison" and winced whenever someone else said it. Freddie could understand why, but he wasn't sure it was healthy for him. Maybe he should mention it to Timothy because Damon was still talking to him.

"The guy who picked you up that day. They must've been paid for it. Where was that money coming from?" he asked instead.

Damon shook his head. "I don't know. They're bloody

clever. No monetary amount is ever the same value, whether it's income or expenditure. BG Construction might get ten thousand pounds in, but they spend eleven and a half. On a smaller scale too. If you watch the money go in, no matter what money goes out, it's always different amounts. It's harder to say what they used for what. Not impossible, mind. Difficult." He sighed. "Going back to the photo. I don't think Charles was supposed to send that." He stared at Freddie.

"You think he was gloating?" Freddie said.

Damon nodded. "I think he was supposed to keep quiet and let Charlotte distract you while we languished away, but when he sent that photo…"

"It was full steam ahead in trying to find you." Freddie frowned. "Do you think that's why Charles and Elizabeth were there when we arrived?"

"What do you mean?"

Freddie paced away from the table, trying to gather his thoughts. "Collateral damage. She might've known the moment we mobilised to get you and didn't tell them we were on our way. Scapegoats?" Freddie glanced at him. "It might account for why she's not making much noise about Charles's supposed innocence."

"Do you think she'd give him up when she was so vocal the last time he was arrested?" Damon asked.

"Maybe she has no choice. Everything was recorded." Freddie smirked. "Well, almost everything." He chuckled, then sobered. "There's no way she can get him off the charges when he was on the video. It's possible she didn't account for that. She might've thought she could get him free again, but those recordings are damning."

"It makes sense in some ways. Is she willing to let us know she's behind it all?"

Freddie scoffed. "It's not like she keeps her hatred a secret. I don't think she cares anymore, provided we don't have any proof pointing to her, which we don't. No physical proof anyway. Only witnesses, who might not all be reliable."

Damon sighed and winced, resting a hand on his ribs. "I'll give Charlotte something. She's clever."

Freddie frowned, something his father once said coming to mind. "Not *this* clever," he murmured, trying to grasp where his thoughts were going. They'd been discussing one of Freddie's younger cousins, who had been struggling with school at the time. Andrew had mentioned that Charlotte had been the same, unable to follow a question to its logical end until they hired a tutor to work with her. When she went to university, she met Ernest, who was an assistant there, and he helped her. Shortly after meeting, Ernest asked her to marry him, and she agreed without consulting anyone else. From what he remembered, Andrew said his father had been furious because Charlotte and Ernest had already announced it, but he couldn't find a reason to deny them.

"Freddie?"

Freddie blinked. "Sorry. Lost in a memory. What did you say?"

"I asked what you meant by 'not this clever.'" Freddie explained his memory. "You need to speak to your father."

"Why?"

Damon stared at him. "What if she's not the head of the snake? What if she's just the face of it?"

"She's a puppet?" He raised his eyebrows.

Damon shrugged. "It's possible. And it's something we've not considered before."

"A scary thought." He cleared his throat. "Have you heard the latest results from the public?"

"Yes." Damon gathered the paperwork into a pile. "Could be better."

Freddie stared at him, sliding his hands into the pockets of his trousers. "Could be worse."

"Are they still wanting a heterosexual couple on the throne?"

"Sixty-five percent do." Damon paused briefly, then continued straightening the papers. "Damon?" Damon stopped but rested his hands on the table, not looking at him. Freddie swallowed against the lump in his throat. "Don't leave me," he whispered. "I can't do this without you now." Damon dropped his head forward. "I want to live my life for *me*. I want to make the choices *I* want. And I want you." He licked his lips, scared he couldn't find the right words to explain what he needed. "I'd never had to face the possibility of life without you in it until we started pulling away from each other last year. At the time, I didn't realise why the thought scared me so much, but I knew, deep inside, that I couldn't lose you. Every day brought me closer and closer to the truth until I couldn't do anything but face it." He cleared his throat. "When Father told the world that his love for Mother was different to his love for his children because he *chose* her, it resonated with me. I don't have children, obviously, so I can't compare, but the fact is that I've chosen you to stand beside me, to have my back, to help me stand strong in front of the world, and I would do anything for you. Anything. Including…" he inhaled, "stepping back from my duties and abdicating when the time inevitably comes."

Damon gasped and stared at him, tears streaming down his face. He sobbed and raced to Freddie, throwing his arms around him. "I don't want you to…abdicate. You'll be a fantastic king." He cupped Freddie's face. "I'm scared, Freddie. Of what they'll do to you. To your family. But if you're sure, I'll be with you every step of the way."

Freddie kissed him, threading his fingers into his hair and holding him still to ravage his mouth. Damon groaned and stepped closer. He pulled away, resting their foreheads together.

"I love you so much."

"And I love you," Damon replied. "And I was considering leaving. I don't know how you knew, but I thought I should admit it."

"I know you, D. You're my best friend."

They kissed again, this time slow and meandering. Not to increase their arousal but to be there for the other person. Freddie lost track of how long they stood there, but eventually, he pulled away.

"I need you beside me, D. I can't do this without you," he whispered.

"I'm there. Every step of the way."

The door slammed open, and Damon spun to put Freddie behind him. Freddie's heart raced, and he cursed at George when his brother ran to them.

"What the f—"

"Put the TV on!" George shouted.

Damon grabbed the remote and turned the screen on to the channel George told them.

"—should be made to pay for what they've done! Arresting my son is the last in a long line of things they've done to hide their true plans. Plans I intend to see an end to by removing those bad seeds from the royal family." Charlotte banged her fist on the podium. "We cannot let these murderers continue!" Damon muted it when Charlotte disappeared from the screen.

"What the hell is she doing?" Freddie asked.

"She's inciting uproar," Mav said from behind them, and Freddie jumped, having not realised he'd joined them. "By bringing light to this, she's trying to get on their good side and, in this case, to appeal to them as parents."

"Will it work?" Damon stared at them.

Mav's jaw flexed. "Possibly." He sighed. "I've got Winter looking into it as well. She has a lot more contacts than I do. We'll be able to get a larger spread of how things are looking when she comes back to me."

"I wonder if Father is going to react," he murmured, half to himself.

"I doubt it. Standing up in front of the public every time they lobbed an accusation at us wouldn't be beneficial. If anything, the more often he does it, the more chance there is of something happening at one of them. We can't be predictable," Mav said.

"Are they cancelling the events?"

Mav glanced at him. "Not yet."

He could see that Mav didn't agree and wanted them cancelled, but he wouldn't go against Andrew's wishes, despite his opinion. Freddie wasn't convinced that continuing with the events was the best choice, but he would still attend if his father wished him to. After all, their lives were in service to the public. Freddie's stance on that was changing, too. He wasn't sure who he needed to speak to first: his father or the security team.

Damon grabbed the paperwork. "I'll go to see Brett. You go to your father. We'll meet later to compare notes."

Freddie grinned, reached around to his nape and pecked him on the lips. "Divide and conquer. I like your plan."

Damon returned his smile. "Best get to it then, my prince," he murmured.

Freddie walked out with them but diverted off towards his father's office after another kiss with Damon. He strode down the corridor, a smile on his face, which gradually left when he focused on the conversation he'd had with Damon and the recent news.

"It's not my place, Your Highness, but I'm glad to see you happy," Locke murmured from behind and to his left.

Freddie glanced over his shoulder. "Thank you, Locke. I appreciate it."

He entered the outer office, which should be called

Randall's office, but Randall never liked that idea when they'd suggested it before.

"Is he busy, Randall?"

Randall stood. "No, Your Highness. Go straight through."

That surprised Freddie, but he did what he was told. He entered and closed the door behind him, finding his father standing before the window, hands in his pockets, shoulders slumped.

"Father?"

Andrew smiled and faced him. "Freddie. How's Damon?"

"Damon's healing slowly, but he's getting there. A bit more active each day."

"Good. Good." His father was distracted for obvious reasons. "What did you want to talk about?"

Freddie raised his eyebrows. "Um, Charlotte?"

Andrew sighed and rubbed a hand over his head. "The more we acknowledge her, the more she'll come back. We need to leave it alone and focus our efforts on finding the evidence against her."

He was right, but he didn't have to like it. "Have you heard any more from Christian or Neil?"

"Neil contacted me this morning to give us a rundown, and Christian's on his way to expand on it, but basically, they think they've found the link between the three companies Damon highlighted."

"That's great news!"

Andrew sat in his chair. "Yes, and no. We might have

the link, but we still don't know who owns them. She's far too good at covering her tracks."

Freddie sat opposite him. "That's something I wanted to ask you about. We had a conversation years ago about cousin Philip and how he wasn't doing well at school and needed extra help. Do you remember?" Andrew nodded. "You mentioned Charlotte needed similar help when she was younger. You said she couldn't see the logical steps in working out a puzzle."

"That's right."

"Is that something you can get good at? Or is it something someone would always struggle with?"

Andrew shook his head. "I don't know, why?"

"When I mentioned it to Damon, he wondered if this was her plan at all. In his words, is she just the face of the snake and not the head?"

Freddie watched his father, his expression changing when it sank in what they'd potentially figured out.

"But if she's not the one making the calls, who is?"

Freddie's heart pounded. "I don't know. And I think that scares me more than anything else we've faced."

Andrew scrubbed his hands over his face, then rested his elbows on his desk. "I don't even know where to go with this. If you're right..." He didn't need to finish. A knock sounded. "Come in!"

Christian came in, expression grave, followed by Damon and some of their group, including Kean and a chocolate Labrador inductee. "We have good and bad news."

23

DAMON

"Good first," Andrew said when they settled into chairs around the room or leaned against walls.

Christian stayed standing. "We've found the connection between the three companies. They're all under an umbrella company called 'Kletti Pazo.'"

"That's great. Who are they?"

"That's the bad news. We don't know yet." Christian sighed. "What we do know is what the company's name means. Kletti is Icelandic for 'cliff,' and Pazo is Galician for 'palace.'"

"Cliff and palace. That's a bit...in your face, isn't it?" George said. He wasn't wrong.

"It seems too easy. They're pointing the finger towards them being part of the royal family," Douglas said.

"Or," Freddie stared at them, "they're trying to make it *look* like they're part of the royal family. This could be how they have 'evidence' pointing towards Father."

Christian nodded. "That was what I thought, but if you think about it, it could be both. We already know Charlotte's part of it, and she's part of the royal family—whether we like it or not. It can point to them both, which is a good thing *and* a bad thing."

"What's the latest on the public's response, Mav?" Andrew asked, settling behind his desk once more.

"Not much has changed. Charlotte's rant today has actually harmed her more than us. Some are saying she's unstable, whereas others are saying it's because it's her son and, I quote, 'wouldn't any parent feel that way about their child being arrested?' We've gained some popularity again—verging on seventy-thirty now."

"Better than it was," Damon said.

He didn't know why, but he was still going back to what Freddie had said about Charlotte's school days. It didn't matter that she'd needed extra help—lots of children did. What he kept fixating on was what she needed help with. It was as if she could have a goal but wouldn't know how to plan the steps to reach it. If that was the case, then he was sure there was someone behind her pulling her strings.

"Freddie, tell them about Charlotte."

Freddie settled beside him, linking their fingers. "I've already spoken to Father about this." He continued, explaining their thoughts, and Damon watched everyone's expressions, a mixture of horror, fear and anxiety washing through the room.

"Do you think it's Uncle Ernest?" Douglas asked. "He never struck me as someone who could be the head of something this big. He always seemed..." Douglas shrugged.

"A follower instead of a planner," Freddie finished for him. "Yes. I thought that too. We can't rule it out. He could be a fantastic actor."

"For all these years?" Kean raised his eyebrows, the last of the bruising still visible on his forehead. "I don't think many people could fake it for this long."

"But what if he's only faking it when he's in public? If he is the head of this, he wouldn't have to pretend to be Charlotte's minion when they're at home." Kieren slid his arm around Patrick.

"We need to speak with Albert again." Christian headed for the door, Oreo at his side. "He might not have any more information, but he could give us some insight into Ernest's personality and behaviours. We might be able to figure out from that whether he has anything more to do with this."

"Christian, ask Albert if you can speak with Evanna. She might have picked up on something no one else did, but if he says no, respect it. We don't want to cause them more harm," Andrew said.

"Of course. I'll be back as soon as I can."

Christian disappeared, and everyone was quiet for a few moments. Damon couldn't see Ernest being in charge, but wasn't that the reason to look at him closer? Freddie had said he could be a great actor.

"What else is the public saying about us, Mav?" Andrew asked.

Mav shifted. "In all honesty, they're pushing back and hard. The petition to remove the family from power is growing, but it's still an insignificant number compared to what they would need for it to have any power behind it. At least for now. I'm keeping my eye on it."

"And their opinions on having an LGBTQ+ royal family?"

Mav tilted his head from side to side. "We've gained popularity with the LGBTQ+ community for obvious reasons. They're supporting us vocally, which is great. Unfortunately, some religious segments are not helpful. Those whose religion disagrees with same-sex relationships are vocally opposed, for obvious reasons."

"We've gained some, but we've lost others," Andrew surmised. Mav nodded. "Okay. It's not as bad as I thought it would be." Damon raised his eyebrows at that but didn't comment. Andrew must've caught it because he chuckled. "It's not. Worst-case scenario, we step aside, and Victoria takes over. It then goes to Mary. I'm happy for either of them to take over. They'll continue our work because we're on the same wavelength."

The door opened, and Henry came in, carrying an array of papers and books that looked set to tumble from his hands at any moment. Patrick raced to him and grabbed some of his load, but Henry's gaze was on Andrew, and if Damon had to guess, he appeared scared.

Andrew came around the desk and took hold of Henry's biceps. "What's wrong, Henry? What happened?"

"I... We..." He shook his head, trying to breathe, and

Andrew pulled him into his arms, tucking his head beneath his chin and rubbing a hand up and down his back.

"Okay. Take it easy. Calm down, and we can talk through it." Patrick stood behind Henry, murmuring to him until Henry inhaled deeply and stepped back.

"Sorry."

Andrew waved him away. "Don't apologise. Sit down and have a drink. Then we can figure out what's going on."

Henry settled on a sofa, and Andrew sat beside him while Kieren handed Henry a warm drink. Henry cradled it in his hands after taking a sip, staring at it. When he looked up, he looked wrecked.

"We have a problem," Henry said.

Andrew frowned. "What is it?"

"I have to go back to explain before I tell you what it is; otherwise, it won't make sense."

"Take your time."

Henry sipped his tea. "As you know, I've been researching the family and the club and how it all came about. I was looking at what your father had achieved during his reign," he said to Andrew. "One of his final requests had been to change the law relating to the female descendants of the royal family."

Andrew nodded and smiled. "Yes. Instead of having the line of succession go through all the males in the family first, then to the females regardless of whether they were born first, he changed it to go in birth order. It was one thing he'd been working on for years."

Henry licked his lips. "It was never finalised."

Damon frowned. What did he mean? He glanced at Freddie, then Andrew, and both held identical confusion.

"Yes, it was. We have the document," Andrew said.

Henry shook his head. "Your father died before he finalised it."

Andrew reared back. "What?"

"There had been many people against the change, but Grandfather had pushed for it to happen. He'd been working on getting it completed, but he died before they could complete the change."

Andrew stood and paced to the window and back. "But the document..." He stared at Henry.

"It was a draft of what it would look like or a fake. I don't know. But I checked the laws and everything. *It never went through.*"

Damon didn't know why this made a difference to their current situation, but he didn't want to bring it up when it appeared to be close to Andrew's heart. He'd ask Freddie later.

"I'm sorry. This appears to be a big thing, but I don't understand why," Kieren said, stating exactly what Damon had been thinking.

Freddie tightened his grip on Damon's hand, gaining Damon's attention. He swallowed. "It means the line of succession is different. Those we thought would come into power won't."

Damon's heart skipped a beat.

"Victoria wouldn't be after you four?" Kieren glanced

at the king and three heirs. Freddie shook his head. "Who would?"

The answer shot into Damon's head before anyone spoke. "John."

Freddie's hand tightened more.

Kieren stared at him. "You mean to tell me that with this news, John, who is Charlotte's right-hand man, is next in line to the throne?"

"That's right," Andrew said, his expression grim. "If this information is correct, and I doubt Henry has it wrong, then we have a bigger problem than we thought."

Kean held up his hand. "I'm not understanding right. Other than he'd be king, what does it matter?"

Andrew crossed his arms and leaned back against his desk. "We've been going on the assumption that Charlotte wanted the throne. The evidence pointed towards getting rid of the supposed next in line: Freddie, Douglas, George, Victoria, Patrick, Henry and Mary. That would've left Charlotte the queen." He exhaled. "Under the old laws, the succession would be Freddie, Douglas, George—that wouldn't change—but instead of Victoria, it would be the next eldest son, which is John. Then Arthur. It would've been Christian next, but they've been after him, too. The entire line has been rearranged, which puts Charlotte at somewhere in the twenties instead of eighth."

"Isn't that a good thing?" Kean asked.

"It would be, except, as Kieren mentioned, John is Charlotte's right-hand man. I highly doubt she would allow him to take over what she would've deemed her right."

Kean sat back. "She doesn't know."

"I would hazard a guess she doesn't," Andrew agreed and stood from his lean. "We need to get that law changed quickly. Henry, do you know—"

"What if you don't?" Kean interrupted, flushing when he realised what he'd done. "I apologise."

Andrew smiled at him. "It's not a problem. What were you saying?"

Kean's face flushed, but he moved to the edge of his seat. "If Charlotte doesn't know about this, then something else is at work. Or someone."

Damon watched the back and forth between them, smiling despite the seriousness of the situation.

"He's right," Freddie said. "It pains me to say, but you need to keep it as it is for the moment." Andrew frowned, and Freddie stood. "Several reasons. Aunt Victoria should be safer, as should Patrick, Henry and Mary. If they're after John in the succession line, he might leave them alone. Another reason is we need to find out if Charlotte knows about it. If she doesn't, we know someone else is behind this because she wouldn't agree with it. All this has been done to give her the throne. And if she does know, everything we thought we knew about this situation is dust. Because I don't have the first clue what she's doing if she knows she doesn't get the throne."

Freddie sat beside him again and slid his arms around Damon's shoulders, pulling him closer. Damon didn't resist, not only because he wanted to be close but because Freddie needed the comfort, and this was the only way he would show it in front of everyone there.

Andrew cleared his throat. "Okay. Before we do anything, we need to confirm what Henry's found." He turned to the man. "It's not that I don't believe you because I do. But we need it confirmed officially, but on the quiet. I'll look into it, and I'll ask Randall to help. In the meantime, Douglas, can you contact Christian and get him to ask Albert about this? I doubt he would know anything about it, but he might've heard something."

"Sure." Douglas stood, Mav following suit.

"Damon, can you double-check the information you found on those companies? We need to see what exactly this umbrella company is doing with them and if there are any others linked to it." Damon nodded. "Kean, could you help him? Many hands make light work and all that."

Kean blushed. "Of course."

"Freddie, you need to get ready for the event." Andrew sent him a pointed stare, and Freddie tensed, which was his way of not fidgeting under such a look.

"I'm working tonight, and I know Lottie and Arthur will be there. Do you want me to see what I can find out?" George asked.

Andrew opened his mouth, then closed it again. He sighed. "I was going to say no, but yes. Be careful. We don't want them to figure anything out."

George grinned. "I'll be a super spy."

Andrew groaned and rubbed a hand over his face. "Be gone with you!"

Everyone laughed and headed for the door. Andrew turned to Henry, pulling him into his arms and murmuring something too low for Damon to hear. Henry looked devastated, but he was sure Andrew was reassuring him.

"Shall we get to work?" he asked Kean before they left.

"I'm going to..." Kean thumbed over his shoulder towards Andrew and gave a small smile and a half-shrug.

Damon clapped his shoulder. "Take your time. I'll be in my suite whenever you're ready."

Kean nodded. "Thanks."

Damon slid his hand into Freddie's and followed him out.

"What was that about?"

"What?" he said innocently.

Freddie raised his eyebrows, and Damon ignored the look. "What does Kean need to see Father about?"

"How am I supposed to know?"

Freddie stared at him, then pushed him back against the wall in the corridor, his body flush against Damon's front. Heat flowed through him from head to toe and back again, and his eyelids fluttered. Freddie cupped his jaw, and Damon lifted his chin, expecting a kiss. When it didn't happen, he blinked, seeing a smirk on his boyfriend's face.

"Does Kean want a relationship with my father?"

Damon exhaled and slipped his arms around Freddie's waist. "Confidential information," he whispered.

Freddie brushed his lips across Damon's mouth. "Is he in love with my father?"

"Con... Confidential..." He exhaled heavily, Freddie

brushing the groins together. He could feel how hard Freddie was.

"Hmm." Freddie let go, and Damon grabbed the wall to stop himself from falling, and Freddie stalked back the way they'd come.

"What are you doing?" Damon said.

"You told me to talk to my father. That's what I'm doing."

They entered the office again, and he headed for the door. "Your Highness, he's talking with Kean at the moment," Randall called.

"I know, Randall. It's okay," Freddie said.

Damon wasn't sure it was, but he followed when Freddie opened the office door and entered, stopping over the threshold. Damon peered over his shoulder and saw Andrew hugging Kean to him. They jumped apart, and Kean flushed a glorious shade of red while Andrew frowned.

"Yes, Freddie?" Andrew glared at them.

Freddie stepped closer, and Damon closed the door behind them. "I wanted to say that...you can talk to me. Even if you think I won't be happy or I won't agree. You can always talk to me." He pointed between Andrew and Kean. "This...is all good. I wanted you to know that. Sorry for interrupting."

Freddie spun and left the office, leaving Damon to stare after him.

"You told him?" Kean asked, the hurt audible.

Damon shook his head. "He saw you at the party. Andrew had his arm around you and was holding Kendal's hand. He had questions, but I didn't betray your confidence. He guessed. And though his execution left a lot to be desired, his words were truthful. He doesn't mind. He hates secrets now, which is my fault." Damon gave a small smile, then turned to leave.

"It wasn't your fault, Damon. It was mine, and I'm sorry," Andrew said.

Damon nodded over his shoulder. "It'll take a while for him to forget, but if you can, be open with him. And the others. You'd be surprised who supports you." He grinned. "All *three* of you."

He slipped out, closing the door and racing after Freddie, who happened to be waiting a little way down the hallway.

"Are you okay?" he asked when he reached him.

"Yes. Did I do the right thing?" Freddie said, tapping his thigh.

"You did. It might've been better to wait until a different time, but you got the message across."

Freddie stepped into him, holding him close. "I love you."

Damon smiled into his shoulder. "I love you." He nudged his hips forward. "Do we have time...?"

"Maybe. Depends how long you take to get back to my suite."

It took a second for the words to register, but then Damon tore himself from Freddie's arms and ran down the hallway. He was panting when he arrived but threw the door open, kicked off his shoes and jogged to the bedroom. His ribs and nipples ached, but he didn't care.

He dropped to his knees at the end of the bed, facing the door, rested his hands on his knees and lowered his eyes to the ground. They both needed this. The release of tension. The joy of union. The reminder of what they had and what they could lose.

FREDDIE

Walking into the bedroom and seeing Damon in the submissive pose had Freddie's cock perking up even more than it had been. But he didn't want Damon to be submissive this time. He wanted them on an even level. He knelt in front of Damon, tucking his finger beneath his chin and lifting his head until they locked gazes.

"Here, in this room, it's us. Not me, not you. Us. Equal. Wanting. Needing. Loving. No Dom, no sub. Just us."

Tears filled Damon's eyes, and the first one fell when Freddie captured Damon's lips. His hands grasped the back of his head, and he ravaged Damon's mouth, swallowing every groan, moan and whimper, taking all his air and losing his own. He ripped his mouth away, chest heaving, the oxygen flowing back into him. He kept one hand on Damon, swaying, and grabbed the hem of Damon's T-shirt. The soft fabric barely made a sound as he lifted it and yanked it over Damon's head. The moment his skin was exposed, Freddie's mouth latched onto the soft area beneath Damon's ear. Damon held onto his biceps, Freddie cradling his body in his hands.

He kissed a path along Damon's shoulder, alternating between licks, kisses and nips. He slid his fingers up Damon's spine, a shiver wracking his body and echoing in Freddie's. His fingers reached his shoulder and followed the path of Freddie's mouth down his chest until he halted at his nipples.

"I can't touch these yet, but we'll have fun with them when they've healed," he murmured, kissing a circle around each. Damon raked his fingers through Freddie's hair, tightening his grip every time Freddie nipped his skin, which he did when he kissed his way across to his other shoulder and up the column of his neck to his mouth.

He swept his tongue inside, wanting nothing more than to claim every inch of him. To imprint himself on Damon, so his best friend and boyfriend was never without him, no matter where he went.

Damon's hands released his hair and slid down to his shirt buttons, unfastening them quickly. Freddie rested his hands over them, slowing him down.

"There's no rush, sweetheart. We're not going anywhere."

"What if—"

Freddie quieted him with another deep kiss, and Damon's hands continued undressing him. Damon pushed at the fabric at his shoulders, and Freddie removed his hands, letting it fall over the back of his legs. He lifted his head, cupping Damon's jaw and staring into his eyes.

"You're perfect."

Damon's hands skimmed across Freddie's skin, and Damon licked his lips, and his mouth curled. "You're far from shabby yourself." He leaned forward.

Freddie chuckled against Damon's cheek, his eyes closing at the scent invading his lungs. His fingers explored the ridges and valleys of Damon's back and teased the waistband of his trousers, his nose nuzzling him. The goosebumps following the path of Damon's hands, travelling the expanse of his skin, had shivers lighting his body.

"Freddie..." Damon gasped, arching his back when Freddie grasped a handful of his ass. "More," he breathed.

"Be patient, D. It's coming."

Freddie's hands loosened, and he rose on shaky legs, pulling Damon up with him and wrapping his arms around him again. Damon slid his arms around his neck, resting his face in Freddie's neck. The heat emanating from him was toasty, but his focus was torn between that and his groin. Freddie could feel Damon's hard cock brushing against his own, and he grabbed Damon's ass, pulling them tighter against each other.

Damon hummed, let go and grabbed Freddie's trousers, unfastening them before Freddie had even realised he was going to. He pushed them off Freddie's hips, and they pooled around his ankles. One minute, Freddie had Damon in his arms; the next, Damon was on his knees, mouthing at Freddie's boxers-covered cock and trying to remove Freddie's shoes. Freddie shook his head with a smile and lifted one foot at a time so Damon could attend to him. When he was free, Damon went back to nuzzling his cock, but Freddie gripped him under his arms and lifted him to standing.

"But—" Freddie pushed him gently backwards onto the bed, and Damon glared at him. "That wasn't nice."

Freddie raised an eyebrow and crawled up the bed over him until his mouth was level with Damon's groin. "Are you sure about that?" he said, blowing a heated breath through the material. Damon groaned. Freddie undid and unzipped his trousers, dragging them down his legs but leaving the briefs in place. He moved to the side to pull them off completely and threw them to the floor somewhere. He straddled Damon's feet, smoothing his hands up the toned legs to the edge of his underwear.

Tilting his head, he stared at Damon, his hands hovering over his cock, which was trying to escape its confines. Damon's pupils were blown wide, his chest heaved, and his hands gripped the covers. When Damon's knuckles turned white, and he bit his lip, Freddie leaned down and kissed his stomach, painting circles with his tongue. Damon arched into him, and Freddie slipped a finger between the waistband and his skin, stretching the elastic so the tip of his cock could peek out. Freddie placed the waistband back, securing it beneath the bundle of nerves that made most men weep when it was played with.

"Please..." Damon moaned. "Take them off. I need you."

Freddie slid his body up Damon's, being careful of his nipples, and fastened their mouths together again. He rubbed their groins together like they'd done at the club until Damon's moves became jerky and uncoordinated—a sign he was getting close to the edge. Although edging was not on the agenda for that night, he wouldn't deny himself a little pleasure at the mew of disappointment from Damon.

"Shh," he whispered, pulling away. "Soon."

"Please!"

Freddie moved back to Damon's groin, hooking his fingers in the waistband and removing the briefs. A naked Damon was a sight to behold, and a frisson of jealousy reared its head. How many people had seen Damon naked? His jaw tightened. How many had touched what was now his?

A hand touching his cheek startled him, and he blinked at Damon. "What's wrong?" Damon asked, sitting up and sliding an arm around Freddie's waist to anchor himself. "Your frown line is here, and I don't want that."

Freddie sighed and rested their foreheads together. "A flare of jealousy that I'm trying to swallow. Sorry."

Damon smiled, eyes lighting up. "I like you being jealous." He bit his lip. "What were you thinking about?"

"You with other people. At home. At the club." Freddie shook his head. "I have no right."

"You don't, but it doesn't stop it from aching in here." Damon pressed a hand against Freddie's chest. "And to ease the ache, all you need to do is look at me. See where I am and who I'm with." He pressed a kiss to his lips. "You. It's always been you."

Freddie couldn't take it slow any longer. He needed Damon. Kissing him, Freddie pushed him back again and kicked off his own underwear. The lube and condom were waiting in the drawer of the bedside table, and he nudged Damon higher on the bed until he rested on a pillow and the bedside table was within reach. Freddie grabbed the lube and slid down Damon's body again, pushing between his thighs.

"Hurry!" Damon said, and Freddie grinned.

He slicked his fingers and massaged Damon's pucker before licking a stripe up the underside of his cock and sucking on the head. He licked and sucked while he rubbed against his hole, and when it relaxed a little, he slid his finger inside. Damon exhaled as he did, one hand coming to rest in Freddie's hair, the other reaching above him to hold on to the headboard.

"That feels...fuck..."

Freddie slid his finger in and out repeatedly, stretching him until there was no clenching at all, then he added a second finger and sucked Damon into the back of his throat.

"Holy shit!"

He kept his fingers in a steady rhythm while he lifted and fell on Damon's cock, hoping to take away any lingering pain in his channel at the stretch. He refused to bring Damon any pain. With that in mind, he pulled off. "Colour?"

"I thought…we weren't…doing that?"

Freddie growled. "Colour?"

"Neon freaking green!" Damon shouted.

Freddie grinned and removed his fingers, reaching for the lube and slicking them some more. "Glad to hear it. Here we go again." He pressed three fingers to Damon's entrance, took one of his balls into his mouth and used his hand to stroke his shaft.

"Holy…Jesus…bloody…oh!"

If Freddie hadn't got a mouthful of balls, he would've laughed, but instead, he concentrated on stretching Damon and alternating his attention on his sacs. This time, he crooked his fingers, grazing that pad inside him and receiving more guttural cries in response.

"Okay! Stop! Fuck, stop! I don't want to come yet!" Damon yelled, pulling at Freddie's hair.

Freddie lifted off. "You had to say."

Damon panted and glared at him. "Come here. Now."

Freddie pulled his fingers free and wiped them on the cover, rising over Damon. His boyfriend grabbed his face and smashed their lips together, thrusting his tongue into Freddie's mouth. Freddie met him strength for strength, and their hips joined in with the battle, thrusting and rubbing against each other until Freddie was delirious.

"Inside me, now!" Damon demanded.

Freddie enjoyed his bossy side as much as his submissive side. He grabbed a condom, and Damon covered his hand. "Do we need one?"

They stared at each other for a moment, then Freddie lowered his mouth for a brief kiss. "I haven't had any kind of sexual relations since way before my last test." Damon raised his eyebrows, and Freddie's heart pounded. "You don't believe me?" He moved back, but Damon caught him.

"No! I mean, yes! I do believe you. I'm surprised. I thought you…did with your subs."

Freddie shook his head. "I cater to their needs and my need for the medical side of things, but more recently, I've kept sex out of it for me—until you."

"I never realised…"

Freddie shrugged. "I didn't exactly advertise it."

Damon slid his arms around Freddie's neck and smiled. "I love you. So much."

Freddie pecked his lips. "I love you."

He slipped into place between Damon's spread legs and held his cock at Damon's entrance. "Are you ready?"

"I've waited forever for this," Damon murmured, staring into his eyes.

Freddie pressed forward, the muscle trying to keep him out, to begin with, but then he slid inside, exhaling hard at the surrounding warmth. He watched Damon for any twitch of pain but could only see pleasure. He sank deep, then slid his arms around Damon's back and kissed him.

"Did you know," he murmured against Damon's mouth, "you're the first man I've slept with?"

Damon cupped Freddie's cheeks and pushed gently, putting space between their faces. "Ever?"

"Ever." Freddie smiled.

Damon frowned. "I thought we told each other everything?"

"Everything that mattered." Freddie let that sink in before rolling his hips and enjoying the gasp he received from Damon and the trill of pleasure streaking up his spine. "And in case you haven't realised yet, no one mattered but you."

He withdrew and slid deep again, peppering kisses over Damon's face until Damon caught his mouth and devoured him. Their kiss intensified, and so did Freddie's thrusts. He rose to his hands, changing positions but not letting go of Damon's mouth. He slammed deep, again and again.

"Come on, D. Give it to me. I want to see what I do to you when I'm inside you."

Sweat dripped down his temple and chest, dripping and joining with Damon's on his stomach. Damon stroked himself to Freddie's thrusts, his moans and whines getting louder the closer he came.

"That's it. I'm almost there, D. Come for me, sweetheart. Come on my cock."

Damon's mouth gaped, and he stiffened before ropes of come streamed from his dick. His ass clamped down on Freddie, and he pounded into him before growling his release and holding himself deep inside. When his orgasm abated, he rested his forehead on Damon's chest, panting.

"Jesus, D. I want to go again already."

Damon laughed. "I don't think your—Ah!" His eyes widened when Freddie rolled his hips with his still half-hard dick. "Fuck! How...?"

"Must be because I'm younger than you, but we don't have time." Freddie winked. "Later."

He kissed Damon and pulled free, jumping off the bed and dodging the pillow that came flying at him. He laughed, entering the bathroom and wetting a cloth before returning to the man he loved. Damon lay on the bed, eyes closed, legs akimbo, arms above his head. The epitome of fucked. If Freddie could've chanced it, he would've taken a photo of him and kept it with him. Unfortunately, there was always the chance someone would steal his phone, and finding photos like that would be a hefty payday for whoever that was.

He cleaned Damon, threw the cloth in the washing basket and climbed onto the bed beside him. He slid his arm underneath Damon and threaded their fingers on the other side of him, then tucked himself into his side. Pressing a kiss to his temple, he said, "You get ten minutes of sleep, then we're getting up. We have work to do."

"Yes, Sir," Damon mumbled, nuzzling his head into Freddie's neck.

"I love you."

"Love you," Damon murmured, drifting off.

Freddie would've loved to be able to go to sleep as quickly as Damon could, but it had always taken him at least half an hour of relaxing in the dark before he could even contemplate it. His best friend, however, could sleep whenever and wherever.

They really shouldn't have taken this time to themselves because they had a lot of work to do, but he couldn't regret it. He would apologise to his father for commandeering his boyfriend for an hour—or however long it had been.

Freddie hadn't lied when he'd told Damon he'd not slept with anyone in a while, but he might've fudged the truth about exactly how long. In fact, he'd stopped sleeping with the subs the moment he realised he had feelings for Damon, and even he couldn't remember how long ago that had been. Just because he hadn't been willing to admit it to anyone else didn't mean he couldn't subconsciously admit it. He religiously got tested every month, regardless, because he wanted to ensure he, and anyone he played with, was safe, and Damon did the same.

He smiled at the ceiling. He had shocked Damon with his admission of having not slept with a man. He'd played with plenty, but he'd never had intercourse with them. Why he had no idea. He hadn't wanted to. Maybe his feelings for Damon had been there for even longer than he'd realised. No matter what, there would be no other for him now. Damon was everything he could've wished for and more. He could only hope that he could make Damon as happy as Damon made him.

Which brought him to their jobs. He pecked Damon on the lips, slowly bringing him to the surface after too little sleep. Damon startled but settled immediately when Freddie murmured to him.

"Time to work, sweetheart."

"No." Damon put his arm over his face, and Freddie smiled. He'd always hated waking up.

"Yes. If you get up and into the shower, I might suck you off before you have to go."

He waited, and sure enough, between one heartbeat and the next, Damon was scrambling off the bed and stumbling towards the bathroom. Freddie laughed and followed at a more sedate pace. He knew exactly how to get Damon to do the things he didn't want to do from now on.

One pleasurable act at a time.

Twenty minutes and two orgasms later, they exited his suite. Their guards were waiting, all wearing identical smirks, but said nothing. He faced Damon.

"Behave. If you need me, I'll be with Randall or Portia."

"Okay. I have no idea how long this'll take, but you know where I'll be."

Freddie kissed him. "Say hi to Kean for me."

Damon chuckled and turned away. "He'll probably be cursing me out for leaving him alone for so long," he called over his shoulder, Hudson falling into step beside him.

"Tell him to get his own man… Actually, never mind!" Freddie shook his head to rid himself of the image of Kean and his father. It was more than he needed to see.

Laughter floated back to him, and Freddie smiled.

"It's nice to see you happy, Your Highness," Owen said, starting towards Randall's office.

Freddie clapped him on the shoulder. "You should try it. It isn't half bad."

"Nah, I'm good. The single life is all I need."

Locke snorted. "No one will put up with us, Your Highness. We're too high maintenance."

Freddie laughed. "That's not a bad thing, Locke. Save yourself for someone who's worth it."

"I'll keep that in mind."

2 5

———

DAMON

*D*amon entered his suite and immediately apologised to Kean. "I'm sorry for taking so long."

Kean snorted. "I have a feeling I know why. I don't mind. Anyway, it's been nice to sit in silence for a bit, but I can't do it forever. I'd drive myself mad."

Damon wandered to the table where they kept the kettle and clicked it on. "I know the feeling. Especially when we all get together. You've been a part of this family since you were a child, like I was, but it's still overwhelming." He set up two mugs.

"Yeah, once they get going, we've got no chance."

Damon chuckled. "Damn right." He stirred the drinks and picked up the two mugs, carrying them over to the table Kean was sitting at. "Wouldn't be without them." A wave of sadness washed over Kean's face, and Damon winced at his off-hand remark. "Shit, I'm sorry."

Kean gave a small smile. "It's fine. It hurt at the time, and I didn't understand why Henry pushed me away, but now everything's clear." He sighed. "It was a difficult time, but we got through it." He huffed a laugh. "It seemed like a decade rather than a year."

Henry had pushed Kean away after they'd shared a kiss two years ago because Henry had seen what Charlotte was capable of and hadn't wanted that for them. He'd done it to keep Kean safe as well as himself. In doing that, they'd lost their friendship for a year but had managed to rekindle it after Henry had found Robert and come out to the world. But during that year, Kean's brother had died, and Henry hadn't known. They were friends again now, but Henry still hadn't forgiven himself for not being there for him.

Damon settled on the opposite side of the table and wrapped his fingers around the mug. "Time is made up of seconds, minutes, hours, but how we perceive it varies depending on our moods. When we're sad, time stretches out. A blanket of infinity laid out before us with no end in sight. When we're happy, time condenses. Makes it feel like there's never enough of it. Like we have to make every second count, but those seconds slip through our fingers too fast." He exhaled. "It's a no-win situation."

"Never had truer words been spoken."

They shared a smile, and Damon said, "What do we have?" He nodded towards the paperwork.

Kean shrugged. "Not a lot. I can't see any connection between Kletti Pazo and any other companies within the royal business list other than those three you found. I guess that's a good thing, but it doesn't help us much."

Damon pulled some paper towards them. "No, actually. That helps us a lot. It means we can focus on these three companies. We need to figure out what's happening between them." He pulled his phone from his pocket. "Bear with me a second." He dialled, putting it to his ear. "Hey, Neil. It's Damon. I'm here with Kean, and we're going through the paperwork from the audits. Are you okay if I put you on speaker?"

"Sure thing. I've got Daniel and Gia with me."

Damon pressed the speaker button and put it in the middle of the table. "Okay, Kean's been through the information and can't see a connection between these three companies and any others. Therefore, for now, I think we need to focus on these."

"I agree," Neil said. "Once we find out what's going on, we can cross-reference the rest of the businesses."

"I saw that money was moved from BG Construction to Jamison Investments, and I assumed it was to hide the money. You know, make it look like the construction company was investing its money."

"The money going into the investment company, what happens to it?" Daniel asked.

Damon pulled the accounts towards him. "From what I can gather, they're not good at investing. Every account has gained a significant amount of money and then lost the majority of it."

"Lost how?" Neil asked.

"There are several places that had money invested in it

that didn't work out. It lost money across several accounts," Kean said.

"Large amounts?" Neil said.

"Significant."

"Damon," Gia said, "from what you've seen from the information you've gathered, is there any trail from one company to the other?"

Damon stared at the papers, a thought trying to materialise. "Okay, bear with me while I talk through this. I might ramble." He pointed to one paper. "If we think logically about these companies, ignoring the financials for a minute, but concentrate on what they do. BG Construction is a construction company. Jamison Investments is an investment company. Elemental Financials is an accounts company. Now, on a basic scale, the accounts company would do accounting for other companies, for example, BG Construction and Jamison Investments. The investment company would take money from other companies and invest it, hoping to gain a profit. I don't see the accounts company needing to invest money, but BG Construction might. And the construction company would receive payments for building." He paused, trying to gather his thoughts. "If we put that on a linear scale almost, BG Construction might give money to Jamison Investments, and Jamison Investments might invest in BG Construction. And Elemental Financials might do the accounts for both."

"Are you thinking that they're fudging accounts? Moving money around?" Neil asked.

"Why not?" Kean said, getting out of his seat to stand

beside Damon. "Those losses from the investments could easily not actually be losses. They could say they were but, instead, move the money to BG Construction."

"Jamison Investments is embezzling the money, Elemental Financials are amending the accounts, and BG Construction is what?" Daniel said.

"Building the prisons," Kean said.

The moment the word hit his brain, Damon tuned out. He heard the clang of the doors, the scent of the earth, the dryness of the sand on his tongue, the shadows reaching towards him as he clutched at his ribs. The laughter. The pain. The cold.

"Damon?"

Damon jumped and stared at Kean, blinking. "Sorry, what?" He wiped a hand across his forehead and slowed his breathing.

"Neil had to go, but Gia's going to cross-reference the details and see if she can find a connection to any other company," Kean said, taking his seat across from him again.

"Great." Damon inhaled.

"Are you okay?"

Damon smiled and nodded. "I will be. One day."

"I have nightmares," Kean said, wringing his hands on the table. "Every night, there's at least one. And in most of them, we don't get out."

Damon swallowed. "But we did."

Kean met his gaze. "Doesn't make it any easier."

Damon sighed and rounded the table, pulling Kean to stand and wrapping his arms around him. "I wished I'd been able to do this while we were there." He rubbed Kean's back as they gripped each other, sharing in silence the memories of what happened to them. "We'll get them if it's the last thing I do."

"*We'll* get them." Kean pulled back, staring at him. "We'll get them all."

"We can't find any answer to if Charlotte knows about the law or not. My only guess would be that she doesn't because it doesn't make sense for her to do this to get John on the throne. She's too self-serving for that," Andrew said a week later.

They'd worked hard, talking to their contacts, their family and everyone they could think of besides going to the source to see if they could figure out if Charlotte knew the law had never been passed. Also, they'd been through the companies' accounts and found a few links to each other but nothing concrete. The few bits they had found had wormed their way through several shell companies before ending up at the next stop, but it was tenuous proof, if nothing else.

"I'm calling Charlotte in for a chat."

Andrew's words were met with silence for several seconds before Freddie, Douglas and George shouted their denial. He let them have their say before holding up his hand. When they quietened, he said, "I'm going to do it under the guise of discussing her accusations and seeing if we can't come to an agreement."

"I don't think that's a good idea," Freddie said, his fingers tapping a fast rhythm against his knee.

"She won't try anything because there'd be too much of a chance for her getting hit in the crossfire. If anything, I'm safer when I'm with her."

Damon could see his point, but none of them had to like it. "You'll have to have guards present. Meaning in the room," he said.

Andrew grimaced. "I don't know if she'll agree to that."

"She'll have no choice," Douglas said.

"Do you think she'll speak to you?" George asked. "I doubt she'll be loose-lipped."

Andrew chuckled. "She will talk around the houses about anything she doesn't want me to know, but I'll be able to see if she knows anything about the law if I ask her about it. She's never had a good poker face with me."

"I want to be there," Freddie said.

Andrew shook his head. "She won't talk with you there."

"She might gloat about it," Freddie argued. "If I can antagonise her a little, she might let something slip."

"It's not a bad idea, Andrew," William said, speaking up for the first time since their greetings. "She will take it one of two ways. She'll either think you're scared of her and need Freddie as backup, or she'll think you're trying to intimidate her. Regardless, she'll be off-kilter. Especially if you add guards inside the room too."

"I'll contact her and get it done."

"No," Damon said before he realised he intended to

speak. "Sorry." He flushed. "It's Douglas's birthday today and Freddie's event tomorrow. Wait until afterwards. If anything happens at the event, she'll think we're reacting to what happened."

Andrew stared at him, a small smile in place, before nodding. "Good idea. I'll wait. Let's make sure everything's in place for Freddie's event. I've never been happier that we didn't throw you a huge party Douglas." He chuckled.

Douglas pouted. "It's not fair." He crossed his arms, then ruined it all by laughing when Mav poked his side. "I honestly don't mind. I think I prefer our little get-togethers." He frowned. "Although they're not little anymore."

Freddie grinned. "We've certainly grown from our Scandalous Six days."

George threw his arms in the air. "I knew you'd take on the names, eventually. Thirsty Thirteen is here to stay."

"But what about all the others that have joined us?" Damon said, thinking about the potential for Kean and Kendal to join them.

"I've been keeping it to the central group and their partners," George said. "I suppose we could open it up."

"I like having the core group, but maybe we can play it by ear?" Freddie said, glancing at Damon with a curve to his lips as if he'd caught the direction of his thoughts.

George shrugged. "Sure."

"Right, you lot. Get to work," Andrew said, clapping his hands and standing. "I have important business to attend to."

"Meaning you're going to be gossiping with Uncle William," Douglas said.

Andrew winked. "Wouldn't you like to know? I'll see you for dinner this evening. Happy birthday, Douglas."

They filed out of the room, saying goodbye to Randall as they left and leading Douglas down the corridor to the receiving room. They'd commandeered it again for everyone who was coming for Douglas's birthday celebration, but they'd all agreed beforehand that they were going to start the celebration early. The thirteen of them. Though Douglas didn't know that.

"Where are we going?" he asked when Mav linked their arms and forcibly steered him where they wanted him to go.

No one said a word until they entered the receiving room, leaving the bodyguards outside. They were invited to the party later, but this was just for them.

"What's going on?" Douglas asked, standing in the middle of the room, hands spread wide.

"Calm down," Mav said, stopping in front of him. "Happy birthday, Douglas." Mav lifted to his toes and kissed him.

Douglas smiled and slid his arms around his boyfriend. "Thank you."

"This is a little more subdued than our last celebration, but we thought we could start early," Freddie said, reaching for Damon.

Damon went willingly, smiling when he pulled them chest to chest. He glanced around the room, each couple or triad stepping closer together. They made a loose circle, each of them able to see the other.

"Happy birthday, little brother. I wish you an amazing day and an even better year," Freddie said.

"Don't drink too much," Damon added. "We don't want a repeat of what these three got up to."

Patrick chuckled. "Why? It was fun. Happy birthday, Douglas."

Kieren held Patrick from behind. "It was enlightening. Put it that way."

"Remember what happened on your last birthday?" Henry nudged Douglas's arm.

Douglas hummed. "Yeah, let's not have a repeat of that. I'm happy we're staying home today. But," he nudged Henry back, "remember what you gained that night."

Robert squeezed Henry. "You gained Kean back after far too long." Henry smiled and leaned his head on Robert's shoulder.

Christian clapped Douglas on the back. "Happy birthday. Let's forget about everything and have fun."

"Happy birthday, Douglas," Oscar said, snuggling into Christian's side. Was he close to his little side?

"Hey, bro? Heads up!" George called, throwing something towards Douglas.

Douglas barely caught the wrapped box before it hit Mav, and he glared at his brother. "Say sorry!"

George winced. "Sorry, Mav. My aim is worth shit."

Mav waved him away. "It's fine. I wasn't expecting it."

Timothy shook his head and wrapped his arm around

George's shoulders. "We'll practise," he said, winking at Eddie, who flushed.

"Not sure how much practice he truly needs," Eddie murmured, hiding his face in George's neck.

Damon chuckled, and Freddie groaned and rubbed a hand over his face. "That's more info than I want, Eddie."

"Three cheers for the birthday boy!" Christian called.

They cheered and, once they'd grabbed a drink, toasted Douglas, then settled around the room. It wasn't much different from the other nights they'd spent together, and Damon had fun. Officially, he supposed, this was his and Freddie's first get-together as a couple. Not that he'd remind any of them about that. He doubted they'd hear the end of it if he did. Damon had been around long enough to become part of the furniture, but it was nice to be able to touch Freddie however he wanted while they were in company now, instead of it being in his head.

As if sensing Damon's thoughts, Freddie pressed a kiss to his temple and said, "Are you okay?"

Damon hummed and rested his head on Freddie's shoulder, closing his eyes, contentment settling into him. This was what he'd always wanted, and he now had it. "I'm great."

"I know you are." He could hear the smile in Freddie's voice. "How are your piercings?"

"They're fine, and you know it, Doctor Sutcliffe," Damon murmured low enough that no one should be able to hear him.

Freddie hissed out a breath. "Don't push for something we can't do here, D."

"Wouldn't dream of it." He was tempted.

"I think we need to book an appointment with the piercer again soon," Freddie said, slipping his arm around Damon's back and pulling him closer. "I have something I think would look pretty on you."

Damon's breath hitched, and he sank into Freddie's chest, nuzzling his nose into his neck. "I can't wait."

"You don't want to know what it'll be?"

Damon shook his head. "You can do anything. I trust you." He lifted his head, taking them nose to nose, so his eyes crossed trying to get Freddie into focus. "No matter what you do, I trust you."

Freddie's eyes both softened and heated at the same time, a feat Damon hadn't seen before. Freddie tilted his head and joined their mouths, palming the back of his head to deepen it. Damon closed his eyes and let Freddie have him however he wanted him. He would take everything Freddie gave him without complaint, and he would give whatever Freddie wanted from him. He trusted his prince to the depth of his soul and would not let anything harm him if he had anything to do about it.

Catcalls and whistles drew his attention, and he pulled away, laughing. It was nice to have the distraction, even for a little while, because the event tomorrow terrified him. There was a higher risk of something happening, whether or not it was royal-related, because it was an LGBTQ+ event. The security team—meaning Brett—had tried to persuade Freddie to cancel, but he'd refused. It had been a long time in the works, and he hadn't wanted to mess things up for them when they needed the funds they were hoping to raise from the event. Damon could understand it, but quietly, he agreed with Brett. Unfortunately, Freddie could be stubborn, which was something he loved about him. Most of the time.

But as Douglas's guests began arriving, he pushed aside all thoughts of what tomorrow might bring and focused on the celebration. He'd mentioned to Kean that time was their enemy in more ways than one, and god forbid, if this ended up being one of the last moments with Freddie, he wanted to be present. He wanted to remember everything about it. And if Damon were the one to leave, he wanted Freddie to remember this night, too.

If luck was on their side, they'd all survive to fight Charlotte and take her down. It was the one thought that kept him going. They would take her down until everyone was safe.

26

FREDDIE

Freddie stared at himself in the mirror, smoothing his hand down the front of his black suit jacket. There was nothing different in his appearance from any other event, but his heart rate hadn't calmed since he'd begun getting ready. The event itself was for a charity that supported the LGBTQ+ community. Even before his brothers and close cousins had found boyfriends, they had supported them, but it felt closer to home now. He now understood, first-hand, what uphill problems they faced every day, and it made him sad that it had taken experiencing it for him to truly understand. But, as in the ways of a lot of things, someone explaining it or watching it on TV would never show the exact feelings, emotions, behaviours and everything else involved in a situation because everyone's experience was different.

Hands came around his waist, and a chin rested on his shoulder. "Are you okay?"

Freddie covered Damon's hands, inhaled and exhaled before answering. "I am. Too many thoughts circling in my head, that's all."

"You don't have to do this."

Freddie twisted in Damon's arms and cupped his face. "I know, but it's important. I want to be there for them. They deserve all the support we can give them."

"I doubt they'd want that at the potential cost of someone's life." Damon's bottom lip protruded, and Freddie thumbed at it.

"We will be fine." They had to be. They'd lost enough already.

Damon sighed. "Are you ready to go?"

"As I can be." He dropped a kiss on Damon's mouth, linked their fingers and tugged Damon along behind him.

"I can walk, you know." Damon settled into step beside him.

"I know, but if I'd stayed there much longer, we would've been late." He winked, and Damon flushed. It never got old, seeing that pink blush fill his cheeks.

There were extensive bodyguards on duty that night. Not only were Freddie and Damon attending, but so were Patrick, Kieren and Christian—having requested Oscar to stay home, understandably. Mainly as added security because all were well-trained, but they could hide in plain sight while also showing royal support for the cause. It made them more of a target, but they'd all decided to go ahead with it. They had secured the venue, and although Brett wasn't happy, he was there with them, not only as Christian's guard. He was the one in charge, as always.

Freddie greeted everyone as they entered, but he refused to let go of Damon's hand and ended up shaking everyone's hand with his left hand instead of his usual right. He introduced Damon as his boyfriend, much to the man's delight if his blush was any indication, and squeezed his hand whenever he said it. They chatted with the charity's trustees and drank before it was time for dinner.

The security team had ensured their table was at the side, close to an exit and near the stairs to the stage. Freddie didn't have far to go when he made his speech. They all sat at the same table with one guard, who blended in with them dressed in a suit. They'd chosen the relatively unknown Hudson, who was officially Damon's guard, to take this role because he was new to the team and would not have been photographed as much.

When dinner ended, and the servers had delivered the desserts, it was time for Freddie to stand before them and persuade them to donate their money. When the charity trustee announced him, he stood, fastening his jacket buttons. He stepped away, then turned back and touched Damon's shoulder.

"Will you come with me?"

Damon raised his eyebrows but nodded. "Of course."

They climbed the steps to the stage, and Freddie shook hands with the man before approaching the podium. Damon settled to his right and a little behind him. Freddie wanted to hold his hand, but he'd never needed that before, and he couldn't start now. He inhaled and, before he spoke, felt Damon's hand rest against his lower back. His shoulders immediately loosened, and he started speaking, thanking the guests for being there and reminding them what the event was for. Then he took a sip of water from the bottle Damon handed him before continuing, this time taking Damon's hand and bringing him closer with a small smile.

"Damon has been by my side for my entire life, but it's only recently that I realised how much more love I had for him than just being my best friend. He means everything. I chose to support this charity because it's not only a worthy cause that supports so many people in need, but it's central to who we are as individuals and as a family.

"We hadn't expected to be a gay and bisexual royal family, but it doesn't detract from who we are as human beings. The same goes for everyone who finds themselves second-guessing their orientation. This charity helps people who don't have easy answers to hard questions. They offer various ways of support to anyone who needs it, even if that person realises it's not who they are after all. You can only be true to yourself, and that is the hardest lesson of all because the weight of what *could* happen is heavy. Without help, that weight can be overwhelming. But help is available. All you need to do is ask.

"Life throws us curveballs, but it's how we react to them that makes us who we are. Damon and I stand before you to show you what's possible if you believe. If you take a chance. If you live for yourself rather than those people who want to mute you. But you might need help. Be strong. We will stand beside you, we will stand up for you, we will stand in front of you until you are capable of standing strong. And even then, we will never leave you by yourself. We must all stand for those who cannot, especially in times of upheaval and strife.

"Tonight, we hope you have an amazing time, and please, be generous—with your money, but also with your time and patience. You never know who needs it."

They descended the steps to applause and settled back at the table while the trustee wrapped up the talking portion of the evening. Once the meal had ended, they wound their way back into the room, where they would mingle for another hour before they gave their leave. Freddie held onto Damon's hand throughout and stuck close to the rest of them.

"Are you sure you're okay?" Damon whispered in his ear when guests distracted the others.

Freddie gave a small smile. "I'm fine. I guess the stress of waiting to see if something would happen made me tenser than I thought it would." He sipped the last of his champagne, glancing around the room, trying not to meet anyone's gaze, so they didn't think it was an invitation for them to come and talk to him—he'd done enough of that already.

When a waiter came near, he placed his glass on the tray, but the waiter didn't move away. He glanced at his face and saw wide, panicked eyes, tears welling in them. Damon stepped between them, holding Freddie in place behind him.

"What's wrong?" Damon asked quietly.

The man opened his mouth several times before the

words came out. "Were you telling the truth?" he asked Freddie.

"About what?" Damon answered, but Freddie couldn't keep his eyes from the man whose tears streamed down his face.

"Standing beside us?" The words were whispered.

Damon tilted his head. "Absolutely. What's your name?"

The man swallowed hard. "Kevin. I don't want to do this. They made me, but I don't want to."

"Do what, Kevin?"

Kevin closed his eyes and opened part of his jacket, and Damon hissed. Freddie couldn't see what he'd seen, but Damon stepped back.

"You don't have to do this. You have a choice," Damon murmured.

"It's on a timer. There are about fifteen minutes left." Kevin's eyes overflowed.

"Fuck," Damon said. "Kevin, are you the only one?"

"I don't know. If there are others, I don't know about them."

Damon stepped back again, encouraging Kevin to come with them. "Do you know how to stop it?"

"I was told it needed to stay cold before I used it. The moment it warmed to my body temperature, the count-down would start, and if, for any reason, I needed it to stop, I could cool it down again."

"That's good," Damon murmured. Freddie saw Christian glance at them and figure out something was wrong.

He motioned to Brett, who stepped closer but to the other side of the waiter.

"No, I don't think it is! When I put it on, there was a click. I wasn't told about that! I don't know what that was!"

"It's okay. It sounds like a trigger switch," Brett said, making Kevin jump. "We can look at it." He stared at them. "Your Highnesses need to get out of here. I'll deal with this." He spoke into his radio, requesting evacuation from other guards, and squeezed Kevin's nape, focusing back on him. "Right, let's get to work. See what we can do."

Brett led Kevin away while the guards converged on them. Damon took hold of his hand and tugged him behind him, entering a corridor that led to the exit. Freddie glanced behind him, saw his cousins behind him and exhaled. They reached the foyer, there was a rumble and a loud bang, and the bodyguards flew into action, dragging them out of the building as another explosion happened. Screams and shouts erupted. People raced from where Freddie had been moments ago. The guards manhandled them into their cars and drove away before they could even sit on the seats properly.

"They were suicide bombers?" Freddie asked Damon, his hands clenching to stop them from shaking.

Damon met his gaze, eyes sombre, and nodded. He sighed. "The cummerbund was filled with explosives.

"How many of them do you think there were?"

"I don't know. There were two explosions that we

heard. It could've been Kevin and another person or two other people."

"Do you think Brett…" Freddie swallowed hard.

Damon linked their fingers. "I don't know. If it was Kevin…Brett would've been too close."

Freddie rubbed his face with his free hand, warmth curdling inside him until a ball of fury churned. "This has to end." He clenched his jaw. "I don't care what we have to do. I will end her if it is the last thing I do."

Damon slid his arms around Freddie's shoulders. "I'm right there with you."

Throughout their journey home, which was over an hour, Freddie seethed while Damon fielded calls from several people. Freddie wasn't coherent enough to converse with anyone, and when they finally arrived, he stormed through Windsor towards his father's office but met his father on the way. Andrew pulled Freddie into a hug.

"I'm glad you're here. I can't believe what I was told. Even with the best security measures in place, they still get through." He hugged Damon and, when the others came into view, did the same for them.

"Father, we need Charlotte here now," Freddie said. "I won't stand by anymore. It ends now."

Andrew sighed. "I understand, Freddie, but we have to be careful. If we don't get the information we need, it might continue, even if she's incapacitated."

"She needs to atone for what she's done!" Freddie threw his arms wide. "Everyone I love has been hurt by this…this…evil twisted plan of hers. I can't…" He could feel the emotions building up to overflowing, and Damon wrapped his arms around his waist. Freddie exhaled and dropped his face to Damon's neck.

"Come on, son. Let's go to my office. Make no mistake, Charlotte is going to be at the end of my anger. Tonight. But we need information from her as well."

Freddie stayed where he was for a moment, and when he lifted his head, he and Damon were alone, save for their guards, who were likely not to let them out of their sights for the foreseeable future.

He glanced at Locke. "Have you heard from Brett?" Locke's jaw clenched, and she shook her head.

Freddie's stomach churned, and he closed his eyes. A hand cupped his cheek. "Let's see what we can do about the witch, okay?"

Freddie cracked a smile at the words and followed Damon's lead. Before they entered the office, Freddie pulled him to a stop. "Kiss me?"

"Always."

Damon slid his arms around Freddie's neck, brushing their lips together, but Freddie needed reassurance. He clutched Damon to him and devoured him, sliding his tongue into his mouth and exploring every inch. Pulling back when he needed air, they rested their foreheads together and panted while they regained their equilibrium.

"I love you," Freddie whispered.

"I love you."

They entered the office to Andrew's raised voice. "—here, immediately. No, Charlotte. You do not have a choice in this matter. If you are not here within the hour, I will send guards for you and see that you are arrested and locked up, and I will ensure they lose the key." He paused. "One hour, Charlotte." He slammed the phone down and leaned his hands on his desk, exhaling. "She should be here soon," he said in a softer voice. "Do you want to get changed before she gets here?"

They agreed and went to shower and change quickly. When they resumed their seats, Freddie said, "How are you going to play this, Father?"

Andrew sighed and settled in his chair. "We need information. We need to know if she knows about the law, first and foremost. When we have that answer, we'll have the answer to whether or not she's the head of the snake."

"If she is?" Christian asked.

"We'll be able to focus on her and find the evidence we need—"

A knock sounded before the door opened and several people crowded in. It took a moment for Freddie's heart rate to slow enough to register it was his brothers and cousin. There was a round of hugs all around, and then they settled back again.

"And if Charlotte isn't the head of the snake?" Christian continued their previous conversation.

Andrew sighed again. "We need to figure out the connection between Charlotte and whoever it is."

"Do you still think it's not John?" Damon said.

Andrew scrunched his face. "I'm not convinced, but that doesn't mean anything. It would've never crossed my mind that Charlotte was capable of this, and she is. If only I'd seen—"

"No, Father. This isn't your fault," Douglas said, resting a hand on Andrew's shoulder.

"Isn't it?"

"No," Christian said. "Something sparked her hatred into a full-blown plan of attack, and I doubt it was anything you did or didn't do. Personally, I think John is more than capable of this." It was hard for Christian to say such things about his father, despite how the man treated him for years. "He beat his child. He shot his wife." Christian's voice cracked, and Oscar hugged him. "There was always something I thought I was missing whenever I tried to follow his plans, but maybe that was because I was looking at them as if he was a follower, not a leader."

"Until we know for definite, we can't choose a course of action," Andrew said. "I don't think it's wise that you're all here. She'll be more defensive if you're present."

"She might mess up if she feels threatened," George said.

"She also might not say a word," Freddie said. "Father's right. Let's stick to the original plan." He glanced at Christian. "Have you heard from…anyone?"

Christian shook his head. "Not yet. I'm going to check when we've finished here."

"Go!" Andrew said, waving them away. "Do whatever you need to. When Charlotte's gone, we can get together again. No, actually. Come back in the morning. Get some rest."

Freddie said goodnight to most of them until there was only Andrew, Damon and him left. "Are you bringing the guards in?"

"When she gets here. Those who escort her in will stay." Andrew settled beside him. "What happened tonight?"

"A waiter approached us," Damon said. "He wore explosives hidden in his uniform, but he didn't want to do it. From what I could gather when we spoke to him, he was within the LGBTQ+ community because he spoke of *us*. Do you think this is her version of conversion therapy? Suicide bombers who can't be 'treated' are then used in a different way."

"I don't want to think of it, but it sounds likely. What better way to get rid of those she deems pests?" A knock sounded. "Come in!"

Randall cracked the door and slid inside. "Her *Highness* is here, Your Majesty."

Freddie didn't miss the inflexion in his voice, and he grinned.

"Send her in, Randall."

Randall opened the door, and Charlotte strode in, four guards behind her.

She sighed. "To what do I owe the *pleasure*?" She grimaced.

Randall left, closing the door with the guards still inside. Charlotte glanced at them, frowned and stared at Andrew. None of them had risen to greet her.

"Take a seat, Charlotte," Andrew said. "We have plenty to discuss."

27

HENRY

Robert led Henry down the hallway to the exit, and it wasn't until they were ensconced in the car that Henry started talking.

"How can they be like this? I don't understand how Charlotte can not only be so mean as to want people like us dead but to turn them into living bombs. I can't fathom it."

Robert pulled him into his arms again, tucking Henry's head beneath his chin. "That's because you have such a pure heart. The crimes of others make no sense to you because you love everyone as they are." He sighed. "I wish people weren't like this, but unfortunately, they are, as you well know."

"Charlotte has always been nasty, making threats and snide comments, but suicide bombers? It seems completely overboard, even for her."

"People escalate, Henry. She's taking the next step up the ladder, that's all."

Henry closed his eyes and let the warmth of Robert's arms soothe him. By the time they reached Bagshot Park, Henry was exhausted, but he wouldn't be able to sleep.

"Do you want to visit with Patrick?" Robert asked.

"No, you need to sleep."

Robert tugged him in the direction of his brother's room. "I can sleep, but you won't. Let's see if Patrick is still up."

They knocked on Patrick's door and were told to enter. Patrick and Kieren sat on the sofa, curled up with some music on in the background. When they entered, Patrick stood and held out his arms. Henry hugged his brother, barely keeping the tears from escaping.

"Would you be able to keep him company until he can sleep? I want to be with him, but I need to work tomorrow." Robert's voice sounded pained, and Henry held out his hand, even as he stayed within his brother's hold.

"Don't feel bad. Your shop means a lot to you, and you have people relying on you. Get some rest. I don't mind," Henry said.

Robert's expression told him he didn't believe it, but Robert nodded. Henry disentangled himself from Patrick and hugged Robert. "Truly. You might think I'm more important than your shop, but it's not a competition. I know what I mean to you, and I know what the shop means to you. Get some sleep. I'll be in when I've calmed down."

Robert kissed him. "All right. But promise you'll wake me if you need anything at all."

"Promise."

Robert left, and Henry settled into an armchair. "Thanks for letting me drop by."

"You know it's never a problem," Patrick said. "We couldn't sleep either."

"I don't know what to think about all this."

Patrick leaned forward. "What do you mean?"

Henry sighed, trying to collect his thoughts. "I don't know everything Charlotte has done in her past, but what I do know about has never been this..." He shook his head, unable to think of the word he needed. "It's as if two people are trying to run plans alongside one another, but they're getting tangled. Does that make sense?"

"How we're saying Charlotte isn't the head of the snake?" Henry nodded at Kieren's words. "I can see that, too. Some incidents have a different feel to them than others."

"It doesn't stop Charlotte from being an evil, conniving —" Kieren pressed his hand over Patrick's mouth before he could continue, and Henry chuckled.

"She is," he agreed.

"We'll figure it out. We might be a few steps behind at the moment, but we'll do it. We'll bring them all down." Patrick rested against Kieren's side. "After all, we deserve our happily ever afters, don't we?"

"We do. Especially Freddie and Damon." Henry grinned. "They were clueless before. Well, Freddie was."

"He threw himself into it once he'd figured it out. I'll give him that," Kieren said.

"That's Freddie for you. Once he's decided, that's it. Like Uncle Andrew."

They lapsed into silence, and Henry wondered what was happening at Windsor.

"I hope Uncle Andrew is giving Charlotte hell," Henry said.

"I guarantee it," Patrick said.

28

DAMON

Charlotte curled her lip and settled into an armchair towards the back of the office, not as far away as she could've chosen but far enough to stay outside of their physical reach. Good job, too, because Damon could tell it would only take the wrong word, and Freddie would be on her. Andrew, too, maybe.

She crossed her legs and rested her arms on the arms of the chair. "And what might that be?"

Andrew stared at her for a moment, then said, "Do you remember the law Father was trying to change before he died?"

The subject must've shocked her because she stared at Andrew for a long moment before shaking her head as if to wake herself up. "Um, no. He had many... Yes!" She held her hand up and leaned forward. "He was changing the line of succession. Or rather, he *changed* the line of succession, making females as important as males." She smirked. "Quite right, too."

"I agree," Andrew said. "It was a big deal."

Charlotte nodded. "There were many people against him if I remember." She hummed. "I hadn't thought about that in a while." She frowned. "Is that why you brought me here? To discuss Father's legacy."

"No, but I've found out they did not change the law." Andrew sighed and shook his head. "I have to get working on it again, but it won't take effect for a while yet. Too much red tape to go through."

Damon observed Charlotte, but even if he hadn't been, he wouldn't have been able to miss the widening of her eyes and the dropping of her chin.

"What?" she finally said.

Andrew paused his mumblings to stare at her. "What?" he asked, feigning ignorance.

"What did you say? About the law?"

"Father died before they passed the law, and the female line of succession is still as it was. It means after me and mine, it would go to John, not Victoria. I'm sure Victoria wouldn't care either way, but it's a shame." Andrew kept his musings up, but Damon could tell he was saying stuff to keep her off balance.

Charlotte stared off to the side, her forehead creased, her mouth pursed. She looked like she'd eaten a sour fruit and truly like she had no clue about the law. Damon's stomach rolled. Looks like they had their answer. He glanced at Andrew, who closed his eyes briefly. They had a much bigger problem than Charlotte, it seemed.

"The event Freddie went to tonight had a security problem," Andrew said abruptly.

Charlotte blinked, then smiled. "I heard." She glanced at Freddie. "I'm glad you survived."

She didn't sound glad, and Damon clenched his fists to stop him from throttling her.

"Thank you," Freddie said, the hostility in his voice clear.

"This has to stop, Charlotte. What you're doing is hurting people who don't need to be hurt."

Charlotte leaned back in her chair again, though not quite as poised as before. "I don't know what you're talking about. I have nothing to do with that."

"Someone else was in charge of that event, were they?" Damon asked.

Charlotte flicked a glance at him and then ignored him. "You keep pointing the finger at me, brother dear. What about those around you? Have you seen what you've surrounded yourself with? It's no wonder you're confused."

"Confused?" Andrew scoffed. "I've known who I was before you even knew what the options were. It's not a recent epiphany."

Charlotte glared. "It's unnatural, Andrew. The Lord made a man and a woman to procreate. There's no procreation between men or between women. It's not possible. Procreation is important to our line. It's necessary."

"Gay people can still have children, Charlotte."

"But not of a true bloodline. There's only one set of

genes from the parents. That's not a true line." She scooted forward in her seat.

"It doesn't need to be," Andrew countered. "If they are deemed the parents, the child doesn't need to be blood bound."

Charlotte stood, and the guards stepped closer. "That's the problem! Diluting the line! How can you expect true royal heirs when they're not even of our blood?"

Andrew sighed. "Blood doesn't mean anything, Charlotte." He pointed at her. "Case in point."

"What do I have to do with it? I'm of royal blood."

"I know, but that doesn't mean you're fit to rule. I'm quite glad the law hasn't been changed. You won't get your hands on the crown unless something takes out over twenty people who are there before you."

Damon held his breath, wanting to laugh at Andrew's audacity. Freddie didn't have any qualms and snorted. Charlotte glared at them again but spoke to Andrew.

"You're wrong about that law. You must be."

Andrew stood, heading for his desk. "Here. You can see for yourself."

Guards stepped behind him when Charlotte moved closer. Andrew handed her the paperwork, and though Damon could only see her profile, her jaw tightened, her eyes narrowed, and her hands shook. She had no clue about the law. No clue at all. Which meant they were in deep shit.

She handed the paper back. "I'm assuming you're working to change it?"

"I am, but it took Father over three years to work towards this. It won't happen any time soon."

"Times have changed." Charlotte crossed her arms.

"They have, but not enough. I'll get it done as soon as I can, but there are no guarantees."

"You would be surprised. The public isn't taking too kindly to having *gay* heirs. Bringing this law to light would make it easier for them to trust us, knowing that women could rule if they deemed the men...unfit."

Andrew and Charlotte stared at each other for a long moment before Andrew said, "Have a lovely evening, Charlotte."

Andrew turned her back, and Charlotte's hands clenched. Damon assumed she didn't like the dismissal and tensed, ready to intervene if she tried anything, but she glared at him and Freddie and left, the four guards going with her. When the door closed, they all relaxed considerably.

"Well, good news and bad news," Andrew murmured, settling behind his desk. He rubbed a hand over his mouth. "How did she get played? Who did it? John? And when did they get to her?" Andrew paused, frowning. "Victoria asked me if Charlotte had met Ernest earlier than when she went to university. Apparently, Kieren had asked her the question, and she wanted to double-check. None of us recognised him or his name when she introduced him, but other than a feeling, Father had no reason to deny them the marriage. He couldn't find anything in Ernest's background to suggest foul play."

"Maybe we could get those checks done again?"

Damon said. "I'm not saying he has anything to do with it, especially with how he acts around her, but it wouldn't hurt."

Andrew nodded. "Yes, I'll get Brett..." He picked up his phone. "Randall, have we heard anything..." He listened for a moment, asking a few questions, then closed his eyes and sighed. "Thank you." He replaced the receiver. "Brett's fine. He took that waiter into the freezer to cool the explosive, and it did stop the timer. Then they got the bomb squad to diffuse it. The other bombs were from two other waiters. Because of where they were, they didn't get the brunt of the explosion."

"Were there many casualties?" Freddie asked.

"Nine dead, seventeen injured. Several of those are life-threatening."

Freddie dropped his head into his hands, and Damon held him for a long moment. When he raised his head, his expression was fierce. "Father?" He waited until Andrew looked at him. "I want all royal events cancelled. We're putting everyone in danger every time we attend. I thought it was the best idea because we didn't want to show them we were scared. But people are dying. I'm not willing to let another person die because we were at an event when we could've stayed home."

Andrew stared at him, and Damon thought he'd disagree. "Agreed. I don't think Victoria will be happy. She was looking forward to her event at the end of the month." He frowned. "We will make one exception."

Freddie shook his head. "No, Father. She wouldn't

want you in danger." Damon frowned, unsure who they were talking about.

"She would know I would do this, regardless. It's not just about us, as you mentioned. I'll make sure I'm not near anyone. If they aim for me, no one else will get caught in the crossfire. I promise."

Freddie stood. "No. She'd want you safe."

Andrew smiled. "She'd want me to do my job, which is to grieve with the country."

Damon understood. Next month was the one-year anniversary of the queen's death. They were arranging a celebration of her life, but Freddie was right.

"I don't think it's a good idea." He gave his two pence.

Andrew stood. "Probably not, but it will happen. It's non-negotiable."

Freddie stared at the floor before going over to hug his father. They murmured too quietly for Damon to hear, and he wandered to the door to give them privacy. When they pulled apart, both had tears in their eyes but smiles on their faces.

"Goodnight to you both," Andrew said.

Neither said a word until they were behind the closed doors of Freddie's suite. And even then, they stayed quiet, but only because Freddie's mouth was on Damon's, stealing his breath. He could feel the fear in Freddie's movements, and Damon held onto him, proving to them both that they were still alive and well.

Damon pulled his mouth away. "Bedroom, please. Need you."

"No. Right here." Freddie pulled at Damon's clothes, buttons flying until Damon was naked with his hands pressed to the door. Freddie dropped to his knees and tapped Damon's feet to widen his stance. He gripped Damon's ass cheeks and spread them, blowing on his sensitive skin, and Damon's breath hitched. Freddie licked from his taint, over his pucker and down again before focusing on his hole.

Damon rested his head against the door as Freddie rimmed him, his tongue sliding inside and making him shiver. He lost track of time, Freddie taking him higher and higher but never allowing him to fall.

Freddie stood and slid his arms around Damon's front. "Bend over the table," he whispered in his ear, biting the lobe.

With help because of his shaky legs, Damon rested on the table, hissing when the chilly surface touched his skin. It wasn't particularly comfortable because of his ribs, but it didn't hurt. He listened, trying to figure out what Freddie was doing. All he could hear was rustling, and he assumed Freddie was removing his clothes. At least, he hoped he was.

Warm skin met the back of his legs and ass, and Damon bit back a moan, wanting to feel every inch of Freddie's skin against his own.

"Let's get you ready for me," Freddie murmured, and Damon gasped at the sudden coldness on his crack. It took far too long for Freddie to stretch him, and if he'd had his way, Freddie would've been inside him way earlier. Freddie hummed, and he pressed his cock against Damon's pucker. "I wish we could video this so you could see what you look like taking my cock." Freddie hissed, his hips rocking back and forth until he was balls deep. "Fuck, D. You're tight and hot around me." He withdrew, groaning. "I'll never tire of this."

"You better not," Damon growled. "You're mine."

Freddie chuckled, deep and low. "I enjoy hearing that." His hands bracketed Damon's body, but he didn't rest on top of him. "You tell me if your ribs hurt."

An order, not a request. "I will." *Maybe.*

Freddie rose again, his hands gripping Damon's hips. "Hold on."

Damon had barely braced himself when Freddie started a punishing rhythm. He countered every thrust forward by pulling Damon's hips back. He'd expected his lower stomach to ram into the table, but because of Freddie's diligence, that didn't happen. What happened was Damon flew. Higher and higher until he worried Freddie wouldn't let him come. But then Freddie said the magic words.

"Come for me, D."

His ears stopped working, his vision went blank, and his entire body convulsed while his orgasm thrashed through him. When it released him, he slumped to the table, gasping for air, his ribs screaming at his deep breathing.

"Fuck, D. That was…magnificent. You're gorgeous when you come."

"Did…you?" he panted.

Freddie pushed forward, and Damon could feel him inside him, but he wasn't hard. And when Freddie withdrew, his come dribbled out, too.

"Are you going to keep that in for a bit?" Freddie asked, sliding his finger up and into his pucker as if wiping his come and pushing it back inside him. Damon clenched around his finger, and Freddie groaned. "Fuck. I want to suck it all back out of you and fill you again."

"No," Damon said. "Mine now."

Freddie chuckled, the sound vibrating through him. "Maybe next time." He helped Damon to stand and led him to the bathroom. "You won't be able to keep it inside you for long."

"Don't care. Mine."

Freddie kissed him, and Damon barely kept his eyes open while Freddie washed him. "Come on, sleepyhead. Let it go now."

Damon pouted but relaxed enough to let the come dribble from his ass. Freddie washed it away, laughing when Damon glared at him.

"There's more where that came from. Don't worry."

By the time they settled into bed, Damon was already half asleep, and it didn't take long for him to slip away to dreams of him and Freddie.

Three days later, the public response was still on their side, but barely. It hadn't increased since the last test, but it hadn't decreased either.

"I want to speak to the public," Freddie said when they met with his father later that morning.

"Whatever for?"

Freddie rose, sliding his hands into his trouser pockets, and paced the length of the office before continuing. "You're always going to bat for us, which is great, and we appreciate it, but only Henry ever spoke out about his love for Robert to the masses. No one else has. I think we need to change that. What I said at the event at the weekend needs to be said to everyone, not just a group who wants to appear as if they care."

Andrew shook his head. "I don't think it's a good idea."

"What better way to share with the world than on Valentine's Day? We don't have to do it in front of an audience. We do it similarly to how you do your Christmas speeches. From the comfort of home. If we get everyone together, we can show solidarity."

Damon had to admit it was a good idea, but they wouldn't have much time to put it together. Andrew was wavering, but the smile that lit his face came through.

"Oh, hell. Why not? Go for it."

Freddie grinned. "Thank you. Damon, can you speak to Brett to make sure he knows about this? I'll call around everyone to get them here."

"I'll call my lot, too. May as well get the entire family in on this," Andrew said.

"Can we pull it off on short notice?" Freddie asked.

Damon snorted. "Once we tell Mav, it'll be all over the news and social media. Pick a time."

Freddie glanced at Andrew. "You usually broadcast at 3 p.m. on Christmas Day, don't you?"

Andrew nodded. "It's neither too late nor too early and accounts for many time zones. Not all, but many."

"We'll do that then."

"Let's do it," Andrew said, smacking his hands together.

It took a couple of hours to get everyone there and everything set up because no one had expected a TV broadcast that day, but Damon could see the idea behind Freddie's choice. It certainly couldn't hurt their ratings. Initially, they'd decided to do it in the same room where Andrew broadcasted his speeches, but when the entire family arrived, they realised there wasn't enough room for them, despite the size of the room. They moved everything to the receiving room, which was far bigger—a lot more comfortable.

When everyone settled, Freddie sat on the sofa off to one side. The idea would be to have him talk, then join the rest of his family in wishing everyone a happy Valentine's Day. But Freddie beckoned Damon over with his finger. Damon crouched in front of him.

"What's wrong?"

"I want you beside me."

Damon swallowed and shook his head. "This should be you—"

"I'm telling the world how much I love you. Why would I not want you by my side?"

Damon's heart pounded. "I..."

"Please?"

When Freddie looked at him like that, Damon was

hopeless to resist. He glanced at Andrew, who nodded at him with a smile.

"Okay." He slipped onto the seat beside Freddie, sitting straight and smoothing his suit.

"Don't be nervous," Freddie murmured. "I'm here."

Damon stared at him and smiled. The love in Freddie's eyes was clear to see; it often mesmerised him. They'd spent many years trying to find the one they believed was their soulmate when that person had been right there in front of them. Naturally, Damon had realised first, but he wouldn't hold that against Freddie. They were there now.

Damon cupped Freddie's face. "I'm not going anywhere."

"Two minutes, Your Highness."

Damon inhaled and blew it out. "Here goes nothing."

"Remember one thing," Freddie said.

"What's that?"

"I love you."

29

FREDDIE

Freddie might've been putting on a brave face, but inside, he was a mess. His stomach churned, and his palms were sweaty, but he was making the right choice.

"Go get 'em, Freddie," Douglas said with his usual smirk.

The rest of them grinned or chuckled, dropping silent when the thirty-second mark was given. He inhaled and pasted a small smile on his face.

"Good afternoon. Valentine's Day is a celebration that has grown more popular throughout the years. Its origin has been debated by different events in our history, but today, the celebration is of love. The love of family and the love of those you have chosen to share your life with. But love is not always a choice. When we are born, we have our parents' blood running through us, but for those unfortunate among us, they may not have their love.

"For me, love can be given by anyone. They do not have to be 'blood' family or your chosen partner to be allowed to love you. People who have adopted choose to love those children no matter whose blood is in them. Bloodlines have always been used as currency. Those with so-called perfect genes are given more opportunities, more support, a higher standing within the community. But blood doesn't stop anyone from committing crimes. Blood doesn't stop children from being abandoned. Blood doesn't stop families from falling apart.

"Love, however, can heal. Love can overwhelm and bring joy and bring comfort. Yes, love can hurt, and if you are alone this Valentine's Day, remember you are loved. Love is something everyone strives for. Even those who deny it, deep inside where no one can hear, they want to be loved. Since my mother's death, I have never gone a day without feeling her love for me. My father loves me. My brothers love me. My cousins, my uncles and my aunts love me. It doesn't change who I am.

"The man sitting beside me is my best friend. He knows everything about me, and I about him. Does having his love mean I am unable to do my job? I don't believe it does. Does having his love mean I am unable to see what is good for the commonwealth? I don't think so. But if you, the public, can prove that my love for Damon makes me an unfit heir, I will step aside."

Soft indrawn breaths went around the room, but Freddie didn't react, only tightened his grip on Damon's hand.

"Before you consider this option, think to yourself...

Would you stop your family from finding love? I am so happy that my family has found love." Freddie glanced at the group, smiling, and he understood the cameras would show them while he spoke. "Douglas has Mav, George has Timothy and Eddie, Mary has Nathaniel, Patrick has Kieren, Henry has Robert, Christian has Oscar, Albert has Evanna, Alice has Xavier, William has Sophia, Louis has Beatrice, Helena has Bailey and Margaret has Quentin. Before these people found their love, my father found my mother, Louisa. Aunt Victoria found Uncle Patrick, Uncle William found Aunt Lou, Uncle Arthur found Aunt Sarah, and Aunt Catherine found Uncle Francis.

"Love makes every day worthwhile. Whether it's love for people, love for the job you do, or love for the food you're eating. It doesn't matter. Blood is what runs through our veins, but love is what keeps our hearts beating."

He paused, knowing he should wrap it up, but he made a split-second decision and hoped it was the right one.

"With that in mind, I wish to share something with you." He inhaled and slid off the sofa onto the floor on one knee, gasps sounding around him. He slipped his hand into his pocket and pulled a small velvet bag free. He tipped the contents into his hand, then held it up and met Damon's wide gaze. "Damon Philip Winchester, will you do me the honour of becoming my husband?"

Damon's eyes watered, and he wiped at the tears and nodded. "Yes. I most certainly will."

Freddie grinned and slid the gold band onto Damon's

left hand and pressed a kiss to it—personal displays of affection be damned. He wanted to kiss him, but he didn't want to push too far. He slipped back onto the sofa and faced the camera again.

"Love is sometimes beyond expression, but find it in the little things in your day, and one day, you'll be rewarded by more than you ever thought possible. Have a wonderful Valentine's Day from all of us."

The producer signed that the cameras were off, and the room exploded into chaos. Freddie ignored everyone but Damon. "I didn't mean to do that on camera, but I didn't want to hold back any longer. I wanted them to see how much you meant to me and what I was willing to do to have you. Are you sure you mean yes?"

Damon laughed, teas still overflowing. "Yes, yes, yes. I definitely mean it." Damon cupped his face. "I love you."

Freddie touched their lips and sealed the deal. He rested his forehead against Damon's and sighed. "I hope I don't have to do another speech any time soon. I'm worn out."

"Frederick Alexander Andrew Sutcliffe!"

Freddie froze and then stood, facing his father, whose neutral expression worried him. They stared at one another until his father broke into a grin and dragged him into a hug.

"You silly, silly boy. What have you done?" Andrew pulled back, holding the side of Freddie's neck, worry blazing from his eyes.

Freddie swallowed. "What do you mean?"

Andrew sighed. "I love you, and I am happy you're engaged. But you've painted a target on your back."

"I hadn't planned—"

"I know. I know." Andrew smiled. "Forget about it. We'll deal with it. No matter what. I love you."

"I love you, Father."

Andrew turned to Damon. "It doesn't need to be said because you're already part of it, but I'll say it, anyway. Welcome to the family." They hugged, and Andrew whispered something in Damon's ear before pulling back.

"You sneaky son of a gun," Douglas said, clapping him on the back.

"Talk about taking the limelight," George said, elbowing him.

Freddie shrugged. "Well, when the opportunity presents itself, what can you do?" He glanced at Damon, who smiled over Mav's shoulder at him.

"I guess we need another party." George sighed, but he loved the idea of it—the social butterfly that he was.

"Nothing big, just us together like normal," Freddie said, smiling when Damon threaded his arm through his and rested his cheek on his shoulder. He spotted the ring, and his cheeks ached from how hard he grinned.

"You won't get away with that," George said.

Freddie brought his attention back to his brother. "Yes, I will. Reduced events, remember?"

George's mouth opened and closed, and he pouted. "So unfair," he mumbled.

"When are you thinking of having the wedding?" Christian asked.

Freddie huffed a laugh, opening his mouth to say that they'd only just decided, but he paused and stared at Damon, who seemed to know something was on his mind. "I'd like to do it on Mother's birthday." He hadn't realised that was what he was going to say until the words came out, but once they had, he knew they were right. His mother would want something happy to happen on a day that would be difficult for them all. Last year, it had been difficult keeping a blank expression on his face while the country mourned her loss all over again because it had only been six months since she'd died. She had always tried to spread happy memories over sad ones, and Freddie was sure she would've approved of his idea.

"Are you sure?" Damon whispered.

Freddie nodded. "She'd want that. Something happy to help with the sadness."

"But that's only seven months! Royal weddings usually have at least a year, if not more," Henry said.

Freddie raised his eyebrow. "Says the man whose wedding is in two months, which will be seven months since he proposed."

Henry's cheeks coloured, and he peered at Robert. "Oops. I wasn't even thinking of that. I hadn't worked out how long it was."

Robert laughed and slipped an arm around his waist. "Doesn't matter how long it is. We'd make sure everything was perfect, even if the date was tomorrow." He glanced at Freddie. "I wouldn't recommend it."

"Duly noted. I need to check with Father, too. He might not like the idea."

"It'll be fine." Douglas squeezed his shoulder. "Doesn't matter that it'll be the biggest wedding of the century. We can do it in seven months." He blew out a long breath, and everyone laughed.

Mav slipped in beside Douglas, his tablet at his side, and Freddie asked him without asking him. Mav chuckled. "Initial reports are favourable."

Freddie's muscles unclenched, and Damon rubbed his back. It was good news.

"We're going home, boys." Aunt Victoria stepped up to Freddie and cradled his jaw. "Your mother would be proud of you. Congratulations to you both." She kissed his cheek and then Damon's cheek. Uncle Patrick gave them both handshakes, and they disappeared.

Most of their guests had vanished, leaving their group.

"Is it a good idea to have a wedding so soon?" Henry asked, dropping back to walk beside him as they wandered away from the receiving room. "I don't mean yours. I mean mine. Two months is…soon."

"Is that your nerves talking?" Freddie asked.

Henry shook his head. "I'm not nervous. Not about marrying him. Only about whether we survive it."

Damon tutted. "You can't think like that, Henry. We'd never do anything if we believed we wouldn't live through it."

"He's right. We would've stopped all these events the moment the first incident happened if we were too scared. Besides, I'm sure there will be far too many people that attend who are on her side. She wouldn't want them to die. She'd lose followers."

"But what—"

Randall came racing down the hallway. "Your Highnesses, His Majesty would like you in his office as soon as possible."

They all quickened their pace and followed behind Randall, entering the office and being waved straight in. Andrew stood behind his desk, resting his hands on the back of his chair. For once, Freddie couldn't interpret his expression.

"Father?"

Andrew blinked, then stood upright. "Kletti Pazo is registered to John Ernest Dyer."

Freddie frowned. "Who's that?"

Andrew sighed. "Two people. Also known as John and Ernest Sutcliffe." He glanced over to the side, and Freddie followed his gaze to Christian, who had gone pale. Oscar wrapped himself around him.

"I knew he would be deeply involved, but I thought he was a follower," Christian whispered.

"It seems as if he might be the head of the snake," Andrew said. "I'm sorry, Christian."

"What of Ernest's involvement?" Damon murmured.

"He's her husband. I'd be surprised if he didn't have his hand in it, too. We have proof now, I assume. Can we get the police involved?" Freddie said.

Andrew rounded the desk and leaned back against it, crossing his arms over his chest. "Not yet." He sighed again. "The reason I'm concerned is that Charlotte didn't know anything about the law. She's working under the assumption that if she wipes out those before her, she'll get her hands on the throne. We know that's not the case, and if John *and* Ernest's names are on the company, then does Ernest know?" He paused, and Freddie let that sink in. "We need to see if there's a connection between John and Ernest that goes back before Charlotte or if it started after."

"What does Ernest gain from siding with John against Charlotte?" Freddie said.

Andrew shook his head. "I don't know. Maybe John said he'd take Ernest to the top with him. I've no idea. But John and Ernest are working together, and Charlotte is out of the loop on that bit."

Freddie straightened. "When you told her about the law, you clued her in. She looked mad, but maybe it goes further than she didn't know about the law. Maybe she's figured out what John's motives are."

Randall poked his head through the door after knocking. "Your Majesty, I have Commissioner Thomas on the phone for you."

"Thank you, Randall." Andrew picked up his phone. "Brady, how are things?" He listened, staring at the floor, but Freddie could see the tension creeping into his posture. "You're certain?" Andrew rubbed a hand over his face. "Thank you, Brady." He replaced the receiver and moved closer to Christian. "I'm sorry, but Elizabeth is dead."

"What? How?" Christian said, stepping forward. Oscar went with him, gripping his arm.

Andrew held Christian's shoulders. "There was a

scuffle where she was being held. She was stabbed in the thigh. I'm sorry."

Christian closed his eyes. "Foul play?"

"Brady thinks so. They'd been working on getting her to confide in them. Brady said they were close. She'd given them bits of information, which was why we know who owns Kletti Pazo. He had planned on trying again this afternoon, but…"

Christian swallowed and lifted his head, tears shimmering in his eyes. "I shouldn't care because she was too much like my father, but…she's my sister."

Andrew drew him into his arms and held him as Christian silently cried. Robert went to Oscar and hugged him, Christian's little sobbing beside him, still holding Christian's hand. Oscar didn't know Elizabeth like the rest of them, and his tears were for Christian's pain and nothing more.

"It doesn't matter what she's done. You feel how you feel, and I, for one, am sad that I've lost a niece, regardless of what she did," Andrew said. "Any loss is painful."

They fell into silence, grieving in their own ways. Charlotte, or whoever, knew Elizabeth was going to give them everything she had, so they had her killed. Would they be able to prove it? It was doubtful, but they knew. But they hadn't got rid of Charles or any of the others involved, like Talon. Why? Were they still useful, or were they next? Were they cleaning the board?

Christian, Oscar, Henry and Robert disappeared after a few minutes. No doubt Henry and Robert would be there in case Oscar dropped into his little space, which he did in stressful situations sometimes. Henry would look after Christian while Robert took care of Oscar.

When they'd left, Freddie voiced his thoughts.

"I would certainly consider getting extra guards or something for Talon and Tobias. They were the ones with the most contact with Charles and information about the situation. We could use them as witnesses if this ever went to court," Kieren said. "But only if they survive."

Andrew nodded and made a call to Commissioner Thomas. When he hung up, Andrew dropped into his seat.

"If John is aiming for the top, why go through all this subterfuge?" Damon said. "Surely it's more difficult to kill eight royals than to kill four. It can't be because they're trying to hide it. There are too many ways this could've gone wrong, and they would've been found out."

Freddie agreed. "If you think about it and include the helicopter crash, I was first, then they tried to have Douglas removed, but then it went to Henry. Why did they skip George?"

"They didn't."

Freddie stared at George. "What?"

George sat forward, eyes wide. "Remember the break-in on my birthday? It wasn't long after your accident, and they hadn't even taken anything before the guards caught them."

"You think he was waiting for you rather than a payday?" Douglas said.

George shrugged. "It's possible. If we're going back to Freddie's crash, how many more things have happened that we brushed off when we should be looking into them?"

Andrew nodded. "We need to get a list together of all the incidents that have happened over the years and see if there's a pattern. For now, rest. We don't know what tomorrow will bring."

They said goodbye, but before Freddie left, he approached the desk. "Father, would you object to a short engagement?" He swallowed. "I was hoping to get married on Mother's birthday."

He held his breath while he waited for his father's answer. Andrew had a fantastic poker face when he wanted to, but privately, he didn't hide his feelings. A wave of sadness washed over Andrew before he smiled.

"She would love that," he whispered. He stood, holding his arms out to Freddie. "I would love that." They hugged, and Freddie had to swallow the lump in his throat. When they pulled back, Andrew had tears in his eyes. "What a celebration." He chuckled. "I'll let you break the news to Randall." He tapped Freddie's cheek and winked.

Freddie groaned. "Really? I was hoping you'd do that."

Andrew shook his head. "Not on your life. You can tell him he has seven months to plan the biggest event of the year."

"Henry and Robert are getting married, too." Freddie pouted.

"Yeah, but Henry isn't the first heir in line to the throne. His wedding will be huge, no doubt about it, but yours..." He glanced behind Freddie and grinned. "I hope you're ready for this, Damon. Despite how long you've been with us, I doubt you've seen what you're in for with this wedding."

Freddie glanced over his shoulder in time for Damon's eyes to widen. He nudged his father. "Don't scare him off. I've only just caught him."

Freddie joined his boyfriend—fiancé—and said goodbye to his father. He stopped at Randall's desk. "Randall, we'd like the wedding to be on 5 September."

Randall smiled. "Perfect. That gives us a good eighteen months to get things organised." He rubbed his hands together.

Freddie scraped his teeth over his lower lip before breaking the news. "No, I mean, this year."

Randall blinked, and his mouth gaped. Freddie was sure he had stopped breathing. "That's... That's..." He exhaled. "Okay." His voice actually squeaked.

"Thank you, Randall. You're the best." Freddie stopped outside the door and stared back at him, grinning when Randall's head lowered to the table. "I think I broke him," he whispered to Damon.

30

DAMON

*D*amon kept moving his fingers, wanting to feel the ring. How had Freddie had the courage to do that on live TV? He hadn't expected it at all, but his answer would've been the same no matter where they were. He hoped Freddie wouldn't regret it.

They hustled through the hallways, Freddie's hand clasped around Damon's and almost dragging him along beside him. Damon couldn't hide his smile as they passed the household staff, and they received more than one large smile, which he appreciated. When they arrived at Freddie's suite, the man opened the door, pushed Damon through and slammed it closed behind him.

"You have two minutes to get undressed and in our bed," Freddie said, eyes darkening to the colour of a stormy ocean.

Damon exhaled, but the moment Freddie took a step closer, he raced for the bedroom, stripping as he went. His heart pounded with what his fiancé would do to him, and he couldn't wait. He threw his clothes into the washing basket by the bathroom door and climbed onto the bed naked, waiting on his knees with his head lowered and palms resting on his thighs. His breathing increased while he waited, a flush heating him from the inside out, and his cock lengthened the more he thought about what they might do. Would they play, or would they go slowly? Either would satisfy him, but he trusted Freddie to know what they both needed.

"Beautiful," Freddie murmured, and Damon sighed when Freddie touched his shoulders with both hands, his body letting go of any tension it held.

His fingertips glided across his skin, leaving a trail of goosebumps in his wake, down his biceps and inner forearms, and Damon shivered. Freddie touched the ring, and Damon's mouth curled, turning into another long exhale when Freddie continued his path along the inside of Damon's spread thighs, around his groin—much to Damon's groan of displeasure—and up his stomach to his pecs. Freddie kneaded them, but Damon wished he would touch his nipples, but knowing he was unable to—until Damon could barely stay still, and he had to tense his body to stop himself from pushing into his touch.

"Good boy." He could hear the smile in Freddie's voice. "I have something special for you tonight to celebrate our upcoming nuptials. What's your safe word?"

"Cheesecake, Sir."

"Good. But first." Freddie hooked a finger beneath Damon's chin and lifted his head. "Kiss me, my love."

Damon leaned forward and sealed his mouth over Freddie's, unable to stop his arms from tangling around his neck as their tongues danced. Freddie's arms banded around his back, holding onto him tightly. Damon's head grew lighter, but he couldn't pull away. Instead, Freddie tore his mouth free, and they rested their foreheads together, breathing into the space between them.

"I love you, D. No matter what happens. I will always love you."

Tears pricked at Damon's eyes, but he refused to let them fall. "I love you with everything I was, with everything I am and with everything I will be."

Freddie pressed their lips together once more but pulled back far too soon. "Face the headboard."

Damon licked his lips, trying to keep the taste of Freddie in his mouth, and did as he'd asked. He kept his gaze on the intricately designed wooden headboard, his eyes following the designs, but his ears on the sounds in the room. Drawers and doors opened and closed, and fabric rustled, but everything else was too quiet for him to figure out what it was.

The bed depressed beside him, but he didn't look away, though he could see Freddie from the corner of his eye, holding a length of rope, and Damon's heart kicked up its rhythm. Freddie's hand rested on Damon's knee and slid along his inner thigh, squeezing.

"Hands behind your back." Damon did. "Lift a little," Freddie murmured, tapping Damon's leg.

Damon leaned to the side and lifted his right knee. Freddie wrapped the rope around his upper thigh and calf, tying them together with intricate knots that Damon would never learn himself but loved seeing on his body. Freddie tested the tightness by sliding his fingers between the rope and Damon's skin.

"Perfect. Leg down." Freddie rested the rope over his other leg, climbed off the bed and slid back on the other side of him. "Up." He tapped Damon's left leg, and Damon repeated his lean, feeling the rope pressing into his skin. His cock jerked, and Damon breathed through it.

Freddie ignored it and tied his other leg, effectively stopping Damon from standing. He could still spread his legs, but only a little. When Freddie finished tying that leg, he rose to his knees and slid the rope underneath Damon, wrapping it around where his leg met his groin and to the side of his leaking cock and tight balls. He followed it around the other side and then his hips and waist, slowly rising. Freddie moved behind him, decorating both his upper arms.

"Cross your wrists."

Damon swallowed down a moan. Freddie slid the rope around his wrists, securing them to the rest of the design.

"One last bit," Freddie whispered in his ear.

The rope settled loosely against his throat, and Damon panted as his cock pulsed. He'd trusted no one enough to do this, but Freddie was completely different. Damon trusted him with his life. Freddie secured the rope and tugged a little, and it tensed against his throat. Freddie's fingers skimmed across the rope, following its path along Damon's skin.

"You're beautiful."

Damon wanted to thank him, but the words caught in his throat with the emotion overflowing him. His heart was full of love for this man, and he couldn't express how much he loved him. Words were not enough.

Freddie climbed off the bed and disappeared, but Damon wasn't worried. He closed his eyes, letting everything sink into him to remember it for years to come. Memories of their years together played in his head, and he smiled at the love he saw in them. Even if it was platonic at that point, the love was still evident.

"Drink," Freddie murmured.

Damon didn't open his eyes, but he parted his lips and a straw settled between them. He drank the warm, sweet liquid. He pushed the straw with his tongue when he'd had enough, and Freddie removed it.

The bed depressed behind him, and warm skin pressed against his hands, a solid cock resting against his ass cheeks. Freddie's hands covered his stomach and chest, reaching up to tilt Damon's head towards him.

"Open up." Freddie's finger brushed against his lips, and Damon opened his mouth. Freddie chuckled. "I meant your eyes." Damon blinked, locking gazes with the crystal blue orbs and never wanting to stop. "There you are."

He lowered his head and kissed Damon, his hand cupping his face, their tongues tangling. Freddie's free hand lowered to Damon's cock, encircling it with a firm grip and stroking. Damon's lungs stuttered, and his eyelids fluttered. He was already closer than he wanted to be because he didn't want this to end. He never wanted any of it to end.

"Are you ready for the rest of your present?"

Damon could barely understand his words, but Freddie didn't need an answer. He knew him. He knew when Damon was at his limit, and Damon wasn't anywhere close to wanting to stop.

A cool finger pressed against his pucker, and Damon rested his head back against Freddie's shoulder and bore down. The finger slid inside, and all the while, the slow stroking of his cock sent him higher. He wanted to squirm, but the ropes held him fast. It didn't stop him from trying. He lost track of time, Freddie preparing him until he took three fingers easily, and his body was on the edge. Sweat beaded on his skin, slicking where his skin rested together and trickling down his chest and back.

Freddie let go of his cock, and Damon hissed, biting back his begging but unable to withhold the whimper that came after. The orgasm that had been creeping up on him ebbed, and he panted through the need to reach for his dick and stroke himself to completion. He couldn't do anything, tied up as he was, but the wish was there.

Until Freddie pressed his cock against Damon's entrance, his legs bracketing Damon's so they were skin-to-skin. "Are you ready for me?"

"Always, Sir. Always."

Freddie slid his arms around Damon's waist again, holding him close while he slid his cock into his channel. Damon wanted to push back, to have him deep straight away, but Freddie slowed until it seemed like he would never fully settle inside him. Damon moaned, licking his lips, while Freddie withdrew and thrust in small increments. It was only when Freddie's groin met Damon's ass that he let his body relax. He didn't want Freddie to withdraw, though he would. He loved the full feeling of being one with his man, and it would never get old.

Wrapping his hand around Damon's cock again, Freddie said, "Colour?"

"Green, Sir," he half-moaned.

"Good."

Freddie made a long, slow, torturous withdrawal, barely touching his cock, but enough for a steady leak of precome. When the tip remained, Freddie pushed back in the same way, rubbing at the underside of Damon's dick, and Damon couldn't help the whimper of need falling from his lips.

"You feel amazing. Hot. Tight. Mine," Freddie growled and thrust harder, sending tingles of pleasure along Damon's nerves. He stopped when he was fully inside, and Damon sobbed, needing more.

Freddie held Damon tight in his arms, one hand still wrapped around his cock, and circled his hips, grinding his shaft deeper and grazing Damon's prostate.

"Fuck," Damon whispered, not sure if he could take any more. "Please."

"It feels good to be wrapped around you, holding you, knowing you're mine and I can do anything to you, and you'd accept it. You're perfect."

"So are you, Sir," Damon gasped.

"Perfect for each other, then."

"Definitely." Damon's voice caught on the last part of the word when Freddie tightened his hold on his cock.

Freddie's hand released him, and Damon cried out from the loss, but Freddie encircled his throat. Damon dropped his head against Freddie's shoulder, losing himself in the sensations of Freddie's cock impaling him, the ropes tugging at him, the warmth of Freddie's body behind him, and now the heat of his hand around his throat.

"Let's see how high we can go," Freddie murmured.

Damon opened his mouth to answer, but Freddie's grip tightened, and he moaned instead. He could still breathe, but it was harder. He swallowed, feeling Freddie's hand as his Adam's apple bobbed. Still, Freddie's hips circled, and Damon's cock pulsed with need. The hand around his throat let go, and breathing became easier. Freddie took his mouth, stealing that breath he'd taken, and Damon gave as much as he took.

"Fuck, D. You're amazing." Freddie nipped at his bottom lip. "Ready for more?"

"Yes, Sir."

Freddie grinned and increased the speed of his thrusts, tightening his hand again and cutting down Damon's air supply. Damon stared into Freddie's eyes, taking small sips of air. Freddie's free hand stroked Damon's cock, and his mouth opened as his climax tingled down his spine, lifting his balls.

"Ready, D?" Freddie panted, their lips grazing.

Damon blinked in answer, his head going light, but at that moment, Freddie released his throat, gripped his hips and sank deep and hard, nailing Damon's prostate.

The sensations bombarded him all at once. The influx

of oxygen, the stroke of his cock, the pressure against his prostate, the tightening of the ropes, the expression on Freddie's face. It all culminated in an orgasm that blew his mind. His vision narrowed to Freddie's face and nothing else. His mouth opened, but nothing escaped. His body tensed and released, tensed and released. He could only hear a rushing sound while his body exploded.

When he came back, he leaned back against Freddie, secure in his arms, with the man's cock still in his ass.

"Fuck," he whispered. "When can we do that again?"

Freddie chuckled, the vibration sinking into Damon. He flattened his hands and rested them against Freddie's stomach, feeling the slickness of his sweat-soaked skin. If he had a choice, he wouldn't move. They'd stay there forever.

Too soon, Freddie pulled back, and Damon smiled at the feel of the come trickling out of him. He wanted to keep it inside, but he thought he'd tease Freddie with the sight. He pulsed his ass, letting more escape, and when Freddie came back, it was mission accomplished.

"Fuck, D. I wish I could get a photo of this," Freddie growled from behind him.

Damon opened his mouth to answer but moaned when Freddie's mouth and tongue cleaned him. The ropes held him immobile, and he groaned, wanting to fuck himself on his tongue. A warm cloth replaced Freddie's mouth, and when he was done, Freddie rose to kiss him. Damon could taste them both on Freddie's tongue, and it was as much an aphrodisiac as the man himself.

"Let's get you free."

Freddie untied Damon's body with careful movements, rubbing the feeling back into each limb as he did.

"I'd love to see these ropes around you all the time," Freddie murmured, helping Damon to lie down.

Damon glanced at him. "Next time you do it, follow the rope pattern with a pen. I'll get it tattooed on."

Freddie chuckled and shook his head but stopped when Damon didn't laugh with him. "You're serious?"

"Without a doubt. I'd love to have a reminder of your work on me every day. Whenever I look in the mirror. Whenever I look down. I'd have you with me always."

Freddie lifted Damon's left hand and kissed his ring. "I'm with you always, anyway."

"But this would be for us. Not for anyone else."

"And if you ever went swimming?" Freddie asked, stretching out beside him and avoiding the mess Damon had left.

Damon shrugged. "No one would know what it was. It doesn't have to look like ropes unless we want it to. It could be lines."

Freddie exhaled, his pupils expanding. "I'd love that."

"We'll do it, then. Maybe we can ask Helena to do it?"

Freddie grinned. "Is that because you know I won't like a man with his hands on you?"

Damon kissed him. "Of course. Plus, she's good. Very good, and you know it."

"She is." Freddie slid his leg over Damon's, twining them together. "Did I hurt your ribs?"

Damon shook his head. "I'm fine." He pushed his fingers through Freddie's hair. "I love you."

"I love you." Freddie rested his head on the pillow next to him and sighed. "I wish we could stay in our bubble forever, but real life calls."

"I'm sure we can have a few hours free. We have just got engaged, after all."

"Oh, I know they'd let us have time, but do we *have* *time*, is the question."

Damon rolled over, pushing Freddie to his back, and snuggled into his side. Freddie's arms tightened. "We have some. Others will put out any fires for now. Let's stay here for a while longer. They'll fetch us if they need us urgently."

"Yes, sir." Freddie ruined it by chuckling.

"I could dominate you, you know."

Freddie laughed louder. "I'd like to see you try."

Damon lifted his head and rested his chin on Freddie's chest. "One day."

Freddie cupped his cheek. "I'd let you do whatever you want to me. All you need to do is ask."

"I know," he whispered.

They shared a long, lazy kiss until Damon shivered. Freddie pulled back. "Shower." He climbed off the bed and tugged Damon up. Grabbing Damon's thighs, he lifted, and Damon automatically wrapped his legs around his waist.

"You'll drop me."

"Never going to happen. Ever. You're safe with me."

Damon kissed him, and Freddie stumbled. "Except when I do that?"

Freddie's cheeks flushed. "Maybe."

After a hot shower, they changed the sheets and climbed into bed, wrapping themselves around each other. If he excluded everything that was happening with Charlotte—or rather, John—life would be perfect. He had a fiancé, he had friends, he had a job he enjoyed and kept him close to his man, and he had a family. That thought took him to his parents. How had they taken the news? Would they react or bury their head in the sand like they usually did? Would he receive a call or visit from them? Time would tell.

He loved his parents—and would forever—but he couldn't condone their behaviour towards Freddie or the royal family. They were scared, he knew that, but it didn't mean they could ignore Damon's wishes. They knew he loved Freddie, but they chose to lose Damon instead of being happy for him. He'd never understand that. He'd never do that to his kids.

He tensed. *His kids?* He loved the idea of having mini-Freddie's running around the place, but he wouldn't be comfortable bringing them into the world as it was. They'd need to get rid of Charlotte, John and Ernest, plus any of their hangers-on, before it was safe enough.

For the time being, he was content with his prince charming. *And everyone that came with him.* He chuckled when someone knocked on their door, and Freddie shouted, "Go away!"

31

FREDDIE

"You've won the public back," Mav said when they met two weeks after Freddie's live proposal.

They'd had a blissful couple of weeks because Charlotte had gone to ground, and they'd heard nothing from her or her "followers." Freddie and Damon had spent more than enough time in bed and at the club and also celebrating with their family. They didn't think Charlotte —or John—had finished their attack, but nothing had happened since Freddie's event the previous month. It could also be that none of the royal family had attended events, but if that's what needed to happen, then it would. Although, they couldn't keep up with that. They had jobs to do, after all.

"I suppose that's something," Freddie murmured, grimacing and changing position on the sofa. "I still can't believe we've heard nothing from Charlotte or John. Is anyone mentioning it on social media?"

Mav sniffed. "There are calls from Charlotte's followers for her to come back into the 'light' and show them what they should be doing to help her, but she's not responded."

"Father was right, then. She didn't know about John and Ernest's involvement, and she's having to regroup." Freddie sighed. "I don't know if that's a good thing."

"Me either." Mav stood. "Are you ready for tonight?"

Freddie scoffed. "Are we ever ready for the Thirsty Thirteen to get together?"

"Point taken." Mav laughed and left.

Freddie hissed when he stood, rubbing his lower back. Most days, he was fine, but occasionally, he felt like someone had pliers in his back and was twisting them in his spine. He headed for the shower, hoping the hot water would soothe the ache.

He'd pulled his shirt off his shoulders with a groan when hands slid across his shoulders.

"You hurting today?" Damon asked, kissing his jaw.

"Yeah. I twisted wrong when I stood up earlier, and it's twinging now."

Damon tapped his shoulders. "On the bed. Let me help."

Freddie stripped to his boxers and lay on his stomach, pillowing his head on his arms. Damon grabbed the massage oil they kept on hand since Damon had begun regularly massaging him. The image that bombarded

Freddie every time they did this came back, and he decided to thank Damon in his own way.

Damon settled to Freddie's right and poured the oil into his hands, rubbing them together to warm them. When he placed his hands on Freddie's upper back, Freddie sighed and closed his eyes. He enjoyed the pressure, allowing his muscles to relax under Damon's manipulation. When Damon reached towards Freddie's back, his groin met Freddie's shoulder, and Freddie grinned. He unfastened Damon's trousers, pulling his cock free before Damon could protest.

"What are you doing?" Damon's smile was audible.

"If you're asking that, I'm doing it wrong."

Freddie stroked his length, and it thickened in his hand. Damon's breath stuttered above him, but his hands continued to massage his back. Freddie groaned at a particularly sore spot, and Damon concentrated on that area, but Freddie distracted himself by sucking Damon's cock into his mouth.

"Fuck!" Damon said.

It wasn't the best position with Freddie's head to the side, but he could work Damon's dick no matter where they were. He licked at the head, slipping into the slit and coaxing precome to the surface. He flicked the tip of his tongue against the sensitive underside, making Damon curse and tremble, but despite that, Damon's hands worked on him.

"Bloody hell, Freddie. How am I supposed to concentrate when you're doing that?" Damon groaned.

Freddie removed his mouth and tapped Damon's hips.

"Move in front of me."

Damon moved, but Freddie couldn't get his cock into his mouth without craning his neck back too far. He grabbed a couple of pillows and put them beneath his torso, lifting him from the bed a little.

"Scoot forward. Put your knees on either side of the pillows," Freddie ordered.

"I can't massage properly from this position." Damon did what he'd asked.

"Try." Freddie didn't give him any more words, just sank his mouth down on Damon's shaft. The heat and scent of him sent Freddie's head spinning, and he wanted this more than anything at that moment. He didn't care if Damon didn't finish the massage, but he had to have his man.

When Damon leaned forward to rub his hands on Freddie's back, it pushed his cock deeper into Freddie's mouth, and Freddie moaned around it.

"Fuck, Freddie."

Freddie held Damon's hips and encouraged him to move in and out in time with his hands. A mixture of the massage and sucking Damon's dick was enough to have Freddie on the edge, but he had more control than that. Damon would come first.

Damon's hands pressed into Freddie's back, pushing him into the pillows and thrusting his cock into Freddie's mouth. His movements increased as he neared his release, and Freddie sucked harder. Damon had stopped all pretence of the massage and instead fucked Freddie's mouth, releasing increasingly erotic sounds.

"Freddie!" Damon's warning wasn't necessary—they'd discussed it previously—but he gave it all the same.

Freddie swallowed every bit of Damon's orgasm, pushing his hips into the cover to release some of the need for his own impending climax. When Damon finished, Freddie pulled off and wrapped a hand around his own cock, stroking until he was right on the edge. Damon lowered his head, sucking the tip into his mouth, and that was all it took for Freddie to go over. He held Damon's head, thrusting through the contractions.

He panted as if he'd run a marathon by the time he was done, and he settled onto the bed with Damon beside him. "Hmm. That was fun."

Damon chuckled. "How is your back?"

"Can't feel a thing at the minute. It's perfect."

They lay entwined in silence until Damon asked, "Are you ready for tonight?"

"Why do people keep asking me that?"

"It's a bachelor party. Why do you think I'm asking?" Damon rose to his forearm, grinning.

Freddie rolled his eyes. "I don't know why we need one."

"It's not like we're going out separately to watch strippers, Freddie."

Freddie narrowed his eyes. "You better not be."

Damon smirked. "The only person I want to see stripping is you, my love."

"Glad to hear it." He paused. "I have a gift for you."

Damon's head lifted like a dog hearing the word "treat." "What?"

Freddie grinned. "Lay back, legs straight and close your eyes."

He grabbed the items he needed from the drawer where he'd hidden them and pulled on some gloves, holding up an item in front of Damon. "Open your eyes." Damon did, his eyes widening when he saw it, and a flush deepened the colour of his cheeks. "Do you want it?"

Damon nodded. Freddie sat on the bed beside him and sterilised the area. He inspected Damon's cock, noticing the thicker ridge which he would avoid, and marked with a black dot the spot he intended to pierce. Grabbing the needle piercing tube, he said, "Deep inhale for me, then exhale quickly." Damon did, and when he exhaled, Freddie slid the tube into his urethra. He checked the spot, feeling for the end of the tube, and rested it against the black mark from the inside. The piercing needle was next, and he held it near the dot and repeated his earlier request. When Damon exhaled, Freddie pierced the skin, and Damon hissed. Freddie put a captive bead ring on the end of the needle and slid it through the newly made hole before pulling the needle tube and the needle free. He turned the ring and secured the bead on the end. Grabbing some saline, he cleaned away the blood. Then he inspected his work. It looked amazing on him.

"We won't be able to have too much fun for a little while, but it'll be worth it." Damon stared down at it, and tears overflowed. "Are you okay?" Freddie panicked.

"Yes, sorry. I'm good. Oh, god. I love you so much!"

Damon threw his arms around Freddie, and Freddie chuckled. "I love you." He kissed Damon's tears away.

"Now, remember the rules to keep it from getting infected."

"Yes, Doctor."

Freddie stood, heading for the shower. His back was better than it was, but not perfect. But then, it never would be. It was something he'd have to live with.

"I'm still doing the barbecue, aren't I?" he heard Damon say while Freddie dressed. "Good. I want cheese-burgers." He laughed, and the sound soaked into Freddie's chest. "Henry will have to put up with it. He doesn't have to eat them."

Freddie exited the bedroom to where Damon sat on the sofa with the phone to his ear. Damon smiled at him and stood.

"Yes, I know. He'll be there." Damon listened for a minute. "Okay, see you soon." He ended the call. "Everyone thinks you're going to bail."

Freddie sighed. "I'll be there. I always will be. Regard-less of the mischief you all get up to." He dropped a kiss on Damon's lips.

"Good. I'm going to get changed." He strode for the bedroom, stripping his shirt off along the way.

Freddie smiled as the black lines came into view. He loved putting his mark on Damon, and Damon was more than happy for him to do so. The tattoos weren't finished, but the initial lines were in place, and Freddie could imagine the ropes being against Damon's skin. He hadn't thought Damon would go through with it after they'd first spoken about the tattoo, but the following day, he'd brought it up again and asked Freddie to call Helena. Freddie's cousin had agreed immediately and arranged for the initial visit. No one but the three of them knew, and Freddie was happy to keep it that way. He didn't need the ribbing from his family about it.

A knock sounded, and Freddie called for them to enter. "Father! I wasn't expecting to see you yet."

Andrew hugged him. "I'll be there tonight, don't worry. Although I'm still concerned about what my kids get up to when they think no one is watching."

Freddie scoffed. "You know exactly what we get up to. You get reports from the guards."

"Not *full* reports, I have a feeling." Andrew raised his eyebrows, and Freddie raked his teeth over his bottom lip to contain his smile. "Exactly. Being part of your shenanigans will make me feel old."

"It'll be fun." Freddie stared at him. "And besides, Kean and Kendal will be there."

Andrew glowered at him, and Freddie chuckled. "I have something for you, but I wasn't sure when to give it." He pulled an envelope from his pocket, tapping it against his hand before handing it over. "There were no specific instructions as to when, but I think now is a good time."

Freddie glanced at the front of the envelope and saw "Freddie and Damon" in his mother's handwriting. He stared at his father. "I don't understand."

Andrew rubbed his jaw. "Your mother made sure to write a letter to each of you to be given to you when you're due to be married in case she wasn't present. She had rewritten the letter every year for…I don't know how long. This was the last version before…" He swallowed. "I didn't know if I was supposed to give it to you on the day of your wedding or not, but I thought it was better that I don't upset you on that special day. Today is as good a day as any." Andrew squeezed his shoulder. "Read it with Damon."

"How did she know?"

Andrew chuckled. "She knew everything."

His father left, and Freddie dropped to the sofa, staring at the white envelope, tracing his mother's words. He had many memories of her that he brought out whenever he needed comfort, but this was something more. Damon settled beside him.

"Everything okay? Was that your father?"

Freddie nodded, his heart not knowing whether to pound rapidly or break. "Mother wrote us a letter."

"What?" Damon leaned over his shoulder. "Okay. Do you want to open it?"

"I'm not sure."

Damon's hand rested on Freddie's nape, and his other hand gripped Freddie's chin, bringing them face to face. The moment their eyes met, Freddie's shoulders relaxed. "You don't have to do anything."

"I can't believe she put our names on it."

"What do you mean?" Damon let go of Freddie's face when he moved his gaze back to the letter.

"Father said it was for when we got married."

"You and me? How did she know?"

Freddie snorted. "That's what I asked. Father said, 'she

knew everything,' which is true. There was never a time I could get anything by her."

Damon chuckled. "Don't I know it?"

Freddie stared at it for a moment longer, then turned it and ripped it open. He pulled the pages free and set the envelope aside. His chest ached, the scent of honeysuckle rising from the paper, and he closed his eyes and soaked it in. Damon rested his head on Freddie's shoulder.

Inhaling deeply, he blew it out and unfolded the pages.

Dearest Freddie and Damon,

If you've been given this, then your lives have changed irrevocably, and I'm sorry I can't be there with you. I would love nothing more than to celebrate your happy day and the days of your future. That I can't hurts my soul.

Undoubtedly, you're wondering why I wrote a letter to you both when I can't have been sure you'd be together. But I know you both. You are two halves of a whole. You always have been. Neither of you would've been happy apart, and marrying someone else would've made you miserable.

I'm glad you've finally seen sense, Freddie. Damon has loved you for so long, and I know that you have loved him, even if it was difficult to admit. You always were stubborn, like your father.

Times are difficult, and you'll be facing an uphill battle, not only for yourselves but for your family. Keep fighting. The result is worth it, though it might not seem like it right now. Changing the public's opinions is the long game. It's not a short hustle. Show them your love. Show them your devotion. Show them everything you can because only then will you win their hearts again.

Damon, look after my boy. You know what he's like. Tear down his walls and build a picket fence around you both instead.

Freddie, take care of Damon's heart. He deserves everything, as you well know.

My boys... You carry a piece of my heart no matter where I am. Take it and use it as you see fit. I love you all so much, and I wish I was there to tell you all this in person. But fear not. I will never not be there. Look inside you, and you'll see me waiting with open arms.

I'm happy that you've found each other, and I love you.

Love,
Mother

Freddie finished reading with tears streaming down his face and a lump in his throat he couldn't swallow. The paper trembled in his hands, and Damon's arms held him.

"She was psychic. I'm sure of it," Damon said.

Freddie turned, burying his face in Damon's neck, and cried. Damon held him, Freddie's heart breaking open once more. It was ten days until the anniversary of his mother's death, and reading her words was like flaying open a wound that had barely healed. But in some ways, it helped, too. He'd never believed she was truly gone from this world, and her words rang true. She was inside them all, her words, her actions, her love. It was all there waiting for them.

He inhaled and wiped his face. "Thank you."

"You never have to thank me, love."

"Shall we go?" Freddie said.

"Let's wash your face first. Are you taking the letter with you?"

Freddie stared at the papers, then folded them and replaced them in the torn envelope. "No. Father implied Douglas and George would have one, too. I don't want to ruin theirs. Plus, it's a time for celebration."

Damon kissed him, and Freddie slipped his arms around him, deepening the kiss until they needed to breathe.

When they arrived at the receiving room, which had been arranged to be the Thirsty Thirteen's party room again, everyone was already there. The moment they entered, confetti, rice and poppers were thrown over them. Freddie ducked his head, trying not to swallow anything he shouldn't.

"Freddie and Damon, sitting in a tree, K-I-S-S-I-N-G!" George shouted. "I knew you would get together in the end."

"Not earlier than I did," Christian said, throwing some rice at George.

"Did too," George argued.

"I distinctly remember Oscar mentioning it," Christian said.

"Yeah, and everyone brushed it off, including you," Douglas said.

"I think I might win this," Timothy said. "I knew a year ago."

Andrew stepped forward, throwing rice at them all.

"Well, you all lose. Louisa knew from when you were kids." He chuckled.

Damon squeezed Freddie's hand at his mother's name. "She was psychic. I'm telling you."

They received hugs all around, and Freddie settled on the sofa with a drink while Damon went outside to start the barbecue food. He loved doing that, and Freddie loved what he cooked, so he'd never make him stop. Except if there was a good reason for it. Several of the group peeled off after him, and Freddie noticed it was the princes' partners. He narrowed his gaze on what he could see of them outside the window and watched as they animatedly spoke and laughed.

"They started a group for themselves," George said. "They won't let me name them, although I've already come up with The Princes' Hearts. No one has to know," he said with his finger over his lips.

"They have to be able to let off steam about us to someone. May as well be someone else in the same situation," Douglas said.

"We can be a little heavy-handed sometimes," Patrick said, joining them.

George snorted. "Says the man who loves impact play."

"That's not what I meant, and you know it!" Patrick laughed, throwing a napkin towards him.

Freddie soaked up the company. He had never been as happy as he was at that moment. He had the love of his life, he had his family, and he had his job. Despite wanting more privacy, he still wouldn't change it unless he had to.

He could weather anything if Damon was by his side.

32

———

PATRICK

Patrick watched Freddie relax, and he smiled. He couldn't be happier that he and Damon had finally given in to their feelings. But to propose on live TV was something Patrick couldn't imagine doing.

"How did you get the courage to propose during your speech?" he asked when he couldn't stop himself.

Freddie chuckled. "I had no plans to do it then. At all. I'd had the ring in my pocket for a few days, and I'd thought I'd do something special like a candlelit dinner or something romantic." He snorted and rubbed his nape. "Instead, I did it in the most unromantic way, in front of millions of people."

"It wasn't unromantic at all, love," Damon said. His arms came around Freddie's neck, and their cheeks touched. "I'd have said yes, no matter where you asked."

"That's not the point." Freddie kissed his cheek. "I was sitting there, ready to say the last paragraph of my speech, and I couldn't. I had to ask him. I have no idea what came over me, but I wouldn't change it." He tilted his head. "Well, maybe I'd get them to turn the cameras off first. We could've done without the drama afterwards."

They chuckled.

"Four of us are engaged now," Patrick said. "We're all grown up."

"Possibly five," a voice whispered in his ear.

He glanced over his shoulder at Kieren. "Who else?"

"I see Mav sporting a ring, but I don't remember getting the memo."

Patrick stood. "Douglas Sutcliffe! Have you got something to tell us?" he shouted across the room.

"Subtle," Kieren murmured.

Mav's eyes widened, and his cheeks flushed, and Patrick wished he'd kept his mouth shut. Douglas put his arm around Mav and led him to where they were sitting, a smirk firmly in place.

"Maybe. What's it to you?" Douglas grinned.

Patrick whooped. "I wondered when you were going to propose. When did you do that?"

Douglas settled into a chair and pulled Mav onto his lap. "It took you lot long enough to notice. He's been wearing that for four days."

"Four days!" Freddie said. "Why didn't you tell us?"

"There's been a lot going on. We were going to wait until it calmed down," Mav said. "Maybe tomorrow, after this bachelor party."

"I can't believe you're engaged," Patrick said. "I'm

happy for you." He hugged them both and sat in the chair closest to them. "How did he do it?"

"Now, that is a story for when hell freezes over," Douglas said, covering Mav's mouth.

"Ooh, what did you do, Douglas?" George asked.

"Nothing. Besides, don't you have news of your own?" Douglas said, raising his eyebrows at George.

Patrick ping-ponged his gaze between them. "There are no secrets in the Thirsty Thirteen, guys!" he said.

George rolled his eyes. "We're not getting married, for obvious reasons." He glanced at his two men, both resting their hands on his shoulders. "But we have decided to do a promise ceremony for family and friends."

Patrick's heart expanded at the love he felt through the room. He wasn't overly emotional most of the time, but when it came to these people, he couldn't help it. They'd all found the person or people they were supposed to be with, despite the problems in their way. Charlotte couldn't take this away from them. No one could.

3 3

DAMON

*D*amon hid his smile behind his hand while the king and the heir went head-to-head.

"I don't think that's a good idea, Father. It's too soon—"

Andrew interrupted Freddie. "It's the perfect idea. Go. Have fun. Relax. Get away from this mayhem for a little while."

"Can I at least do a visit or two while we're there?" Freddie asked with a sigh.

"No. This is for you and Damon." Andrew glanced at him. "Damon, tell him."

Damon laughed. "As if he listens to me."

"He listens to you more than you realise." Andrew clapped them both on the shoulder and headed for the door. "You're leaving at three o'clock. Make sure you're ready because they're ordered to take you whether or not you have underwear on."

Damon snorted as Andrew exited. That imagery would stay with him for a while. He slipped an arm around Freddie's waist. "It'll be nice to have some quiet time."

Freddie sighed. "It would. I suppose we better pack." He aimed for the bedroom, muttering, "If I'd thought we'd have a weekend to ourselves, I would've postponed that bloody piercing."

Damon chuckled, his entire body feeling lighter than it had in months, maybe years. Yes, the piercing was rather unfortunate timing, but they could still have fun. He'd make sure of it. A long weekend in Scotland was just what the doctor ordered. Everything had quietened down, and Damon wasn't sure if that was a good thing or not, but regardless, there had been no signs of Charlotte or John.

The security team and Christian's "boss," Neil, and his team were still going through all the information they had to figure out anything they could to help. Commissioner Thomas was leaning heavily on Charles and the other prisoners, but so far, they'd had no luck. It pained them all, but they needed to wait for the next attack—if there was one.

By the time they'd packed, he'd managed to cheer Freddie up. "Think of this as a holiday from when we were only best friends. We've done that before. This time, you can hold my hand and kiss me, but that's it. Not much different, and we had fun then, didn't we?"

Freddie sighed. "Yes, we did." He sat on the bed and tapped his fingers on his thighs. "I'm worried, that's all."

Damon settled beside him, steadying his hands. "I

know. But even if we were here, we wouldn't be able to do anything. It's still a waiting game."

"I'd never forgive myself if something happened while we were away." Freddie stared at him.

"I know, and I can't do anything to make that better. What would your mother have said?"

Freddie's lips curled. "She would've told me to stop worrying and have fun. What would happen would happen no matter where I am."

"Exactly. We can't change other people's future actions when we don't know what we're looking for. Let's concentrate on ourselves for a change instead of the country."

They lapsed into silence until Freddie inhaled and squeezed Damon's hand. "Okay. Enough moping. Let's do this."

He was putting on a brave face, but hopefully, he would relax more as the weekend progressed. They finished packing and headed out with their bags. Freddie's family joined them before they left, and they gave a round of hugs and well-wishes before they were on their way to the airport. Holding hands in the rear of the car, Freddie watched the scenery while Damon watched Freddie. Regardless of Andrew's order, Damon would turn them around if Freddie truly didn't want to go.

They didn't have to wait at the airport, thankfully, and they were in the sky before Damon could sneeze, as George would've said. They sat side by side, duplicating their car journey, but this time, Damon broke the silence.

"Want to join the mile-high club?"

Freddie's head whipped around, mouth gaping. "What?"

Damon chuckled. "That got your attention." He back-handed his shoulder. "You know we can't do anything." He waved his hand towards his groin. "Someone put his mark on me again. I just wanted your attention."

Freddie rubbed his nape and gave a small smile. "Sorry. I'll try to get out of my head."

Damon ran his fingers through Freddie's hair. "It's okay. Stop apologising. But let's see what we can think of to do this weekend. I would've suggested swimming, but…" He waved at his groin again.

"Plus, it's bloody freezing." Freddie stared at him as if he'd said he was going to wear a fig leaf to a party.

Damon snorted. "It's March, love. It's not freezing."

"It's 3 March. It's still winter, as far as I'm concerned."

"Wimp."

Freddie narrowed his eyes. "If I wasn't certain I'd hurt you, we'd be tussling right now."

Damon grinned. "Luckily, I'm off the hook." He pursed his lips and sent an air kiss to him. "Anyway, what do you want to do?"

Freddie tilted his head and looked off to the side. "I wouldn't mind visiting the distillery. I've not been there for a while. Also, what about skiing?"

Damon laughed. "You were complaining about being cold."

"There's a difference between going swimming in trunks and nothing else to skiing in full thermal gear."

Damon shook his head. "We can't do either of those tonight. By the time we get there, it'll be late."

Freddie threaded his fingers with Damon. "I know exactly what we can do tonight."

"What?"

"It's a surprise."

Damon rested his head on Freddie's shoulder and closed his eyes. He couldn't believe they were there, together. His wish from years ago had come true, and he couldn't be happier.

It was past seven o'clock by the time they reached Balmoral Castle, and instead of the travel making him tired like it usually did, Damon was buzzing. And it had nothing to do with the shot of whiskey they'd had in the car. The household staff took their bags to their room, and Freddie dragged Damon down the hallways to the dining room. When he stepped from behind Freddie, Damon gasped at the sight. He took in the small, two-person table near the window, set up with candles and everything they needed for an intimate dinner.

"When did you arrange this?"

"When you fell asleep on the plane. I sent a few messages." Freddie slipped his arm around Damon, pulling him close. "You deserve this and more for putting up with me."

Damon turned into him, lifting his chin to reach Freddie's mouth with his own. Damon's eyes fluttered closed as they explored each other's mouths, his hand creeping up behind Freddie's head to keep him in place. Far too soon, Freddie pulled back.

"Shall we?" He waved towards the table.

Freddie held the chair for Damon, tucking it beneath him when he sat, and he tugged the seat next to him rather than leave it across the table. At Damon's raised eyebrows, he said, "I want to share this with you, not be away from you. Even for dinner." He rested his hand on Damon's thigh.

Freddie glanced behind them and nodded, and within minutes, the staff placed steaming plates of food before them. Being able to eat without interruption in some form or another was a luxury they didn't often get. Either a family member or their phones interrupted them at inopportune moments, but they'd both sent messages to their family saying they were turning their phones off for the weekend in the car before they'd arrived. If anything was urgent, a message could be given to a staff member.

Once their plates were empty, Damon leaned forward and captured Freddie's mouth for a brief kiss. "Thank you."

"For what?"

"Taking a chance on me."

Freddie cupped his face. "It wasn't a chance, D. It was fate."

They shared another spine-tingling kiss that made Damon want more, but he lifted his head, smiling. "Don't get me worked up. It's not fair."

"On either of us," Freddie growled. "So much for my ideas."

"Don't regret this one, love. I love it and can't wait for when it's healed."

Freddie's eyes darkened, but he exhaled. "Would you like to take a drink to the sofa, and we can decide what we're going to do this weekend?"

"Sure."

Freddie grabbed their wine glasses and carried them from the dining room to one of the many living rooms. The one he chose was a smaller one with more comfortable furniture. He set the glasses on the side table and settled onto a seat, holding out his arms. Damon didn't hesitate and folded himself into Freddie's side, sighing. Freddie draped a blanket over their legs, and Damon watched the flames flicker in the fireplace. They didn't speak initially, and Damon found it wasn't strained at all. He was content that they hadn't lost the ability to sit in comfortable silence. He had worried that when they'd developed a romantic relationship, they'd lose some things he cherished as best friends, but it seemed they were one of the lucky ones—best friends and lovers.

"Are you okay?" Freddie asked.

Damon leaned his head back against his shoulder to look up at him. "Never better."

Freddie pecked his nose. "What do you want to do this weekend?"

"I think we should leave skiing until Monday because it won't be as busy."

"Agreed." Freddie sipped his wine. "Maybe visit the distillery tomorrow afternoon? We can buy some whiskey to bring home with us."

Damon smiled. "Sounds like a plan."

"What about a walk to Loch Muick? We did that a few years ago, didn't we?"

Damon nodded. "I remember. George nearly fell in." They laughed. "It'll be cold," he teased.

Freddie poked his side. "I'll wrap up warm." He held his glass to Damon's mouth, helping him drink. "Besides, the walk will keep us warm. We need to make sure we bandage you well enough to stop chafing."

"That's most of Saturday planned. Monday we're going skiing and home. What about Sunday?"

"Golf?" Damon rolled his eyes. "Fine. How about visiting the town and wandering around? We could go to the pub for lunch."

"That sounds nice, but let's check with Locke and everyone first."

"We could stay here and hibernate."

Damon laughed. "Anyone would think you didn't like being cold."

"I prefer being warm." His voice had taken on a husky quality, and Damon shivered.

"No," he whispered. "You know we can't."

"I know, but I love seeing your eyes darken when you're aroused." Freddie cupped his jaw and took Damon's mouth.

Damon expected him to be hard and dominating, but Freddie kept it gentle, teasing him with his tongue, his lips, his teeth until Damon couldn't breathe. He could feel the ache in his cock, which, unfortunately, had nothing to do with arousal. He pulled back and exhaled, resting a hand over his groin, hoping to ease the ache.

"Getting an erection is not going to happen." Damon grimaced. "Not pleasant at the minute."

Freddie pressed a kiss to his temple. "Sorry. I'll behave."

"You behave? You're as bad as Douglas and George most of the time. You hide it better."

Freddie laughed. "True." He drank some more wine. "Do you want to watch a film?"

Damon sighed. "Yeah. We've not done that for a while, either." He frowned. "It seems we're missing out on a lot of things since all this started."

Freddie grabbed the remote. "Yes, we are. Hopefully, not for much longer."

Damon hoped so, too. They'd all been through enough. It was high time Charlotte and John got what was coming to them.

"You've all found your partners," Damon said suddenly.

"What do you mean?"

"Well, there's only the two youngest cousins—who I doubt will find their true love yet—who are single. The rest of you are loved up."

Freddie tilted his head. "You're right. Now it's a waiting game for the next generation."

Damon's stomach swooped. "Is that...something you want?" He cleared his throat. "I know we mentioned it in passing before, but we've never discussed it properly."

Freddie licked his lips. "Okay, I'm going to be completely honest, and hopefully, I won't freak you out."

Damon's stomach churned, hoping for the answer he wanted but willing to hide his reaction if it wasn't.

"I want plenty of kids."

Damon's lungs expelled the air he'd been holding, and tears filled his eyes as he smiled. "I do, too. I think we have much we can give a family of our own. I'd love a bunch of mini-Freddie's running around."

"And mini-Damon's."

Damon shook his head. "They can be biologically yours. I don't mind."

Freddie picked Damon up and dragged him across his lap to straddle him. He replaced the blanket over them again before answering. "I mind. I want some that are little versions of you, too. We're a family, which means we share everything, including our biological kids. They'll still belong to both of us, no matter whose genes they have."

Damon cradled Freddie's face in his hands. "On one condition." Freddie raised his eyebrows. "The first must be yours. I won't have the crown in jeopardy. I refuse."

Freddie's eyes flickered, and his jaw clenched while he considered Damon's words, and Damon believed he'd say no, but he surprised him. "Okay. I don't agree that it would matter, but if it would settle your worries, then okay."

Damon smiled, a weight lifting from his chest. "Thank you. It might not matter, but why rock the boat when we don't need to? As you said, it doesn't matter what their genes are. I'll still love them, but it will make things easier."

Freddie pecked his lips. "When are we starting this family journey?"

Damon laughed and slid off Freddie's lap again, snuggling into his side. "After we're married at the earliest."

"We need to consider a surrogate. It might take time. We could start looking."

Damon shook his head, a smile he couldn't stop spreading across his face. "You're impatient."

"I want everything with you. Now. I've waited long enough. I want it all."

"And you shall have it, love. But not yet."

Freddie huffed. "Fine. What are we watching?"

"I'm feeling romantic—"

"*Before Sunrise*. Okaaaay."

His fiancé knew him well, and Damon couldn't help but kiss him again. Freddie didn't mind the romance films, even though he pretended to complain about them. More often than not, Freddie was as emotional as Damon by the end. Their love for these films was something they didn't advertise to the rest of the family. The film started, and they rearranged themselves until Freddie was lying against the back of the sofa. Damon cuddled in front of him with Freddie's arms secured around his waist and a blanket over the top of them. They could've moved to the bedroom, but Damon didn't want to. He loved the little bubble they'd made for themselves, and he didn't want to pop it yet.

Nothing in their future was certain except for their love. But Damon was willing to hold on to that love as tightly as he could to ensure they always had it. No matter what their future entailed. Life didn't always go according to plan, but he didn't care. If they had each other, everything thrown their way was manageable.

And as Freddie murmured the words from the film in Damon's ear—showing they'd watched it far too many times—he knew nothing could come between them.

Thank you for reading Freddie and Damon's story. I had high hopes for these boys, and they didn't disappoint. Commanding Royal is next. See if King Andrew can put aside his concerns and be what he needs to be for the two men he loves.

Sign up to my newsletter to get some free short stories and regular updates and exclusive content.

Would you also consider leaving a review?

ABOUT ELOUISE EAST

Elouise East writes sweet and steamy connections in gay romance. She also touches on taboo stories under the name Elouise R East.

Books that tell the stories where friendship and family are the focal point - be it blood family or chosen - are very important to her. That's why she includes a variety of personalities, talents, ages, situations and abilities as she believes a story or character needs. She wants her characters to be real, to be relatable, to be free to have whatever views they tell her they have. And trust her, most of the time, she does not have *any* say in the matter!

Her characters come to life on the page for her as well as her readers. Their stories unfold in front of her as she writes, and she has very little input into how they want to be shown. Just like real life, the lives of her characters change with every choice, every interaction and every conversation. And she wouldn't have it any other way.

She writes books that are emotionally realistic, even if liberties are taken with other aspects of the stories. She doesn't know any other way to write. It comes from deep inside.

Who is she? A single parent to two children living in the UK. An avid reader who still tries to devour every book she can get her hands on. A student of learning about any subject that takes her fancy. An author of books she would read herself. And a romantic at heart who loves anything cheesy.

Who's joining her on her journey?

Stalk her here… ;-)
Website https://elouiseeast.com
Newsletter https://readerlinks.com/l/2368814
All links https://linktr.ee/elouiseeastauthor

BOOKS BY ELOUISE EAST

<u>CLUB ROYAL</u>

Royal Firsts (prequel)

Rogue Royal

Secretive Royal

Grieving Royal

Disowned Royal

Trained Royal

Awakened Royal

Commanding Royal

<u>ILLUMINATE MATCHMAKING</u>

Ignite

Blaze

Kindle

<u>BOYS, DADDIES, SNUGGLES & MORE</u>

Need Him

Trust Him

<u>DADDY</u>

Love Me, Daddy

Soothe Me, Daddy

Spoil Me, Daddy

The Complete Daddy Series

LOVE IN FLAMES

Out of the Frying Pan

Smokescreen

Breathing Fire

CRUSH

Love Conquers

Crush Series Page

Crush Box Set Series Page

JUST A LITTLE CRUSH

First Kiss

He's Behind You

A Special Love

STANDALONES

Treehouse Whispers

Star-Crossed

Protecting the Thief

Sizzling Chauffeur

BOOKS UNDER ELOUISE R EAST (TABOO)

DARK & DIVERGENT

Forbidden Temptation

Too Many Secrets

<u>COLLIDE</u>

When Fantasies Collide

When Dreams Collide

When Pleasures Collide

When Cravings Collide